Roejay the poet's

# The Stick

# Up

By James R. Johnson

Copyright © 2004 James R. Johnson

ISBN-13: 978-0615772981 (Roejay The Poet)

ISBN-10: 0615772986

# DEDICATION

*In memory of Darren Singleton*

# CONTENTS

## The Stick Up Begins

# The Stick-up

The conversation starts with the placement of an extremely large and uncomfortably heavy hand gun to the rib cage of an unaware, unsuspecting hustler.

"Oh shit!", says the hustler as his head drops and shakes side to side. He knows he has been caught slipping.

"Shut da fuck up nigga", says the stick up kid as he pokes his victim with the cold barrel of his piece; the hammer is now cocked, evident by the long sinister sound of the pistols' click.

"What the fuck you want man? I ain't got shit!"

"What the fuck I want?

Nigga you know what the fuck I want," the jacking thug replies.

He pulls the hustler closer. His inner arm wraps around the baller's throat, squeezing so tightly that for a second the gangster chokes. The gun now placed at his temple, the conversation gets really short.

"Aw'right, Aw'right! Shit! Awww fuck! Aw'right. You got it man, my shit's in my pocket."

"Dat's right nigga!" I got yo ass is what the stick up kid says. Then he firmly presses the cold steal with varying pressure to the youngster's head. Slowly releasing grip of his pray, the sinister thief says.

"Punk turn yo ass around slow, and remember bullets run fast."

The once cool dealer turns to the sight of a shining Colt 45 pointing straight at his face.

*The Stick Up Begins*

He empties his pockets all the while trying not to look this man in his face. Instinctively he glimpses. Oh shit! He thinks to himself; straight killer is embedded all in this mothefucka's face.

"Man please. Please don't kill me!", he starts to beg.

"Shut da fuck up bitch!" The stickup kid exclaims as he violently smacks the nickel-plated canon to the side of the hustler's head.

To his knees he falls clasping his hands, while for his life he continues to beg.

"Man I got a wife and three kids. Man please, please don't take my life."

"Motherfucka! Diss all the money you got!", he yells as he yanks the hustler's chains from around his neck. At that exact moment he kicks the player in the center of his chest.

"Gi'me dem rings too nigga!"

Now crawling, shaking, sobbing and bleeding the once composed Lexus driving, rock slanging killer is shook to the core of his heart with fear. Nothing is on his mind but a fleeing specter of hope. Hope he looks for in the cold, bloodshot eyes of this stick up demon.

Two-shots ring out! Two copper coated hollow point culprits scream through the stale night air. One strikes the gun welding robber in his lower back, the other brings eternal rest as it enters the back of and explodes from the front of the stick up kids head. Lifeless his corpse falls to the ground coming to rest aside the humbled hustler. Now crawling in a pool of mixed blood, the stunned hustler rises. With trembling effort he composes himself. His life he owes, but to whom?

# Chapter 1 *Pitch Black*

He kicks the lifeless body of the- would- be robber and killer then bends over to recover his blood soaked money and jewelry which are scattered about the crime scene. He begins to rant, occasionally pausing to disrespectfully kick the corpse of this now dead motherfucka.

"Mother fucker dats what's up! Dats what you get! Bitch you didn't know who you was fucking wit? I'm Kenny Nobles. The baddest motherfucka ever!"

(*He kicks the body three final times*)

Standing over the dead he unzips his pants exposing his massive black dick. The ultimate disrespect, Kenny relieves himself of a hot stream of fear produced piss. It soaks directly into the exposed, seeping brains of this demon; this jacking- lowlife- thug. Laughing Kenny continues to talk shit.

"Look at ya now trick. You look thirsty. Here, take a drink bitch!"

He continues to taunt the dead. He continues to piss.
(*A loud voice calls out*)

"What the fuck you doing? Man come on we gotta get the fuck outta here. Comm on man!"

The voice comes from a Jeep parked on the side street.

"Come on man, what the fuck you waiting for, the police?"

Kenny runs and hops onto the front passenger's seat of the Jeep; its tires spin and rapidly they drive away.

"Go nigga! Go nigga commands' Kenny!

The driver's response is swift.

"Shut the fuck up! Nigga I tell you what the fuck to do! Now talk some shit and see if I don't put yo Lil simple ass out."

Whatever, says Kenny in a sarcastic tone.

Concern is written all over the drivers' face. He is a veteran hustler and he knows shit is about to get really deep. You see that stickup motherfucka they had just off'd was a nigga by the name of Black. People call him Dirty Black as not to get him confused with the other two local katz using that nick-name.

Anyway this dead man's street connection run deep; his Father is a kingpin. I mean this old player has shit on lock, from numbers to heroin to prostitution. His cousin is the ex-governor and his wife's brother is the chief of police. If that ain't enough to worry about Black also has six cut throat brothers and twelve renegade cousins. They run all the crews on The Westside. They stopped associating with him when he got strung out on his own Drugs.

But, blood is blood. Chances were that if Black had planned to rob Kenny then it was highly likely that he had told somebody. He had probably run his mouth about it all around his way trying to enlist help. After all Kenny ain't no easy mark. Takers would not be easily found: this situation is critical.

There is silence as they ride; that's until Kenny decides to speak.

"Johnny, main I got to thank you for saving my life.

Main I could see dat shit in his eyes."

"See what K", calmly asked Johnny?"

"Man I could see the dope, main it's like dat nigga was possessed on dat shit. Man I can't sell this stuff no more. Main I got to get the fuck out of town. I know we got the North Side on lock but damned. "I gotta jet."

Johnny slams his foot to the brake pedal hard, bringing the Jeep to a screaming halt. Quickly he pulls a Black Hand gun from under his seat and sits it on his lap; Its barrel pointing at Kenny. He taps it nervously on his thigh while gazing intensely into Kenny's eyes. It is a look Kenny understands. The dice have been rolled; Johnny has killed for his nigga. They are cousins by blood but this new bond is beyond that of kinship.

"Say again nigga", Ask Johnny.

Kenny's response he sincerely rethinks.

"I got you back in diss. I ain't going no-where." Johnny resumes the drive.

He hands Kenny's his gun when they arrive at Kenny's house telling him.

"You know what to do with this right?"

Kenny says consider it ghost. They give each other pound then Johnny drives off.

Kenny sits on the stoop; his head hangs low as he smokes a Newport. The lights in the foyer are on, so he knows his wife Cheryl is awake and awaiting his return. So many thoughts and feelings course through the hustler's head.

"What the fuck?" Gods please don't let this shit be happening he thinks then speaks aloud. He is afraid for his wife Cheryl and their three kids, Darren, William and James. He stands concealing the Black, 357 hand gun in the back of his pant's waist before he revolves approaching the front door. Never has the placement of his key in the lock had such a comforting feel. He is alive and he is home.

As soon as he steps across the doors' threshold he's rushed by Cheryl. She embraces him tightly, showering him with passionate kisses (*She is crying*).

"What's wrong", ask Kenny.

Cheryl fights to regain her composure, and then speaks.

"Oh my God; are you OK, are you all right?

I heard you and Johnny had killed someone."

Kenny's heart sinks to the pit of his stomach. If Cheryl knows what went down, than that is it. The word is all over the streets.

Kenny Yells, "Fuck!" as he slams his fist into a wall, shaking the house. "Damn! I gotta call Johnny."

*(The telephone trembles terribly in his hand as he attempts to reach his partner on his cell phone)*

"Shit Johnny man, come on main answer the phone!" Frantically he repeats the call while pacing the floor.

Kenny orders Cheryl to pack the kids with their things ordering her to go to her mother's home. She looks confused and has a thousand and one stupid assed questions. Kenny runs to his safe withdrawing the $20,000 cash he keeps stashed and shoves it into Cheryl's large designer hand bag. Cheryl is still running her mouth.

"Shit! Stop asking questions and just do what the fuck I say Cheryl." He then rips away his blood covered clothing, tossing them into the fireplace. He tells Cheryl she is to burn them before she leaves. The murder weapon he places into a large jar of acid which he keeps locked away in his gun safe. The safe stands about 6'ft high and is full of an assortment of guns, knives and explosive devices. Kenny grabs his automatic shotgun, his A K-47, two fully automatic handguns and three live hand grenades. Just as he slams the door shut, he remembers his bullet proof vest. "Got- damn- it", he mutters as he reopens the safe to acquire the vest.

As Kenny turns around with protection in hand, he's surprised by Cheryl.   There she stands; in her hands she holds his black sweat-suit, a black ski mask and his black Timberland boots. Kenny thinks to himself.

"Now that's a down to ride ass bitch." Cheryl ain't nothing but the truth!

Kenny gets dressed with the quickness then calls' Lorenzo. He's the third lieutenant in their crew. He stepped up when Kenny's best friend Sean was killed in jail.

"Lorenzo. Main we got some problems." Lorenzo responds with his deep low voice.

"Yeah! Some niggas been asking about you and Johnny; I tried to get Johnny but my calls ain't getting through. I sent Kevin to look for him.

" Motherfuck! Shit", exclaims Kenny kicking the glass coffee table, breaking it. He composes himself and commands Lorenzo to meet him at Johnny's night club.

"I can't say over the phone but you know what the fuck we gotta do. Oh, and get some info on dat nigga Black!

"Which one", asked Lorenzo.

"Dirty", replies Kenny.

# (Mischief at the club)

Outside of his night club Johnny sits in his Jeep, his thoughts heavy. "Damned!" he thinks to himself.

"What the fuck! Shit! Fuck me!" Out of all the people, why did it have to be dirty ass Black?

Johnny's conscious is clear but his mental is a wreck. He had bodied many a nigga, mostly youngsters trying to take respect. But like I said earlier, Black had major street connections.

Shaking his head Johnny reaches forward producing a small bag of white powder from the Jeep's ash tray. Slowly and reluctantly he scoops the powder under his long pinky nail then quickly sniffed it up his nostril; this was a past vice. The seriousness of the situation seems to ease with each repeated hit; now coked-up and cocky he exits his Jeep.

He makes his way down the sidewalk swaying hard. Bitches and niggas all on his tip; dap, hugs and mad-crazy love this thug would always get. People call him Superstar.

As Johnny nears the entrance door of his club, he is met by security guards. The head security officer is a brother named Chief. Chief is a big, burly, muscle head motherfucker. Johnny had met him while he was doing a short bit in the city lock-up. Chief was the head deputy there at the time. He was also the man inmates had to go through to get whatever contraband they wanted while in the lock-up: Drugs, pussy; whatever. Johnny always liked Chief, so when he heard Chief got fired behind drugs he put him on at his club as manager and head of security.

"What's up Super Star? Man the Joint is packed and mad ladies are in the house. Ladies loving this ladies night! We about to kick off the thong contest in about 30 minutes. "Man you right on time!" Chief is foaming at the mouth in anticipation of seeing some ass.

Calm down chief, chuckles Johnny as they make their way to Johnny's office to count door money.

"Chief I need you to be on point and put your people on alert. Be on the lookout. If anybody looks suspicious, you let me know; anybody chief. I got some unresolved issues. The shit might be coming this way tonight."

Chief nods and with a stern stare he says. "I got your back." Johnny deposits the cash in the safe asking Chief.

"Did you take out the cops cut?"

" Un hun says Chief. "

OK then. I want Teddy to make the drop tonight. I need you to stay alert and close."

(*Chief gives Johnny pound then exits the office*)

Johnny takes a seat at his desk finishing the powdered Kane which he had in his pocket. He then places an intercom call to the bar.

Danny the bartender answers after six or seven rings.

"Damned nigga: is we busy like that or what?" slyly comments Johnny.

"Man it's jumping out here. You got some thirsty females out here."

"Whatever nigga"; bring me a bottle of 151 and a soda. Even better get Nicole to bring it to me commands Johnny.

Danny yells across the dance floor motioning with his free hand for Nicole as he hangs up the phone. Nicole comes handing

Danny an order. She looks sexy as hell standing there counting her tip money. Nicole is a dime, two quarters plus a penny. She's the type of girl niggas dream about. Danny hands her Johnny's fix telling her to take it to him.

She twists her lips, smiles then proceeds to the boss's office. Nicole walks in without knocking. She is one of few who can get away with this. By nature Johnny is a paranoid fucker.

Nicole is shocked to see Johnny standing there buck- ass-naked holding his dick in his hand. He's smiles ear to ear shaking it up and down. "Get undressed", commands Johnny.

Meanwhile, in another part of the city Kenny is breaking the speed limit and running stop lights in an attempt to reach his cousin Johnny in time. He can feel it. Shit is about to go down; frantically he makes repeated attempts to reach Johnny on his cell; still, no luck. Likewise his phone is blowing up. He's getting hella calls from everybody. All basically have the same thing to say. Strange niggas are checking for him and Johnny everywhere. Kenny calls Lorenzo to see how close he is to the club.

"Shit! Fuck! Now this nigga ain't answering his phone." He bangs his fist on the dash board then tosses the useless cell phone to the back seat.

*(Back at the club Nicole is giving Johnny shit)*

"Nigga how the fuck you going to disrespect a bitch like that! Just because I let you have a sniff of this good stuff from time to time don't mean you entitled to it. And besides, you know I got a new man now."( Johnny and Nicole used to be a couple).

Johnny holds a fist full of crisp $100 bills in his free hand. He flicks one to the floor toward her feet. With confidence he flips another and says.

" Girl you know it's all about the money. I told your ass to strip!"

When Johnny is coke-up he's on some extra special, obnoxious, hype trip.

He walks toward Nicole slowly shaking his blood-swollen dick. She's getting turned on because in her heart she knows she misses that big, crooked, black dick of his. In bed he is as his nick names suggest: a superstar.

Johnny walks around her flipping hundreds creating a circle of dead presidents around her. Money makes this lady's pussy wet. Nicole slowly pulls her shirt over her head revealing her soft, firm, succulent breast. She then pulls her skirt down dropping it to the floor. Out of laced panties she then steps. Johnny's dick gets even harder and it is now pointing toward the ceiling. Nicole swirls around enticing him as if to say, what do you want?

Johnny places his hands on her shoulders forcing her to her knees. Nicole grabs his dick forcefully cramming as much as she can fit into her mouth. She attempts to casually suck a dick. But Johnny ain't having it, his hands wrap in her hair as he starts skull fucking her face, hard and nasty like.

Nicole tries to pull away. But the more she pushes him away the rougher he gets. He wants to bust hot nut all down her throat. Try as he may; he can't cum. He starts to get frustrated with what he perceives as her lack of dick sucking enthusiasm, or perhaps it's the phone call he received from her earlier tonight that has him tripping. Johnny stops and speaks in an angry tone.

"What the fuck! Bitch didn't your hoe-ass momma teach you

how to suck a dick right!"

Nicole is afraid, in his eyes she can see rape; she can even see murder. But what has she done to deserve this? Johnny smacks the shit out of her; the blow sends her crumbling to the floor like a broken china doll. A rapist approaches her from her rear lifting her smooth, plump, yellow ass toward his dick.

"Bitch it's always about money with you. You tried to fuck my cousin Kenny over? Now Im'a fuck you in yo ass! Do you think Chester can give it to you raw like this?" Jealousy fuels his rage. Chester is Nicole's so called new boy friend. But any man involved with her shares her with Johnny weather he knows it or not. The frightened woman sobs but is afraid to cry out.

She had seen him kill before, and was even excited watching. But when he killed this pregnant girl who stole $2,000 from him that was the end of their relationship; the girl was her niece.

To her he is a monster, but try as she may she can never seem to leave him alone. It's this man's cars and money she truly loves. One could say she is blinded by the sparkle of this superstar. But in her heart she wants this guy and his cousin Kenny dead.

Nicole continues to pull away from him as best she can, but at 5' 7 and 145 lbs it's no contest. Johnny injects the massive head of his 9 and a half inch dick into her moist, tight asshole. He holds her by her hair as he rams until it is all in her. Johnny is in another world. A world of pumping: impervious to pain.

She passes out from pain as he continues to pound in her ass like a jack hammer. Her frail body just couldn't take it.

"AHHH!", roars Mr. Superstar as he releases a well earned jetting stream of nut. He has never cum this hard before in his life.

His energy and rage spent he pulls out of Nicole's now

bloody swollen asshole. He then tosses the remaining money from his hand on to her naked, unconscious body.

"That should be enough to cover the damage he remarks. "

*(This man has issues)*

Johnny calmly walks to his desk where he stands looking back at Nicole lying on the floor: he places a call to Chief on the intercom.

"Hey nigga, clean-up on aisle four, he laughs.

Chief rushes into the office forgetting to knock. He knows how sick his boss can be when he was high.

"Nigga you know to knock first" says Johnny. "Aw'ite Ima let it slide just this once since you My Man".

Chief is disgusted by the way Johnny has disgraced Nicole. He has always had this unspoken crush on her.

Their stands Johnny hovering over Nichole admiring his work, he's smiling like the Cheshire cat. Chief wants to whip his ass, but he contains his rage. He humbles himself.

"Are you OK boss?"

"Never better, never better says Johnny before stumbling to his desk where he takes a seat. He bucks Bacardi 151 Rum from the bottle.

Chief wonders, what could Nicole have done to deserve this. He asks Johnny is she dead? Johnny never answers; he just put his head down on the table and goes to sleep.

"You got my back; right Chief," are the last words he utters.

Chief checks Nicole vitals; she is breathing. He then takes her to the bathroom at the rear of the office where he places her into the shower. With tender- love and care he cleans her up. Fifteen minutes or so pass and a scared Nicole opens her eyes to a concerned Chief.

Looking out of the bathroom Chief can see Johnny, still face down, passed out; wasted.

"Come on baby I got to get you out of here." He rushes, helping Nicole into her skimpy clothing. He then sneaks her out the back door of the office. The door opens into the alley where his car is parked. Chief is weak in his loyalty; he forgets his promise to get Johnny's back. He wants to be with Nicole and he sees this as his chance. He helps her into his car then leaves the club with her. His plan is to take her to his apartment. In his haste he has forgotten his responsibilities. It's Chief's night to lock up the club.

*(It's now 2:30am)*

*(It's now 3:25am)*

Lorenzo arrives at the club. He enters thru the front door; he has questions. Where is Chief and why is security so relaxed? He approaches Danny at the bar. Their relationship is not on the best of terms. They used to be a boy until Lorenzo fucked Danny's wife, Michelle. Danny never confronted him about it. He just keeps that shit inside of him. After all, Lorenzo is a stone cold killer. And that's all he does.

"What's up Dee? Where the fuck is Chief?" Danny shrugs his shoulders indicating he does not know. "Where the fuck is Johnny?"

Danny points to the office door. Lorenzo looks at Danny and shakes his head as he starts to walk away. He had learned that Danny is one of those Keep it on the down low niggas. He was not fucking his wife right, because he has a taste for dick. He had made the mistake of coming on to Lorenzo once when they were getting high. Danny was lucky to still be alive. That's what ended their friendship and led to Zoe (Lorenzo) fucking his wife.

12

"Wait! Calls out Danny," Lorenzo pauses to listen.

"He's got company." Nicole took him a drink about an hour ago."

Lorenzo smiles, He knows not to bother Johnny when he's with Nicole.

"Shit! They done hooked back up Again?" *He smiles releasing a low chuckle.* Still there is this feeling something is not right. He shakes it off as he and his soldiers take seats at the bar. Danny stacks five glasses atop the bar counter and put out a fresh bottle of Hennessy. Lorenzo pulls a fat bag of weed from his pocket and starts rolling fat blunts. These clowns are getting fuck-up as they exchange war-stories. Danny and the other staff including security all left the club at 4:00am. The front door is still unlocked as if was chief's night to close. Lorenzo and his boys are so caught up talking that thug shit and chilling that they make the assumption the club is secured.

*(It's now 4:33am)*

Three strange niggas toting shot guns make their way down the sidewalk. They creep up to the front door of the club. The first gunman peeps into the small window beside the door. He sees six clowns sitting and joking. He smirks than he whispers to the other two. "On the count of three. He starts to count in a low, calm tone of voice; smooth and slow.

"One, Two, and at three his heavy boot kicks the door. Boom! Is the sound made as the door flings open. Entrance has been gained; social thug's hearts lock than race as they dive for cover. Three dive to the floor acquiring there heat as they descend. Lorenzo jumps to the other side of the bar and well let's say the fifth nigga was just a bit more relaxed then his friends. He catches the full blast of the renegade's sawed-off gun. His fucking head just shatters as hot buckshot melts the left side of his once handsome face.

They called him Baby-Boy. He was also Cheryl's kid brother.

13

She tried to keep him from the life but a thug is what he wanted to be. In rush the other two hit-men blasting as they run seeking cover. Johnny's remaining four troopers are laying down mad fire. I mean these niggas are dumping. It's like rata- tat- tat none stop. But those violators are meeting their noise with shot-gun booms.

One hit-man dead, three of Johnny's slipping ass soldiers slain. One minute of fury then dead silence.

In his office Johnny is awakened not by the sounds of the gun battle but rather that of silence. It is an eerie stillness. It's similar to the uncomfortable silence heard only at funerals, that awkward pause just before the minister delivers his eulogy. It is the taste of death's kiss which has awakened the Superstar.

Johnny pours rum into his hands splashing it onto his face.

*(His head he shakes clearing cobwebs)*

He opens his blood- shot eyes; they strain to focuses on the security monitor near the edge of his desk.

"What the fuck!" mumbles a still fucked-up Johnny with slurred speech. This player has a bird's eye view of the drama that is unfolding outside of his office door. He sees his man Zoe pinned down behind the bar holding two Desert Eagle handguns; he's scrambling to reload. Johnny cannot identify anyone else as those mother-fuckers are all face- down dead.

As the surveillance system switches cameras he can see the position of the two remaining intruders. One is concealed in safety in a nook at the entrance by the front door. The other is hiding behind a bullet riddled speaker box approximately 40ft to the left of the bar. A poor choice thinks Johnny as this position is at most 20ft dead center of his office door. I got a clear shot at this clown, or so he thinks. He reaches under his desk and gets his hands on the snub nosed 357 revolver which he has duck taped there. He stumbles and falls as he reaches forward tapping the intercom's button. He speaks with the confidence of a drunk.

"Zoe, count to six my nigga, then come up blasting, that bitch is at the front door. Make Swiss cheese out of his gay-ass. Don't even worry about his hoe ass girl-friend; she's as good as dead. Ya'll niggas here that! Ya'll die in six mother-fucking seconds! Tell Lucifer Johnny says hello." Johnny has sent Zoe the code, six means three to these veterans; they have been here many a time together. Johnny starts to countdown.

"One! Get ready to die; Two: who wants to die? Three!

*(Johnny rushes the door entering the lounge area)*

Two eternal sleeping pills exited the nose of his black steel 357 magnum; their objective is met, one in the head and one in the chest.

*(Lorenzo springs up sending mad cover fire in the direction of the front door)*

*The intruder in the nook is frozen in fear.* Johnny had him shook talking that crazy shit over the intercom.

Fear prompts his speedy retreat; there mission was a success. Johnny's last victim had managed to get off one last shot with his last dying breath. One final shotgun blast had laid the Superstar to rest. Lorenzo's eyes swell to the size of 50 cent pieces in disbelief; Johnny can't be dead. He had been caught off guard and now his nigga is no more. Tears flow as he walks towards Johnny's life-less body. He and Johnny went way back, they were friends before the lifestyle. It all seems so pointless now.

Kenny finally nears the club. He sees a masked shotgun toting male running away from the club. He gives chase on the nearly vacant street. He has the passenger's window down and he's letting off. One hand on the steering wheel, the other steady as his fully automatic hand-gun spit rounds, until it cocks- back, locked and empty.

"Bitch you ain't getting away" he yells as he lobs a hand grenade from the opened moon roof of the car. It lands about 4ft in front of the escaping gunman and explodes. KABOOM!!!!!!! Bits of legs, arms and torso litter the street. The nigga's head comes to rest on his car's hood. Shit, curses Kenny. I know this mother fucker; it's Nicole's new boyfriend. His name is Chester or some shit like that. Stopping the car he gets out, grabs the head and tosses it onto the back seat.

He parks then runs back to the club where he is met out front by Lorenzo.

"Man don't go in there", cautions Lorenzo. He places his hand on the center of Kenny's padded chest stops all forward movement.

"They got Johnny." *Kenny is beyond shook.* "Ok Zoe we gotta regroup, I need to think. Awww fuck! I can't think!  Ok, Ok! We gotta get out of here; come on!" shouts a trembling Kenny.

Kenny runs back to his car and Lorenzo follows on his motorcycle. Follow me to the spot says Kenny. The spot is an apartment leased under Cheryl's cousin's name in Henrico County; only Johnny and Kenny knew its exact location.  This is where they stored and cut their drugs.

Kenny calls Cheryl as he enters a freeway on-ramp. He has to be sure she has done as he had told her to. His concern for his family's safety deepens. Cheryl answers quickly: she has the kids and is on 95 north heading to her mother's home near DC. He tells her that Johnny is dead and that he is going into hiding.  She understands. This is just part of the life they chose. He instructs her to toss the telephone after they hang up. "Look babe I need you to listen real good. Get your cousin Lynette to get you a new phone in her name. Then give the number to Sean's brother Bo Peep. I'll get it from him and I'll call you and the kids on Sunday's at 3pm until this shit is straight. OK baby? I need you to do it exactly like that Cheryl. I love you to baby, but for now I got to go." He hangs up and one tear rolls down her cheek. A loving wife rolls down the window of her White Range Rover and tosses her cell phone to the highway pavement. A single thought haunts her; would this be the last time she speaks to her husband?

Kenny scrambles to get his thoughts together, after all his now dead cousin was the brains of this ring. What's next he thinks? An eerie feeling creeps over him. He feels like he is being watched. He looks over his shoulder seeing the head resting on the leather seat behind him. Its tongue is hanging from its mouth, one eye is missing but the other appears to be looking directly at him. Kenny starts talking to it. "Stop looking at me bitch! I bet you thought you were going to get away, didn't ya! Didn't ya!" He then covers its gaze; tossing the light weight jacket which he had sitting on the passenger seat over it.

## (Questions)

Twenty minutes later Kenny and Lorenzo arrive at the spot. They enter the apartment turning the television on. It is now 6am and the world is beginning to awaken. Kenny tells Lorenzo to turn to the early morning local news. They are not surprise to see Johnny's club live on the box.

*(Reporter speaks)*

"Police are on the scene of what appears to be the aftermath of a gang-land turf war. Police say that local night club owner Jonathan Harris along with several of his associate were found slain early this morning after bystanders say an early morning war raged here on the cities down town streets. This is what on looker Rufus Deon Jones had to say of this morning's event.

*(The camera cuts to a thin, dirty looking man with extremely crooked, yellowish, browning teeth. He is dressed in a stained bright green and red vertically striped shirt with faded Jeans. On his head he has an orange hat, tilted slightly to one side. The hat has an embroidered marijuana leaf with tattered stitching.)*

"Da president needs to look at stuff like diss-hern. Cuz see dem boys ain't got no jobs. They be listening to dat rap music. Dat's why dat one main was throwing dem bombs and stuff. I knew diss was one of dem-dare terrorist attacks. *(He then starts singing God bless America; the camera goes blank for a second then returns to the reporter standing there looking stupidly)*

"Earlier around 12 am the body of 41 year old Leroy Nelson (Black) was found murdered on the East end. Police are being extremely tight lipped but sources say these events may be connected.

"Well back to you Scottie." Lorenzo turns the TV off.

He walks toward Kenny who sitting on the couch where he takes a seat at its far end.

"What's next Kenny? It's on you now. You speak it nigga and I'll bring it to pass. Who you wanna dead first?" This is why Johnny always kept Zoe so close.

Kenny looks confused. With one hand he holds his head which hangs low. In the other he holds the edge of his black ski mask which is on the floor between his boots. Like a Christmas stocking it conceals goodies. He turns it up right and with a shake Chester's head falls out making a dry thud as it hits the floor. He kicks it over to Lorenzo and says.

"Start with this ass hole. He was Nicole's boyfriend. This the nigga that made it out'a the club. Find that bitch and bring her here! Something ain't right about this whole shit! And where the fuck is Chief? This shit all over the news and he ain't call to check in or nothing? And Zoe how the fuck you n yo boys get caught slipping like that? You say them niggas came in the front door?" *(The door is a three inch, steel security door)* Kenny is pissed; his cousin is dead and all he has is a fucking head to show for it. He needs answers.

*(Lorenzo starts to explain)*

18

"Main when I got to the club security was laxed as a bitch. I don't remember seeing Chief at all. I just assumed he was somewhere in dare. Fuck! I thought maybe he was in the bathroom getting his dick sucked or something. Shit, you know he ain't nothing but a big ass trick."

Kenny just looks at Lorenzo with blazing disappointment in his eyes. He then picks up the land-line phone and dials Chief's cell number. Ring.... Ring.... Ring..... *(Chief picks up; Nicole is sitting next to him on an old Victorian style love seat. She had begged him not to answer.)* Kenny speaks very slowly and very seriously.

"Where you at?" Chief pauses as he thinks, this nigga don't sound like his self. He stammers as he answers. "I'm at home. I had to leave da club early. Johnny was tripping tonight! He beat and raped Nicole. I thought he was going to killer her. Main I had to get her out of dare. He was so high he passed out, dats when I managed to sneak her out the back door. Main we gotta do something about him! We need to get him some help. I think he's losing it. *(4 seconds of silence)* "So you left him?"

"Main Nicole needed me."

So you left him repeats Kenny.

"Main, Main, Stammers chief.

"Hold on Chief." Kenny holds the mute button down as he speaks to Lorenzo. "Zoe! That bitch is at Chief's apartment. Take my car and bring them both back here."

"What if they don't want to come", Asks Lorenzo?

"It's not fucking optional nigga! And get Kevin in on this one, we might need his expertise."

*(Kenny releases the mute button)*

"OK Chief, come in an hour early to work tomorrow. We'll talk to Johnny and see if we can get him to go back into a rehab or something. If he's back on that shit it might mess with us getting money." Kenny and chief laugh then they hang up.

*(Lorenzo leaves in a hurry)*

Meanwhile Chief tries his best to put the moves on Nicole. He feels she might feel something for him as he has just saved her life. Nicole's mind is not on Chief in the least, she casually blows him off. Her only concern is in getting him to take her home. She begs him to take her home, but his ass keeps stalling. He fools himself thinking he has a shot at getting some of her high dollar pussy. Chief is old, fat and broke; he couldn't even afford a sniff of her shit. Suddenly there is a knock at the door. Chief looks out of the peep hole to see Lorenzo and Kevin standing there. They are smiling and joking amongst themselves.

He opens the door only to be met by a well placed left hook to his jaw. It is the type of punch meant to bring a man to his knees. But Chief is a big son of a bitch. He sways like a tree in the wind but does not fall. In steps Kevin fast pointing a small 22 caliber hand gun to Chief's ugly, fat face. Lorenzo speaks and there is no love in his voice. He is calm as he tells Chief to "be cool."

Nicole attempts to run to the bedroom at the back of the apartment. Kevin pursues her grabbing her by the back of her hair, he drags her back toward Lorenzo kicking and screaming. Kevin looks at Chief, Chief looks at Nicole. Nicole looks at Lorenzo. Lorenzo looks at Kevin and Kevin blast; So much for sorry ass Chief. Only the smell of gun powder remains as the three exits the building. Two killers and one terrified Nicole.

"Where are you taking me too", she whimpers as she cries.

"Be cool Ma and take it easy. Kenny just needs to talk with you, says Lorenzo pushing her into the car. Nicole loses it; she starts shaking uncontrollably and curls into the fetal position on the back seat of the car. She starts to repeat.

"I just want to go home; please just take me home."

# (The fowl deed)

A Fifteen minute drive and they arrive back at the spot. Lorenzo parks the car to the rear of the apartment complex; Nicole continues to babble and cry. But now she repeats.

"Please take me home Lorenzo. I'll suck your dick, please take me home, I'll suck both your dicks." Lorenzo and Kevin look at each other then burst out laughing.

"Aw'ite Kev I got first." Lorenzo steps from the car making his way to Nicole. He opens the rear door pulling his pipe from his pants. Nicole reaches forward placing his dick into her mouth. She sucks as if her life depends on it. Lorenzo skull fucks the shit out of her pretty face. She gasps for air as he violently rams his rod as far as he can down her windpipe. He is using her hair like a handle to lift her mouth up and down on his throbbing shaft. Saliva runs from the sides of her lips as she is unable to swallow. She's coughs and gags as his hot load pulsates with force down her throat. Her airway open, nut enters and exits her nostrils as he continues to pump. She is drowning in cum but she dares not stop sucking. Exhausted and satisfied Lorenzo pulls from her mouth shoving her head away. Disrespectfully he says.

"Thanks hoe!" then he chuckles. "Look at you hoe! You thought you were so high profile! But now that Johnny's ain't here to protect you, you just another two cent hoe." Lorenzo had always dreamed of doing this to her.

He zips his pants telling Kevin to go next. Kevin's attitude and actions are similar to those of his friend. But there is another factor in doing this nigga. He is HIV positive and everyone knows it, including Nicole. Nicole has to make one of those hard decisions. She wants to live: she does not hesitate to do him. She sucks his infected dick like it is candy. She tells herself she will be Ok as long as she does not swallow his wad.

Kevin's body shakes violently as he releases his demons filling her mouth with what seems to Nicole to be a gallon of distasteful nut. She attempts to spit that shit out when he places his gun to her head.

"What's the matter", says Kevin as he smiles with a wickedly sly grin. "Swallow hoe or you're dead".

Nicole pushes him back and spits it out. Lorenzo and Kevin burst into laughter, and then Lorenzo says.

"Come on girl, you got an appointment to keep."

Nicole snaps. You could say she just loses it. She starts cursing at the two liars.

"You mother-fuckers said you would take me home. Damn-it, I sucked your dicks!!!

"Calm down boo; we will after the meeting", says Lorenzo.

They continue to taunt her as they lead her by both arms to the apartment.

Kenny opens the door; he heard them approaching.

Kenny greets Nicole with a dry, un-welcoming hello then he prompts her to take a seat on the couch. He instructs Kevin to go get her something to drink from the bar.

This bar is the bomb. It is mahogany wood with stained glass inlays of various floral patterns, lit from its inner cabins. This shit cost a pretty penny and fits the decor very well. This pad is laid. Surely they are not going to kill me here, thinks Nicole. Kevin returns with drink in hand. It's a Sex on the beach. He even took the time to put one of those little umbrellas in it alongside of one of those long curly straws. Nicole fells more relieved and she accepts the drink. She thinks to herself, just maybe he doesn't know. She kicks her shoes off and reclines to relax as Kenny starts conversing.

" Tell me where your boyfriend is tonight."

"I don't know. I broke up with him last month. I wanted to get back with Johnny."

"Ok. So tell me who is he getting money with?"

"I heard he got locked up last week. But I think he was working out'a town with some katz in D.C."

"Ok. Tell me what you know about a nigga named Black?"

"Which one?"

"That dirty ass bitch Black."

"I don't know him but I heard he be jacking ballers for they shit."

"Ok. Does Chester know Black?"

"He might. They live on the same side of town and have some friends in common."

"Zoe, Light dat scented candle."

"You got a lighter?"

"Naw; light it on the stove."

*(Lorenzo exits the room)*

"You said he might know him? Well that's not a yes and not a no. I need a yes or a no."

*(Lorenzo returns with the lit candle)*

"I don't know for real. I wouldn't lie to you. Shit you know we go way back. Kenny come on now, this me; Nikkie."

"Zoe."

*(Lorenzo approaches Nicole grabbing her by the head pulling her head back, tilting her chin upward. She starts to feel the heat of the candles flame as he raises it closer to her chin's delicate, smooth, soft flesh)*

"Ok! Ok! Ok! Chester started working for Black's brother

Ricky about a month ago!"

"Keep going."

"Chester and black be getting high together. Chester made me tell him where you were going to be at tonight. He said Black needed some quick cash. Everybody knows how you be flossing. He was going to try to get back in the game with the money. They said they were not going to hurt you! I swear Kenny; I would never want to see anything happen to you. But Chester said he was going to beat me if I did not tell them.  I'm sorry Kenny! I tried to make it right. That's why I called Johnny and told him Black was going to stick you up tonight. I told him where they were going to get you! Johnny's phone went dead before I could tell him the whole story. Kenny you got to believe me. Call Johnny, he'll tell you! Please call Johnny; I just want to go home!"

"Zoe."

*(Lorenzo extinguishes the flame)*

"I'm sorry! Please let me go! Johnny raped me tonight and these two took what little dignity I had left. Please forgive me! I can help you find Chester."

"Chester is not the problem and Johnny is dead because of your stupid- ass."

*(Kevin enters the room and places Chester's head in her lap)*

She breaks down completely. She just sits there rocking back and forth holding her boyfriends severed head. She repeats under her breath as she strokes the head.

"It's going to be alright Boo. They are going to take us home now. You'll see. We're going home."

Kenny motions to Lorenzo with a nod of his head and he leads

24

Nicole by her hand down the hall way to the bathroom where Kevin awaits. He has drawn a warm bath especially for Nicole. She does not put up a fight; she's walking and nervously laughing.

"But I told Johnny."

The bathroom door closes. There is the thrashing of water in a struggle then dead silence. Nicole has been drowned. Kenny does not feel good about what he feels had to be done. But now is not a time to show weakness. He will have to be cut throat if he hopes to make it out of this ordeal alive.

Lorenzo returns to the room. Kevin is supposed to be making preparations for getting rid of the body and head. Lorenzo never liked to watch Kevin do his special work. Kevin is his friend but when it comes to dead bodies he is a strange  Kevin is not a hustler and they never have to pay him for his disposal services. All they know is that he makes problems like this disappear.

Kenny and Lorenzo sit in silence. They can hear Kevin talking under his breath to Nicole's corpse. They try not to hear what he is saying. But they do. Kenny thinks to himself. I can't let him do these things to her body. She was my friend. Lorenzo can see in Kenny's eyes that he is about to confront Kevin. He speaks.

"Kenny I know its sick main but we need this nigga. Don't do it."

Kenny removed his hand from under his shirt where it eagerly rested on the handle of his gun.

"Zoe go tell that nigga to hurry up and get her out'a hear. I don't care where he takes her but he ain't doing that shit to her here.

Lorenzo turns on the radio before he leaves the room to prompt Kevin to hasten the clean up. Kenny turns the volume up with the remote control to drown the sound of Kevin's voice. Kevin continues to talk. This is a one sided un-godly conversation. Lorenzo's curiosity is heightened as he approaches the bathroom. He leans forward pressing his ear to the door to better hear Kevin.

"Nicole I just love the softness of your body. Yes baby you feel so fucking good. Do you like that? Can you feel me? Damn! You feel so good. Give it to daddy. Yes, give it to daddy." Lorenzo has heard enough, this must be stopped.

He opens the door revealing Nicole's dead body, ass-up draped over the edge of the tub. Her head still partially submersed under water. Kevin is attached to her ass like a leach. Kevin stops all motion for a second and stares Lorenzo squarely in his eyes; Lorenzo's look, far beyond disgust.

Kevin rolls his eyes in ecstasy from her loose feel, and then he continues fucking what used to be Nicole. He fucks her corpse harder and faster. Lorenzo begs him to stop. He commands Kevin to stop!

"I can't; not right now, it's too good, it's too good. He freezes; his ass begins to lock while he shoots his load into freshly dead pussy. If looks could kill, Kevin would be dead *(Lorenzo's facial expression is filled with disgust, hate and longing)*.

This encounter has taken Lorenzo to new low. He had seen and done some twisted shit, but this is by far the sickest shit he has ever been a part of! He feels guilty. He feels like he too had fucked Nicole's corpse. He wants to speak but he has not the words. Kevin stands pulling his pants up. He apologizes as he zips his fly.

"Main I didn't mean to disrespect the crib like that but she was just begging for it. She was just laying there looking sexy as hell with her phat ass jacked up in the air like dat. Main come on? Look at her phat ass! You gonna tell me you wouldn't have hit that? Shit nigga, I had to break me off a piece."

This ass hole is excited and proud of his actions. He has no remorse, no ethics and no limits. Lorenzo wants to just grab this nasty mother fucker by his neck and choke his ass to death. He fights the impulse. They still need Kevin. He remains silenced in shock.

Kevin continues to run his mouth

"Shit I can't wait to get her fine ass home: that's when the real fun starts. That pussy should be good and ripe in a day or two." Kevin starts to box the air and give Lorenzo light body taps like fellows sometimes do when they are excited and joking. He taps Lorenzo lightly in the stomach and his body speaks what his mouth dares not share. Lorenzo begins to vomit violently, his stomach cramps, dropping him to his knees. It's not the punch which facilitates the response, rather the sight of cum dripping from Nicole's ass.

*(Kenny feels the thud of Zoe's drop as the floor shakes. He comes to investigate)*

"What the fuck! Diss some sick nasty shit. Ya'll mother-fuckers got two minutes to clean diss shit up and get da fuck out'a here. God so help me Kev!" Kenny bites his tongue then stomps back down the hall way. Shit, he thinks to himself, if I didn't need this bitch!

Lorenzo and Kevin clean the bathroom; wrap the dead in plastic then exit the apartment. They put the body along with the head into a large trunk. The two place the box into Kevin's van. Its apparent Kevin can't wait to shake Lorenzo. He tells him

"I got it from here". A friendship of convince has ran its course. Lorenzo will never see Kevin the same way again. He always thought he was a bit morbid but he thought that was just a side effect of Kevin's occupation. Kevin is an undertaker by trade. Lorenzo thinks back on times when he would joke on Kevin. He would tease him saying that he'd better go fuck some dead bodies because nobody else would fuck him. Kevin would always shrug it off by saying "Go head main, Go ahead." Lorenzo shakes his head showing disapproval as a happy Kevin drives away with his goodies. He knows he is going home to continue what he started; fucking the dead.

Now alone Kenny turns his attentions to getting some sleep. He needs sleep. He makes his way to his bedroom and lies across his King-sized bed. He closes his eyes still his mind races. His mind is flooded with past thoughts of Johnny, Nicole and he. He thinks of better days, recalling the way the three of them used to just hang out and kick- it. Kenny was the one that had introduced the two; Johnny and Nicole.

He had met Nicole outside of her dorm while they were attending Hampton University. She was as green to the street life as she was intelligent. The girl was a nerd and a book worm. All she ever talked about was how she was going to be this big-shot lawyer someday. She felt drug dealers were scum and she wanted to do her part in getting them off of the streets. She was so nivea.

She was raised in the suburbs outside of DC. Her mother was black and her father was white. They had made the decision to move there from Kansas City after her father was convicted of molesting this 10 year old girl. This was one of the girls Nicole used to babysit. He was never able to get another job in law enforcement; he blew his brains out in 1994. Eventually the little girl admitted that she had made the whole story up. But that was after the fact. Nicole's parents loved her and raised her as best they could, but they had failed to school her on the pitfalls of life. Johnny was the pit, Kenny's introduction was the push, and Nicole's life suffered the fall.

Johnny entered Nicole's life and everything changed. He put that big-black dick on her and started her sniffing powdered cocaine. Her girlfriends tried to warn her about hustlers like Johnny, but she wasn't trying to hear anything negative about Johnny. She cut all those bitches off. She felt that they were trying to get her to drop him so they could get at him. She was probably right. Her grades started to suffer and she lost all ambition of becoming a lawyer. She dropped out midway of the second semester of her senior year. This was two months after meeting Johnny.

Other girls would joke about it saying that Johnny's dick was so bomb that he could get a girl to quit school. They used to say he had some superstar dick. That's how he got that nickname, SUPER STAR.

If Nicole was hook on his dick then she was reeled in by his cash. He had purchase Nicole a Benz and he would give her at least $ 1,000 a week in spending money. He was just starting to get big money and he was generous with it; when he bought her a small house that was it. She was his and he was hers. She had a full time job in keeping his ass. This was not easy to do as a hoe was always at this nigga like twenty-four-seven.

Back than ballers had pagers and his shit was always blowing up. He had two, one for business and one for pleasure. She was always searching his pockets finding numbers and calling them. Sometimes he would get mad, grab, shake and threaten her, but he would never hit her. Johnny loved her for real. She was different than anybody he had ever met. She made him want to better himself. He would often joke telling Kenny "she is the one; Im'a quit diss shit when I get enough paper and move to the country. Maybe I'll even start a family with her." He would say that he was joking but you could tell that's what his heart's truest desire was.

Kenny's mind switches gears still unable to rest. He thinks of how Johnny used to encourage and push him to finish school. Johnny had always had such high hopes for his little cousin, Kenny. He was the first in their family to make it to college. Johnny was reluctant to bring Kenny into the thug life.

If Kenny's mother had not gotten sick he never would have. She had mounted hospital bills from her battle with cancer. Kenny needed to pay them. He had been shy and introverted but his introduction to the drug life would change that forever. Experience would toughen him; greed would make him a killer.

Kenny thinks back to the first time Johnny took him along with him too re-up. They had rented a car and driven to Florida. Johnny's connection there was this Jamaican named Charles Sinclair.

He preferred to be called Chucky. At the time the movie child's play was big at the box office. The major character of this flick was a psychotic doll also named Chucky. This doll was a serious killer but he had nothing on this Jamaican. He had a reputation for torturing his enemies. His preferred tool of mayhem was a machete. This dude was large and in charge. He was a jet- setting, high- rolling, eccentric- millionaire.

Johnny had cautioned Kenny not to look this man directly in his eyes. Chucky had this peculiar mental tick. He did not like people looking him in his eyes. Kenny remembers thinking how comically strange it seemed that all of Chucky's staffers walked around with their heads down. They were all extremely jumpy and nervous. He recalls whispering to Johnny.

"Who the fuck does this guy think he is; God?" Fuck'em I'll look'em in his eyes, thinks Kenny! Johnny gave him a serious look, one that said; be cool man!

So there they were at his first major score with a maniac. He had made the mistake off looking Chucky squarely in his eyes while Johnny was in another room attempting to negotiate a better price on the product. Chucky's men surrounded him at the table placing extreme guns to his head. They forcefully pushed it down onto the mahogany hard- wood table and held it there. There he was his first time out and his head was on the chopping block, literally.

Chucky summoned a servant and had her to bring him his machete. Kenny remembers thinking. So this is what fear feels like? Still he maintained his composure and eye contact with Chucky; his gaze even intensified. Johnny spoke not and neither did he. Instead he winked his left eye at Chucky. Chucky slammed the blade to the table missing his head by one inch. He then started to chuckle deep from his gut. Chucky's words were to be remembered for a life time.

"Me likes diss bumble clot. Em real! Em not fraid ta look dem snakes in day eye. Em neva turn! Diss da one, em dat sleeping giant." Kenny had passed a test only few could. Johnny asked Chucky if he was down. Chucky nodded indicating, yes.

They finished their transaction than Chucky later took them out for a night on the town. Kenny was now connected. From that day he was Johnny's right hand. He accepted that drama and conflict were just a part of the game. He was proud of his courage that day.

But years have passed and something in him has changed. Kenny's thoughts spring forward to the stickup earlier tonight. That stick-up kid Black had his head on the table once more and he had begged for his life; like a bitch. Why now was he unwilling to wink at death? Had success and family life made him soft?

Tonight Johnny saved him from the executioner and payee for it with his life. Kenny has to make a decision. He has to step up to the life or step off. But now who will get his back? He trusts Lorenzo only because Johnny had. Kenny speaks aloud.

"There must be a reason Johnny never wanted to introduce Zoe to Chucky. But what could it be?" With that thought he drifts into an uneasy sleep. He's mumbles, "real thugs ride or die."

*(It's now 7am)*

# $\mathcal{C}hapter\ 2$ The Giant

## Awakens

Kenny awakes at 12pm. He gets dressed then eats a large bowl of cold cereal. Still, groggy he calls Lorenzo.

"Zoe! What's the word?"

Lorenzo's long pause is an omen.

"I just left Teddy. He said detective Howard told him that homicide ain't pressed about investigating any of the killings.

"That's not good news is it?"

"Naw", replies Lorenzo.

"I heard it through the grapevine Ricky ordered the hit on Johnny as retaliation for Black. I also heard he wants Johnny's turf. That's what the stickup was about, it was a set up. It won't about you at all. They just used you to try to get to Johnny, and Nicole was in on the whole thing.

"Shit! I guess we got a war", says Kenny.

A blue mini-van approaches the corner where Lorenzo and six of Johnny's corner knot- clocker's are chilling. Its doors are ajar. The van speeds up suddenly and its doors open wide. Hot steal emerges.

Lorenzo and the boys scramble, dodging for cover as they unskillfully return fire. Shell casings litter the streets and the passenger compartment of the blue van. Thirty seconds of fury and screams of chaos then the van disappears down the street.

Kenny shouts, "what's happening Zoe" into the receiver of the black with gold trim telephone. Lorenzo returns to the conversation, he's breathing is hard and fast.

"Man those niggas just made a move on Spot Five.

Johnny had coded his money spots. All together there are 8 get big money spots.  There are more but these are the ones Johnny pays the cops protection money to operate. Kenny shows concern as he asks Lorenzo.

"Any kids get hurt?"

*(Spot Five is a playground on North Avenue)*

"Naw says Lorenzo in an uncaring tone." he then tells Kenny he is coming to the spot. Disrespectfully he hangs up the phone while Kenny is still talking. Kenny has a Lorenzo related thought.

"Naw shake dat shit off nigga" he speaks to reassures himself.

*(Lorenzo arrives at 2pm on the head)*

"What took you so long to get here" asked Kenny?

Lorenzo gives him a look which says; who the fuck are you to question me bitch? Then he slyly comments

"Somebody have to put in work! Kenny could see in his eyes where this shit was heading. He thinks to himself. So now every Indian wants to be a chief? I have to act! How would Johnny handle this?

Kenny tilts his head back, cocking it to one side, he smiles just barley then grin just enough to show his gold tooth; the one with the half carat diamond embedded in it. He taps the top of his pack of Newport's packing it. Casually he removes a cigarette placing it in-between his lips. He lights it as he walks towards Lorenzo. He takes a long, smooth pull, removing it as he stops 3 inches short of Lorenzo's face. He is in his face as if he is about to kiss a bitch. Kenny exhales smoke; pauses then speak in a low voice with firm tone.

"Am I yo bitch Zoe? Do you wanna fuck me Zoe? Do you wanna feel my balls Zoe? Cause I was just wondering if maybe you thought the Magic Ball Fairy tapped my shits with her wand and srunk'em. Oh! Oh! I see, may be just maybe she tapped yo's and made'em grow. Kenny steps back. "Let stay clear in diss shit my nigga he exclaims in a loud and angry tone of voice. "I'm number one now and if you want ta stay number two; you better show me some got-damned respect! Now ain't the time to be fuckin with me. He then turns his back to Lorenzo,

"Go ahead Zoe, you the Man? Put two in my head! "I'm Kenny Noble, the badest motherfucka ever; and you remember dat shit, my nigga!" He turns again facing the serial killer. Lorenzo had his guns drawn; his face cold, no expression only soul piercing, stern killer's eyes. Lorenzo slowly speaks.

"Lil nigga you done come up". He then hands Kenny his guns handles first. He does this symbolizing submission to the new pecking order. Kenny is the new King.

"Johnny was like my brother. He always said you were a

34

sleeping giant. He always told me to get your back if he won't here no more. I got your back boss. Now tell me how you want shit to be. Nigga you speak it and I'll bring it to pass. Kenny accepts the gun placing it atop a table. The two embrace in a brotherly hug with the heavy pounding of thug's hands on each other's backs.

"Zoe. Call the heads and tell them we meeting at Sean's mama's restaurant across from the police precinct. I'm gonna call Shona and see if I can lay- low at her grandfather's farm in Ashland. "I gotta keep on the move." Lorenzo goes into the kitchen to fix himself a sandwich as he starts to place the calls. Kenny calls Shona. Shona was his first baby's mama. They broke up after their daughter was killed in a tragic traffic accident. Shona had a nervous breakdown afterward; mentally she never fully recovered from it. She later married a doctor and moved to Maryland. Kenny avoids seeing her as this dredges up to many feeling and memories. To look at her is to see his deceased child. His stomach quivers as her phone rings.

(She answers)

"Hello."

"Hey Shona, long time no see. So how are you? Look. Is Pappy still living on the farm in Chester? He Is? Well check diss out, I need a favor. Can you call him for me? See if I can stay with him for a week or so." Shona is happy to hear Kenny's voice; she still has feelings for him. She tells him she will set it up. Kenny smiles as he hangs up the phone. He then sits back on the couch and rolls a blunt. He hollars to Lorenzo,

"Yo Zoe, I'm bout ta get zooted and watch some Scar-Face. Come on nigga! Let's kick it like some good fellows." They burst into laughter.

An hour into the movie and Shona calls back. She has good news, everything is set. Pappy is expecting him tonight. He thanks her ends the call then gets back to watching the movie. Lorenzo has finished making his calls as well.

He joins Kenny in the living room. The movie is at the part where scar face takes out his boss Frank. Frank is dead and detective Mel starts talking that crazy shit about scar face working for them. Tony tells Mel maybe he can buy himself one of those first class tickets to the resurrection, and then he pops his pig ass. Lorenzo and Kenny stomp their feet and hop about in excitement as they give each other hi-fives.

Dats what I'm talking about, shouts Lorenzo!

Kenny calls out "dat's my nigga, Scar face!"

Then they sit back down and continue passing blunts until the movie is over.

Kenny packs up his belonging and essentials into a huge carrying bag. He then tells Lorenzo.

"Common Zoe let's get the fuck out of Dodge." He then goes to the bar where he gets a bottle containing a clear liquid.

Lorenzo asked him. "What is that?

" White Lightening answers Kenny as he opens it.

"What you going do with that" ask Lorenzo.

Kenny takes off his wave-cap and stuffs it into the opening of the bottle. He lights it and tossing it to the Mahogany bar breaking it. It burst into flames. The apartment ablaze they leave. The conversation is casual as they walk to their cars.

"Shit I can't wait for you to meet Pappy", comments Kenny.

"Yeah," Says Lorenzo as he continues to take long hits from the blunt.

*They get into their cars and set out for Pappy's farm house. Smoke rises to the skies as they exit the apartment complex; two wayward travelers on the road.*

## (Meet Pappy)

The drive to Pappy's farm is long, but the reward of seeing his face will be well worthwhile. They arrive at sunsets. Kenny and Lorenzo emerge from their vehicles. Kenny goes to his trunk removing a heavy blue carrying bag. Lorenzo approaches him asking. "Is that the stuff? Kenny nodes his head upward indicating it is. The two travelers proceed along a gravel path toward the house. It's more of a shack then a conventional house.

Lorenzo comments, "Damned people still live like this? Shit looks more like a slave shack then a house. "Chill nigga. Chill, replies Kenny as they snicker like little kids. They see movement in the window of the house as a curtain moves. Lorenzo jokes Kenny.

"Damned he can't wait to see yo punk ass.

"Yeah, I know and I won't no punk while I was fucking yo sister nigga.

" Go head nigga. Go head nigga calmly comments Lorenzo as they continue to giggle, snicker and joke like kiddies. Kenny gets serious.

"Pappy is a very private man. He don't like strangers an shit. It's a good thing he knows we're coming.

The window slowly rises to a height of 3 inches. The doubled barrels of a rusty, vintage hunting shot gun gently eases thru the open window crack. Its owner's feeble itchy finger trembles on its trigger.

"Easy now Betsy, Steady now. Steady gurl. Let it go Betsy!!! He pulls and Betsy lets off her load. BLAM!!!! Betsy sings a hell of a solo.

Kenny and Lorenzo rapidly drop to the ground.

"Shit! What the fucks' their common thought! Kenny calls out.

"Got-damn-it Pappy! What da fuck! It's me.

A frail old voice calls back from the house. "Who is ya!"

"Kenny! Kenny Noble! Shona's old boyfriend."There is silence then the sound of a cackling Pappy.

"Hee hee hec ! Com'on in hern boys." Kenny and Lorenzo are hesitant but slowly they rise.

"Shit! Got-damn-it", exclaims Lorenzo! He is pissed. He cracked the face of his Rolex watch in the sudden drop to the ground. "Main what da fuck is wrong with his old ass? "Look at diss shit! It's fucked, exclaims Lorenzo as he points to the watch. Kenny has a smirk on his face.

"My bad dog, I should'a warned you about Pappy. He ain't playing with a full deck.

The two continue to the front door where they are met by a still Cackling Pappy. Papppy looks a mess. He is a tall slender man. His complexion is as black as coal, His hair Kinky and unmanaged. All hell let's just say it. Pappy is an all out country assed motherfucker. From head to toe he is a straight bama.

On his feet he has on muddy old boots. He likes to think of himself as a hip thug so he wears his pants low on his hips. The Dollar General Store has a loyal customer in Pappy. The straw hat he purchased there, he wears with pride. Pappy likes to accessorize. He has a fist full of fake gold and diamond rings. All have changed colors and many a cubic zirconia is missing. About his neck hangs a single thin, twisted herringbone sterling silver chain. Pappy grabs a hold of the charm which is suspended from it; he holds it up to Kenny and asks. "Hey dare boy, how ya likes my new Bling Bling? The charm is a wooden cross Pappy whittled himself. Kenny says nothing.

"Hee hee hee; don't hate on da playa, hate da game says Pappy as he continues to cackle. "Ya'll boys comon in and make ya'll selfs ta home." They enter. It's not much but Pappy makes them feel at home. He makes them a down home meal.

### (Dinner at Pappy's)

The three take seats at the kitchen table ready to partake of this meal. At first there is very little conversation as all are famished. They dig in. A predominant sound overcomes the silence; that being the sound of Pappy gnawing at and sucking on a corncob. Lorenzo looks on in amazement. He wonders how in the hell is Pappy able to eat that corn. It appears to him that Pappy only has three teeth in his mouth. He tells himself there must be more? He counts them again. Three that's right, he thinks to himself. He can see two uppers pushed over to the left side of his mouth and one little brown nubby cracked tooth in the center of the bottom row of gums. Get it Gumby, thinks Zoe as he looks to Kenny and smiles. Pappy is now sucking and smacking so loudly that Kenny raises his left eye brow, a look of curiosity says. Damned is all that necessary?

What ya'll young bucks smilings abouts, ask Pappy. The two refugees burst out laughing. Pappy squints his right eye as he struggles to tear at a gravy covered pork chop which seems to have jumped from his plate to his lips.

"Slow down Pappy, cautions Kenny. The food ain't going nowhere." Pappy takes a break; he is winded from the struggle with the pork-chop. He reaches into the bread basket in the center of the table and withdraws a buttermilk biscuit. He wipes the biscuit across his plate soaking it in gravy; than dips it into his drink. This baked good has seen its last day as it meets its fate at the jagged ends of Pappy's three teeth. Slurps the final sound heard as it dissolves in Pappy's mouth.

"Say dare boy." (*Pappy pauses to have another go at that Damned corncob.*) "So ya'll done let dem city slickers runed ya'll outa yall's town? Dats da ways I hear tell. Hee hee hee." He pauses again to acquire another biscuit which he proceeds to dip into his crumb and liquid filled mug. "See dats what happens when ya gets ta'big fer ya britches. See me, Im'a old school playa. Let'ma show ya'll how'sa real pimp does's it. Pappy gets up from the table and shuffles to the back door with his country walk." He says " Lookee-hern boys. Let me show ya sumfin."

He motions to Kenny and Lorenzo to join him at the window; they do so. He points to a large shack about 100 feet to the rear of the house. Pappy built it himself and Pappy ain't no carpenter. It leans terribly and looks to be made of scrap wood and old rust eaten tin panels. Pappy is beyond proud of his accomplishment. Hee hee heck cackles Pappy.

"See dat dares my liquor house dare!" The two thugged- out onlookers attempt to look impressed. They don't want to offend Pappy who's brimming with pride. Pappy continues to ramble and cackle.

"Hee hee hee, hec hec!  Bouts 9 o clock dat baby dare be a jumpin!

LuLa Mae's boy does ma music and I does' all ma cookin an bartendin. Cept'fin when Shona come stay.

"Shit! I could use a drink", interrupts Lorenzo.

"Hee hee hee", cackles Pappy as he tells them, "com'on boys I gots moe ta show ya'll."

Pappy grabs his lantern as he grabs Kenny by his hand pulling him along they exit the house. The three walk into the woods behind the large shack. "Damn Pappy where you taking us; I ain't trying ta gets bit by no snake messing with you." Lorenzo agrees with Kenny. "I know dat's right." Pappy leads them to his steel which is in full production. Pappy shuffles over to the contraption and milks it. He fills a mayonnaise jar with its clear liquid and hands it to Lorenzo. Lorenzo puts it to his mouth and takes a large swallow.

"Wait dare boy" cautions Pappy. He is too late. Lorenzo clutches his chest gasping for air as he coughs forcefully. Pappy and Kenny repeatedly smack him on his back encouraging him to breathe deep.

"Breathe nigga commands Kenny.

" What da fuck is this, says Lorenzo, still trying to catch his breath.

"Hee hee", cackles Pappy. "Dats dares my moonshine. "Hee hee hec hec" he continues to cackle in joy.

"Dat's what's up. Gi'me some, says Kenny as he takes the jar from Lorenzo's hands. Still coughing Lorenzo say,

"Damn main, don't hog it. Gi'me som'moe." The three start the walk back to the house. They take small sips of Pappy's White Lightening as they pass the jar around. The more they sip the smaller and less steady their steps.

# (Pappy Gets Buck)

Now back inside of the house, Pappy rushes to turn the TV on. "All shucks now, ya'll done made me miss most'a ma picture." He frantically channel surfs until he finds his station.

"All sookee now, dat's ma shit!" Pappy loves those rap videos. He starts to do an old man's dance as he watches a rap video. He holds the almost empty jar in his right hand as he starts to do the Crip-Walk. He pushes his free hand palm- up upwards in a repeated motion. Pappy is in step with the beat and not spilling a drop of his moonshine. "Hee hee", he cackles in joy as he begins to break it down. He is now doing the Harlem Bounce.

He calls out, "Com'on young'uns as he motions for Kenny and Lorenzo to join him. These niggas are through; they are now rolling on the floor laughing hysterically at Pappy's crazy-ass. Pappy is buck-wild. The two manage to partially compose themselves as they join Pappy in the center of the room. "Go Pappy! Go Pappy" they chant to the beat of the music. The telephone rings, bringing the festivities to an abrupt halt. Pappy shuffles to the other room to answer it. Lorenzo remarks to Kenny how cool Pappy is. He wishes he had a father like Pappy. Both of his parents are dead; they never showed him much love so he does not miss them. Kenny agrees; Pappy has much love in his heart.

It was Shona; she was calling to see if Kenny had arrived safely. Pappy returns to the room and they all take seats around the TV. Pappy ask to what does he owe the pleasure of the visit. Kenny explains at great detail the events of the past days. Pappy has a look of sorrow about him as he remarks.

"Das to bad abouts Johnny." He loved Johnny like a son. Pappy is fighting to hide his tears. Johnny would come down on weekends to check on him. Johnny used to give Pappy a little uncut powder to twirl for him. It was more so for Pappy. It was never much but it was enough for Pappy to front like he was in power. Honestly, Pappy sucked when it came to selling drugs. He would give most of it away. He would then give Johnny a case of moonshine and say, "Dat should about make us even." Johnny would play along telling Pappy how he needed it for his club and his after hour spots. The truth be told Johnny never cared much for the moonshine business. He had cases of Pappy's nectar stacked in the storage shed of his parent's home. It was mainly Johnny's pop and his buddies that benefitted from this arrangement.

Johnny loved Pappy because he was so caring and full of love of life. Pappy was the father that his could not be. The two would spend hours hunting and fishing. It was Pappy that Johnny went to when he needed advice. Pappy's wisdom was far beyond his tender age. Pappy will be 75 in November.

"So what's ya'll goin ta do, ask Pappy as he stuffs some dried corn husk into his pipe.  Kenny tells him that he has to leave for a meeting later on tonight.  I'll know after that", answers Kenny. Well its ma nap time says Pappy closing his eyes with his pipe still in his mouth; he fades into sleep in his reclining chair. Kenny and Lorenzo follow. A symphony of snores fills the room.

(It's now 9pm)

## (Back to Work)

Lorenzo and Kenny are awakened by Pappy. They prepare for the meeting and Pappy goes out back to the shack to open his club. People are starting to arrive. Lorenzo jokes Kenny as they walk to their cars. "Looks like we about to miss a hell of a hoot-nanny." See you ain't right says Kenny. They start down the road for home.

Home is The Capital City (Richmond). Once the shining jewel

of the old south it's now the murder Capital of the country. Its inhabitants are down-right southern but their mentality is straight Northern. The drug game here is fast pace, and every hustler knows it's about territory. Fuck Ricky and his punk assed pops sings in Kenny's head as he makes his way down the road. 2 pac's *Hail Mary* plays in the Cd changer. It's on repeat. And as the lyrics repeat in Kenny's mind he becomes that Nigga America fears. He sings out loud.

"I ain't a Killer but don't push me....... revenge is like the sweetest chore next ta getting pussy". Listening to The greatest rapper of all times got a nigga ready to grit on his own mama.

Kenny pulls alongside Zoe motioning to him to roll down his window. Lorenzo taps that power window switch and the sound of 2pac exits Kenney's whip flowing into Lorenzo's Acura. Kenny's hands are up, he's steering the wheel with his knee and his automatic peace- maker is out the window. A nigga's shooting for the moon. KLACKCOW! Kenny's letting off with no regard for the civilized world. KLACKCOW!

"FUCK'EM", he cries out like a maniac.

Heads bouncing in unison Lorenzo (Zoe) calls out, "THE WORLD IS MINE!!!!"

*(His Desert Eagle's screeching)*

BLOOM! BLOOM! BLOOM!

Not the one to be outdone, Kenny pushes the speed past the limit leaving Lorenzo in dust.

He slams his foot to the break petal while spinning the steering wheel.

"DAMN! No he didn't", say Lorenzo as Kenny's Benz enters

into a controlled 360. Kenny's Pistol's steadily blazing the night sky while the car spins like a ballerina. The silver Benz exits its spin and continues with grace down the highway: it has a giant behind its wheel and his name is Kenny Nobles. Lorenzo follows closely, two high status Negroes doing a buck ten (*110mph*).

They arrive at the restaurant in record time. Kenny and Lorenzo park on the street then exit their cars. Lorenzo calls out to Kenny as he approaches him standing at the rear of his opened trunk.

"Wild Wild West My Nigga!" his facial expression that of a playful child seeking mischief. Kenny removes the large bag from the trunk and hands it to Lorenzo.

"Damn cuz, am I your bag boy now." Kenny tells Lorenzo that he needs to get serious. He puts on his game face as he places the carrying strap of the bag over his shoulder.

"Zoe it's all about image now. These people were loyal to Johnny and now I have to win their confidence. If they see any weakness in me or conflict between us, we can hang this shit up." Kenny has no smiles or sly grins, just the stone face of a poker player. Its game time and he is ready to play to win. "Zoe if niggas got questions then I got to have those answers." Lorenzo nods his head upward in agreement. The two give quick pounds then they proceed along the sidewalk toward the entrance of the restaurant. They sway hard as they step in unison.

## (The Meeting)

They are greeted by Shawn's mom Miss Cynthia at the door. She is happy to see Kenny; it's been years since she last saw him. Shawn was Kenny's best friend. He was killed in prison while doing a short bit for possession. No one knew the exact details leading up to his murder, but Kenny has sworn he will find the people responsible someday.

They were like brothers as they had been raised as such. Miss Cynthia was his mother's best friend. After her death she became the closest thing he had to a mother. She and Sean were there for him. She pinches then kisses Kenny's cheek. Such a polite boy remarks Miss Cynthia. Kenny can't help but smile just a little bit. Lorenzo asks if she remembers him. She scrunches her face in disgust, frowning as if she smells dog shit. She remembers some nasty rumors about Lorenzo being involved in the disappearance and killing of some local pets around their neiborhood many years ago when he was a small boy. Lorenzo checks the bottom of his shoes. She does not like Lorenzo as a grown man either. His reputation as a cold blooded, heartless killer proceeds him. It seems to her he merely graduated from killing small animals to people.

She escorts them to the back storage room where the others have assembled for the meeting. The conversation is heated as they approach the powwow. Lorenzo enters first. He takes the bag to the head of the table and places it beside his chair.

Silence takes a hold as Kenny enters the room. All speculation and debate comes to an abrupt halt. They all gaze upon Kenny as if he is an up and coming Picasso and they are art critics.

Eight poison peddlers are seated about an old battered table. It's the old folding type that one can find in any church basement or bingo hall. They all fidget as they attempt to make themselves comfortable in the hard folding metal chairs. Kenny thinks to himself then he speaks what's on his mind.

"These ain't comfortable times and right now comfort is a luxury we can't afford." Lorenzo gives Kenny pound as he takes his place at the head of the table. His air is one of stern confidence as he makes eye contact which each of the eight. The ten call themselves the Black Poison Clan.

# (They Are Poison)

*Teddy*: He had Johnny's complete confidence and trust. Its Teddy's responsibility to make the pay-offs to the cops. Poison pays well so confidential information flows directly from the police briefing rooms to Poison via Teddy. His function is vital so it is imperative that he stays squeaky clean. He never handles drugs or guns. Seated next to him is Kee Kee.

*Kee Kee*: She is an all out hottie and a fine ass'd bitch to boot. She controls the second largest housing project in the city. Raven's Crest is grimy territory but she has that bitch on lock. If she was a dude her nuts would be the size of grapefruits. She is the second highest earner for the crew. Too the right of her sits Tony Boy.

*Tony boy*: People also call him Flavor. He bears a striking resemblance to that ugly ass'd washed-up rapper Flavor Flave. It's kind of scary to think that two ugly niggas like this could exist on one planet. He may be butt- ugly but this little black, crunchy, nigga is the top earner in Poison. He controls all the players on Meadow Bridge Avenue. If Kenny loses this nigga's confidence and respect it could seriously fuck up the unity of the crew. All of their profits go into one pot for an even ten ways split. Naturally Johnny's and Kenny skim extra off the top making their take much larger. Seated to his right is Quan.

*Quan*: He holds down Brooklyn Park Boulevard. It's not a major contributor yet but it has mad potential for development as Gentrification is pushing more displace people into that section of town. At the tender age of 20 Quan is the youngest member. He started scrambling for Johnny at Kenny's spot on North Avenue when he was 15. Shorty boy got's mad heart and he is loyal to his core. Johnny moved him up with the quickness. Johnny was like that; he would see potential and encourage its growth. He had sent several kids from the hood to college, expecting very little from them in return. Kenny harbors a minor resentment toward Quan as at times he felt that Johnny placed Quan before him. Quan was Johnny's pet project; he kept him so close to him that he actually started to look and sound like him. Seated to the other side of Quan is his big brother Blue.

*Blue*: Is a pure mixture of brawn and brains. He works from a house he rents from Johnny's dad's uncle on Moss Side Avenue. Poison mainly trades in cocaine but he also dabbles in selling Lady H. He is their sole connection to heroin. He flips big weight and his clientele is exclusive: they are amongst the most powerful and wealthy people in the state. He is an old head.

He used to run with Black's oldest brother Monster back in the days when Monster controlled the North Side. Monster got torn- off on conspiracy, distribution and murder charges back in 1992.

This nigga Monster was the real deal; one could even say he was untouchable. That he was, that is until he kidnapped this judge's daughter. Her subsequent death was a bad break for him as he did not give the order to have her off'd. His people made mistakes and the shit just happened. He took care of them niggas that did it, but that was not enough.

Even his father's political connections could not save him. He had past the point of no return. Monster was tried, convicted and shipped off to the federal penitentiary. He is now on death row. He continues to appeal the sentence as there is proof of evidence tampering.

Johnny was down with his organization, he stepped up taking over after the guilty verdict was handed down. Monsters brother Mike-Mike was second in command, but was too weak to fill his brother's shoes. He relied on Johnny for everything. Johnny ceased the opportunity of the moment; easing Mike -Mike's ass out. He was

Michael Jackson and Mike-Mike was Teto. A superstar was born. *(The eighth member of Poison is Butter.)*

*Butter*: She is an ex-exotic dancer. Her girlfriend owns the strip club she used to perform at. Now she gets much drug money there. Seated next to her is Mr. Cooper.

*Mr. Cooper*: He used to be a middle school teacher in the Chesterfield County school system. He sells powdered Kane and guns from his home across the street from Battery Park. His customers are mainly law- abiding middle class citizens. Mr. Cooper seems out of place amongst this table of outcast peddlers. He is sweating bullets. He's afraid that Kenny may ask him to participate in some real street shit. He is not down to ride but he will if he must. If he could have gotten a note from his mother excusing him from this meeting he would have. He loves the money but he lives in fear of the possible consequences of the life style. Seated to his left is a thin white character, Chad Harrington the 3$^{rd}$.

*Chad*: He comes from old money and is highly intelligent. He holds a PHD from Princeton University in Philosophy and studied law at the University of Virginia. By day he is a successful and respected criminal attorney but by night he is Super Wigga. He is obsessed with the black urban culture; he prefers his music, food and women black. His dress is designer suits and shoes during business hour but in his leisure time he loves to floss. He is platinum down and iced out; his gear is Phat Farm and Roca-wear from head to toe. Baby from Cash Money has nothing on this white boy. He is not the typical fake ass wanna-be- wigga struggling to spit E-bonics. His speech is proper and he is always real. His political connections are a major asset to Poison. Everyone loves him.

The ten are Black Poison and they have the North side clicking. Their motto is. If one falls they all fall. These are times that will test weather this is true.

Kee Kee is the first to jump.

"Johnny's funeral is Tuesday at 12 noon. I ordered some flowers from all of us. Some will go to his mama's house and the others to the Third Street Baptist Church for the service." Kenny thanks her.

He then asks if anyone will be unable to attend. All have made preparations to be in there. They all had special relationships with him and he will be dearly missed. Johnny had come through for everyone at this table at some point. All looked upon Kenny with compassion as they know he is feeling this lost most. Teddy pets Kenny on his hand which is resting on the table and tells him to keep his head up. Kenny fights the urge to reminisce and to share in the telling of tales of his fallen cousin, but now is not the time for that.

He stands lifting the heavy bag from the floor to the table top. The table flexes under its weight as Lorenzo pushes it to the cents. He then unzips it revealing the 20 kilos of pure, uncut, powdered, cocaine contained therein. The members rise from their seats to help themselves to their allotted packets. There is little commotion or confusion as they pack their goods into their carrying cases. Tony-boy has a question for Kenny as he places his 6 bricks into his large backpack. He asks him,

"What da fuck is up and who is beefing with us?" Tony is crude but the question is valid.

Kenny explains to them that Ricky wants to take back the North side for his family. He gives them as much details of the past nights event as he feels they need to know. The members look surprised as Kenny tells them of Nicole's role in setting Johnny and him up.

Butter shouts out, naw not my girl!

Kee-kee sounds off, "That Bitch!" Let me be the one to do her ass!"

Kenny plays neutral not give his approval.

They have no need to know of Nicole's demise. It could only cause strife as she has friends at this table.

Blue ask Kenny for a damage assessment. He in return hands the floor over to Lorenzo who in turn begins to speak.

"So far we have lost four good people. Poo, Shadow, Lar-key and Baby-boy. Johnny's club is temporarily shut down and spot 5 is too hot to work. Those kids getting shot is all on the news and shit so now the cops got mad pressure on them to clean up over there. Dat spot is history." Teddy asks if they knew Chief was found murdered. Kenny and Lorenzo look surprised.

"Damned, not chief", says Lorenzo putting the appearance as if he is saddened by the news.

Kenny's look is genuine as Lorenzo had left this minor detail out. He starts to wonder what else his 2nd in command may have withheld from him. Kenny did not want chief touched without his approval as Teddy and Chief were brothers.

Aw fuck, thinks Kenny to himself. That was a big fuck-up Zoe had made. He tells Teddy that he is sorry about Chief and that those responsible will be found and made to pay. Teddy's eyes are locked with Kenny's; it appears he is buying this line.

He then instructs Teddy to work with Chad on cutting through the red-tape to get the club up and running as soon as possible.

He then tells Quan that until the club re-opens the cop's payoff money will come from his operation. He tells him to take two additional keys from the bag as he starts to write down a series of phone numbers onto a small note pad. He slides the pad down the table to him. There are three phone numbers written on it. Quan ask him what are they for. Kenny tells him that since business is so slow on the strip that they need to open up new markets. He explains the numbers to him.

The first is that of Johnny's major Marijuana connection, the seconds' that of his Ecstasy supplier and the thirds' is Paulette's. She's one of the neighborhood girls that Johnny paid college tuition for. She attends Virginia Union University; she makes a modest profit there, but with Quan's help it could have mad-stupid earning potential.

The surrounding area is vastly unexploited. Kenny is resolved that he will continue to help the students Johnny backed. He had similar arrangements with students at Virginia Commonwealth University and at Virginia State University in Petersburg. If Quan does well with Paulette than he will consider putting him down with the others as well.

Quan is offended by Kenny's decree and he promptly speaks out.

"What the fuck Main! Main how you gonna play me with this small time nickel and dime shit? " Kenny checks this Lil nigga with the quickness.

" Look Lil nigga! I'm given you diss small shit cuz; I think you can turn it in ta some big shit the family can grow from. If your hustle ain't strong enough, Nigga just say so. You know what, on second thought FUCK YOU!  Coop can handle it better."

Mr. Cooper's mouth drops to the floor. This shit is to high profile for him. He drinks the entire glass of water placed before him in one gulp; perspiration is now pouring from his brow.

Quan has a change of mind. He damned near begs Kenny for the assignment.

"Wait, wait, wait! Not so fast, I want it. I want it! He thinks to himself; Shit! College bitches n shit, I'm down.

Kenny tells him, "cool it's yours." He then tells him Tony-boy will help him as needed.

Kenny warns Quan never to question him again.

There is slight tension so Kenny decides to fuck with Cooper a bit just to lighten the mood. He address's Coop who is relieved that Quan accepted. He asks him if he is alright. *He jokes,* Damned Coop I thought you was going to have a heart attack when I said yo name! They all start to laugh. They know Coop is out of his element when it comes to doing front-line shit.

Blue speaks up on Cooper's behalf."Don't worry about Coop, we all know he is down wit da thug- life. The laughter increases.

Coop tries to put on a game face as he tells them.

"Go head now. Go ahead now. I'm not afraid."

But in his heart he knows they are correct. His deepest fear had always been that Johnny would give him an order to do some grimy shit. As the laughter dies down all he can think about is leaving this meeting with his wears.

Blue ask Kenny who will he take with him when he goes to re-ups. Johnny had shared with Blue the reason he never took Zoe with him to meet his main connection.

Lorenzo is offended as he assumes it will be him. After all he is now second in command. Kenny does not answer him, instead he changes the subject. He poses a question to the group. He asks them if they would be in favor of expanding their distribution of heroin. The answer is a uniform FUCK YEAH!

He tells them to give him a month to deal with Ricky and his family, and then they can open-up shop.

He then puts Blue on the spot.

"Blue. I know you and Monster and his peeps go way back but we need to know where you stand.  Shit may have to get bloody.

Blue stands to address the group. He pauses then he speaks.

"Johnny was my Main and Poison is my family."

Kenny tells his crew that the meeting is over and slowly they exit the room. He tells Lorenzo to stay behind. He asks Lorenzo what happened with Chief and why didn't he tell him about it. Lorenzo answers.

"Kenny its like diss, Chief pulled strap trying to protect Nicole. What the fuck was we supposed to do. I thought I told you dat shit."

"Zoe you know you ain't tell me dat shit. So what's up?"

"Damn Kenny, cut me some slack. You know shit been hectic. Shit main. I just forgot."

"Ok Zoe, but we got to stay on point.

Lorenzo agrees saying, "My bad cuz, it won't happen again.

(They give quick dap than its back to business)

"Ok Zoe, this is what we are going to do."

"I'm Listening says Lorenzo.

I'm going to call Mr. Nelson to see if we can smooth this shit over. If he tells his son (*Ricky*) to back off, he will. We have lost Johnny and he has lost a son (*Black*). I'm sure he don't want to lose another; I hope we can call it even."

Lorenzo's facial expressions betray him; he is not feeling this punk shit Kenny is talking. Kenny asks Lorenzo is something wrong. Lorenzo tells him that he wants revenge for Johnny's murder at any and all cost. Kenny can relate as his heart also yearns for retaliations. He attempts to calm Zoe by rationalizing.

"Zoe I'm with you on dat, but we got ta be smart."

*(Lorenzo has an emotional outburst)*

"Fuck that main! What we need to do is fucking kill Ricky's gay ass first, and then we try to make peace with his punk-ass-old-pops! And if he ain't trying to hear that shit then we X his old ass out to! Got-damn-it! What would Johnny do if it was one of us lying on a fucking slab at the morgue? Calm down says Kenny. "Believe me Zoe, I feel you on what you saying but them niggas ain't that easy to get at." Lorenzo does not like what Kenny is saying but he knows it's the truth, he nodes in agreement.

Mr. Nelson lives in a mansion within a gated complex in the effluent Windsor Farm community. He has around the clock bodyguards plus police protection. To get to him would take some mission impossible type shit. Ricky and his remaining three brothers live at the complex and they seldom leave without tight security. Shit! Killing the president might be easier comments Kenny. Zoe's thought, he sounds weak. He sounds defeated. Shit he sounds like a fucking bitch!

*(Lorenzo taunts Kenny; looking straight into his eyes he says)*

"I bet Johnny would find a way."

Kenny springs forward wrapping both of his hands around Lorenzo's neck. Lorenzo does not move, he doesn't put up a struggle or attempt to break free. Instead he just looks at Kenny with those cold Killer eyes of his. Kenny releases his grip dropping back to his seat. Slowly he speaks.

"Ok Zoe let's do Ricky first." Lorenzo nods his head; he is pleased. He can see himself in the reflection in Kenny's eyeglasses. They are one. He sees that Kenny wants to bathe in Ricky's blood as much as he does. Lorenzo asks, "So what's the plan Giant?"

*(Kenny slowly responds)*

"Give me a minute."

"That's a bet", says Lorenzo as he stands then exits the room.

One man remains in solitude, his only companions his heavy thoughts, his mind's set' unsure. He questions the decision he has just committed himself to. One thing is for sure; the future looks grim.

He closes his eyes in contemplation; visions of blood filled streets flow in his mind, like guilty driven nightmares they haunt him. Kenny seeks comfort even relief in the plotting of Ricky's demise. Immersed in a sea of wicked ideals the outer world ceased to exist. He dives deep into the depths of the darkest recesses of his mind. He's searching. The plot escapes him. Ricky seems invincible. But surely every man has a weakness, thinks Kenny!

*"Think harder", repeats, echoing in his head, teasing and inviting a headache. Then suddenly he has it!*

The plot has been hatched. It's a simple plan. The details began to take form with clarity.

To slay a juggernaut one must attack his weakest point.

The obvious way to draw him into the open would be to use his wife and kids as bait; they are more assessable. But Kenny has a heart, he too has a family. This is not an option.

Instead he will use Ricky's secret lifestyle to his advantage.

He had heard some time ago from a credible source that Ricky is on The Down Low.

He is known to frequent this sports bar in the Shoco Slip club district. It's called The End Zone or something like that. At first glance it appears to be a traditional sports bar with all the amenities of a boys club. There are scores of large screen TV's, pool tables and pinball machines. The theme is well suited to pleasing the most avid sports nut. The walls are covered in sports memorabilia and its shelves are filled with trophies and the typical assortment of sports related nick-nacs. The average man would feel at home here.

This is his secret spot, this is where Ricky goes to relax, this is the place he goes to score. He will not be accompanied by his father's bodyguards or his cousins here. This is where Kenny will catch his prey slipping.

Kenny sits in silence grinning and nodding his head satisfied with the plan.

"Umm hmm. I got yo ass now, fudge packer."

*The intricate details are to be worked out at a later time. Danny's cooperation will be vital.*

Kenny exits the room with the hope of re-joining the other in the dining area. All have departed with the exception of Lorenzo and Teddy. The three take seats at a table off to the side of the kitchen and order their meals. Kenny shares his plan with them. The three are in agreement; this is a good plan. Kenny tells Teddy to loan him his cell phone. He calls Sean's brother Boo Peep, who gives him Cheryl's new cell number. He then instructs Lorenzo to get in touch with Danny who will in turn be required to call him. He could just as easily call Danny himself, but he knows of the fear Zoe instills in him. It's this fear that will make Danny his puppet. Kenny is wrapping up loose ends.

He tells Teddy to pick up his Lexus which is still parked a blocks from where Johnny killed Black. He is to sell it and send the money Western union to Cheryl in D.C. He is then to set Kenny's house ablaze.

Cheryl will need the insurance money as it will be sometime before they are reunited. Kenny is pulling out all stops and leaving no clues or trails behind; Johnny had schooled him well.

The three finish their meal leaving a tip of $500.00 for Ms. Cynthia for her courtesy. They then make their way pass the scores of off-duty cops that frequent the restaurant exiting the building. They can't help but smile at the irony of this meeting place as they look upon the hordes of blue uniforms and badges. What safer place could a nigga on the lamb pick?

They bump into Detective Howard outside. They speak briefly in passing. He tells them Ricky has a $10,000 dollar contract on Kenny's head. 10,000 grand buys a lot of enemies and cuts a lot of friendships. Killing Ricky is now beyond personal, it's now necessary. Lorenzo's short fuse goes off.

"Let's go do dat bitch right now", he speaks in anger.

Kenny calms him saying, "Zoe, chill my nigga: Chill. Last thing they need is this crazy motherfucker making a scene in front of the police station. Kenny thanks Detective Howard for the heads up.

Teddy places some love into the palm of his hand as he gives him quick dap. Gangster's love is best expressed in US Mint Green. Kenny instructs Lorenzo to hold Shit down for him as he is going back to the farmhouse to lay low.

*(The three part company as friends)*

# (Johnny's Story)

Kenny is tired and looking forward to a restful night's sleep, but first he must make a quick stop while he is in the city. There is one remaining lose end. He has to go to the Marriott Hotel on Broad Street. Johnny leases the penthouse apartment there. Kenny always found it peculiar that with all his loot, Johnny never bought a house. However this was ideal living for someone as paranoid as Johnny being he could always pick up and relocate at the drop of a hat. He kept a traveling bag packed at all times. He had always told Kenny that if anything serious was to happen to him that he was to take possession of this bag. Johnny never explained to him what was so damned important about this fucking bag.

Kenny had the spare keys to his crib, plus the combination to his safe. He had his cousin's complete trust. The elevator ride to the penthouse seems to take forever, but finally he arrives. The elevator doors opened directly into the penthouse. He steps into the ex-Superstar's domicile. It's so empty. It's so cold, it's so dead. He expects to see Johnny come from the game room to greet him as he had done a million and one times before. But there are no welcomes to be had.

He walks to the answering machine which is flashing 3 messages. He checks them: Two are from Nicole warning Johnny about the stick up. In hindsight they sound like a set-up. No longer does he feel any remorse about anything that they had done to her. *(He mumbles under his breath)*

"Fuckin- lowly- bitch!"

The final message is from Johnny's mom. She had baked some cookies for him and was concerned that he had not shown up. He was a momma's boy and he was never late for cookies and milk with her. He may have been a lot of bad things but to her he was still her little boy. Tears start to flow from the newly re-born giant's eyes. Despite what many may say about drug dealers being the bi-products of broken homes; this was not the case with Johnny.

He was raised in the suburbs and attended private schools his entire childhood. His mother was a respected school teacher and his father was a long haul truck driver. He was closest to his mother as his father's job kept him away from home for long periods of time. He's a kind hearted man who loves his son dearly. Johnny was not bread for the life; the life style just pulled him in. Johnny would spend many of his summer breaks with Kenny's mother who lived on the North side.

Kenny's mom did not work. She lived off of his deceased father's life insurance, social security and investments. She was always so eager to keep Johnny while his parents were at work. She treated him like a son and he treated Kenny like his little brother.

While visiting Johnny would see Monster and his boys driving big cars and wearing flashy, expensive jewelry and clothing. These Katz had the prettiest ladies and fat bank-rolls to boot. Johnny became obsessed with getting all the trappings of the fast life. Monster was a legend and Johnny wanted to be just like him someday. As he got older he spent more and more time around the way. He would cut school and ride his bike to the pool hall on Meadow Bridge where Monster and his crew hung. Monster took him under his wing and schooled him in the game. Johnny went from running errands to look out, to scrambling on the block, to third lieutenant second only to Monsters brother Mike-Mike. Johnny worked hard and made many an enemy along the way, but he had achieved his childhood dream. He became just like him.

So much so he earned the title Lil Monster. Monster himself gave Johnny a diamond cluster- pinky ring with that very inscription engraved. The ring is identical to the one sported on Monster's hand.

*(Kenny wipes tears from his eyes)*

This vacant space cements a harsh reality to his soul forever. His cousin is gone forever, and nothing will change this.

He makes his way to the safe unlocking it. The safe is loaded. He empties it's of its content of cash and jewelry. He is somewhat surprised by the small amount of cash. There is only $15,000. Johnny had to be a millionaire at least 20 times over. The large denomination of the bills strikes him as odd. There is (1) 10,000 thousand dollar note along with (5) thousand dollar notes. Millions of dollars have passed through his hands and never has he had any bill larger than a $500 bill in his possession. He wonders if they are real.

He closes the empty safe and makes his way to the bedroom; sure enough there it is, Johnny's traveling bag. He opens it examining its contents. There is nothing extraordinary: just some clothing, a toss away gun and 20,000 in travelers' checks along with an autographed copy of a book. The book is titled <u>The Emergence of the Poet</u> and is signed by is author, Roe Jay. The bags contents scattered about the bed he overturns the empty bag shaking it vigorously. The plastic padded bottom drops to the bed along with a sealed white envelope. It is address to a Sleeping Giant. Kenny thinks jackpot as he tears it open. His fingers tremble terribly as he unfolds the letter. The letter is short.

*K,*

*If you are reading this then a nigga got caught up in the game. I'm not much for writing so let's do this my nigga. I got 7 million hidden. You are a smart college boy so I know you can figure this out. Follow my clues to the money. The only people care about is you, moms, pops,*

*Pappy and Nicole. I know you always wanted out of the game. I also know the only reason you stayed in it was to get my back. Well either I'm dead or doing life. You have no more reason to play at this gangsta- shit. I want you to keep 5 and split the other 2 evenly between the others.*

*1. Home is where you find the heart.*

*2. A nigga gotta find his heart behind a wall of steel.*

*3. it's at a place we thugs can find the little kid in us again.*

*4. Just ask and you will receive, it's that simple.*

*Giant, if this riddle got you stumped and you have to stay in the game for a short. Here is some heartfelt advice. Trust Zoe only when you need him to kill and treat Teddy and Chief like gold. You need them. The others heads are solid but without leadership they can't hold shit together.*

*I love you Main. And if I'm dead I'll be holding a spot down with your name on it in heaven. Keep your head up my nigga.*

*Your Man,*

Superstar

*A lump forms in Kenny's throat. He takes a minute to compose himself then he re-packs the bag. He turns off the lights and exits the penthouse. He dares not get excited about the money, as he has not a clue as to where it could be. Those clues made no sense at all to him.*

# Chapter 3/ *The country hood*

T he drive back to Pappy's farm is long and boring, he misses Zoe's company. He listens to the quiet storm and concentrates on not falling asleep behind the wheel. The constant barrage of love songs playing on the radio has him thinking of his lovely wife Cheryl. He misses her dearly. Heat wave's <u>Always And Forever</u> starts to play; he finds himself thinking of Shona. This was their favorite song. He shakes his head clearing these thoughts. He can't go there; surely thoughts of his deceased daughter will follow. He wipes a single tear from his eye. He finds himself slipping in to a mild state of depression as he arrives back at Pappy's. The property is littered with a large assortment of vehicles.

It's now 3:00am and Pappy's juke-joint is still jumping. Kenny finds himself drawn to the back shack as music from it fills the surrounding woods. Lula-Mae's boy is tearing shit up. This boy is cutting, scratching and mixing some wicked music. He's got Kenny's head sprung playing all the latest fire (*The smell of weed permeates the air*).

He makes his way toward the entrance of the club through a sea of honies and homies chilling about their cars in the open field. He thinks to himself, Shit! These are some country ass'd niggas. But damned if they ain't got some of the fattest bitches he's ever seen. He notices some of the wanna-be players mean mugging on him like some bitches.

He is approached by four young ladies as he steps thru the door of the club. They run up to him asking him is that's his silver Benz! They want him to take them for a ride. He tells them to get at him later, than he enters the club. Kenny makes his way to the bar where Pappy is working hard to keep up with the demand for his moonshine. Peoples love that stuff! Dudes try to take it raw and Pappy dilutes it with white grape juice for the ladies in a concoction he calls "Rape –Juice".

Pappy spots Kenny making his way towards the bar and starts to kackle,

"Hee hee hec hec! Damn boy is ya backs sa soon?"

Yeah Pappy, you got me hooked on the white lightening, jokes Kenny.

Pappy hands him one of his mixed contraptions.

"Diss herns whats I makes fur da ladies, but seeing as ya needs ta keep a clear head, diss herns strong a nuff fer ya."

Kenny smiles as he takes the drink and starts to take small cautious sips.

Ms. LulaMae comes from the kitchen to Pappy. She whispers something into his ear and Pappy shuffles off behind her smiling and cackling.

A stranger takes a seat at the bar next to Kenny. He smells of cheap clone and is dressed in mixed urban gear from two years ago. He is adorned with the stereotypical assortment of sterling silver rings and big chains. Most notable is his huge NYC charm with large, imitation, diamonds. This clown is flossing like his ass is dipped in platinum. He thinks he's major league. He pulls a weak grip from his pocket attempting to impress Kenny. It looks to be a mixture of ones, fives and tens wrapped in three or four Franklins.

Kenny smiles as he thinks look, at this small time nigga.

The Country thug opens his mouth addressing Kenny with a fake New York accent.

"What's up son?"

Kenny burst out laughing, spewing beverage from his pink lips across the bar.

"My bad dog", says Kenny as he continues to laugh.

Mr. Prank ass nigga continues to address Kenny in an authoritative tone.

"I see you like Pappy's bitch juice! You must be a bitch! Are you a bitch?

This insult awakens the giant which lay dormant; and in an instant Kenny's look changes. His thought. *(No diss country bitch didn't just call me a bitch ta my face!)*

Kenny decides to shake it off and ignore the pest. He wants to enjoy his drink, but farmers John persist on irritating him like a fucking nat.

"The name is Buck, but you can call me Mr. Buck-Wild!"

He then points to a table surrounded by six similar rodeo clowns and three of the buttermilk fed bitches that were sweating him at the door.

He orders Kenny to send them a round of drinks at his expense. Kenny casually tells him to run along and play. Still Mr. Pussy insists on making his presence know. He continues to press his luck, like a fucking Whammy!  He wants to be fucked!

"See my boys and me don't like strangers around here. What's your name sweet thing?"

Kenny has heard enough. The decision to go raw has been made. The giant explodes, grabbing Buck by the back of his head pushing it downward, slamming it to the rough, hard edge of the bar. Two quick bounces and a rotation of Buck's head and Kenny's fully-automatic, chrome-plated Berretta parks right in this ill nigga's big mouth.

Kenny speaks loudly, "Bitch, you wanna get ta know me?"

Bucks boys pull heat and quickly approach Kenny ordering him to let their boy up.

Kenny rants, " Ya'll wanna fuck with Kenny Noble? So ya'll lil dick niggas wanna fuck a giant?

The music stops and silence takes hold of the party. Kenny's name is infamous and smart-niggas don't want any parts of him.

They put their guns away and return to their table. The only sound heard in the club comes from Buck, gagging as Kenny pushes the barrel of his piece ever deeper to the back of this ill nigga's throat. It is a horrible sound.

Kenny is about to do this joker right in front of everyone.  He looks Buck solidly in his eyes as he is about to pull the trigger. He sees no fear, Buck is resigned to dying. Kenny likes that: Buck has heart. He removes his gun and tosses him a bar rag to clean himself. He motions to Bucks boys to come get him. Kenny then tells Buck that maybe they can do some business in the future. His boys help him to exit the club, bloody and barely conscious.

Kenny decides that he has had enough drama for one night. He makes his way to the kitchen area to say goodnight to Pappy. He opens the door of the kitchen to the sight of Pappy standing with his pants down around his ankles. Ms. Lula Mae is on her knees putting in work like a Las Vegas hoe. Her head is bobbing up and down like a well oiled engine piston. She has Pappy's dick wedged in-between her lips tighter than a food stamp in an Ethiopian's hand. Damned, thinks a shocked Kenny. She's got skills; her down stroke is stopped only by Pappy's balls. Pappy is in heaven. She has him so worked up he can't even manage his patent cackle. Her dentures rest on the floor next to Pappy's feet. There is not a hee hee or hec.

Kenny rushes to close the door as he makes his retreat from this den of sin. Damned that shits got his dick hard as a bitch. He can imagine how good Ms. LulaMae's mouth would fill wrapped around his dick. Damned he thinks nothing but gums and tongue, *he smiles.*

He is followed by two of the girls that had approached him earlier as he exits the juke- joint. They catch up to him and ask him when they can get that ride. He tells them right now, and they follow him to the main house.

Through conversation he finds out that the two girls are cousins; the more talkative is a pretty girl although somewhat homely. Her name is Arlene.

Her cousin's name is Shawnetta. She was a somewhat thick girl with a very attractive face. Kenny can tell by their conversation that the two girls are freaks. And a freak is just what he needs most right about now. This is the first time since all the madness started that he is decisive in his thinking. His mind is clear and he knows exactly what he wants.

## ( Sex'n Cousins)

The three enter the house heading directly to the spare bedroom. This is Shona's room when she comes to visit. The door shuts behind them and it's on. There is no need for further conversation.

Arlene steps to Kenny kissing him as Shawnetta slowly kneels at his feet undoing his pants. Kenny undresses Arlene as Shawnetta struggles to get free of her clothes. Shawnetta places his dick into her mouth and starts sucking in a gentle fashion.

Kenny's stroking Arlene's kitten; his hands are at home in her white panties. He loses himself in the sounds of her purring as she starts to cream. He's enthralled in the taste of her sweet kisses.

Shawnetta gags as she mis-calculates his rate of growth. His rock- hard hammer is swollen to its full length of 8 and half inches. His dick she firmly holds at its base, she removes it from her mouth to recover.

Kenny takes his cream drenched fingers from Arlene's hot, juicy pussy plunging them in to her cousin's awaiting mouth.

She rubs her pussy as she sucks Arlen's creamy liquid from this stranger's forceful finger. In a heightened state of ecstasy she moans as she caresses her own breast.

Kenny withdraws his hand from her mouth and with gentle force pulls her soft pink lips back onto his throbbing dick.

(They continue on in this fashion all the while undressing)

Shawnetta crawls to Kenny's rear and starts licking him about his ankles. Her soft, moist tongue slides up the backside of his leg to the crease of his muscular butt. She pauses. She lingers then she kisses and bites. She continues upward, skillfully she reaches around pulling at his dick with sensual force.

Kenny's mind swirls from the multiple sources of pleasurable stimulation.

He attempts to concentrate on the tenderness of Arlene's kiss as she joins her cousin in pulling at his now dripping pole.

Shawnetta's tongue has left a trail of tingling sensations.

She sucks his neck continuing to his ear nibbling and panting. Her soft body presses even closer as she makes her way to his lips.

Arlene removes her sweet tongue from his mouth, simultaneously Shawnetta plunges hers in; kissing him deeply (*She kisses with passion*).

Removing his right hand from Arlene's warm, tiny breast, Kenny thrust three of his fingers into Shawnetta's big, juicy pussy. His left hand remains vigilant in Arlene's creamy tight love hole.

He can feels their desire for him building as the two cousins' are now rocking and swirling their pussies on his hands. He's works them into a frenzy. He interrupts the flow only to allow the cousins to suck the others juices and cream from his busy fingers.

(*This man's excitement is at its peak*)

Arlene pants hard licking his inner ear. His body contorts from the sensation.

Arlene takes this as her cue; rapidly she drops to her knees snatching his dick from her cousin's grasp.

She engulfs rock hard cock deep within her hot mouth. She licks as she sucks. Her technique is not like Shawnatta's. She's not gentle with this niggas dick. She sucks hard, rough and fast. It's as if she is angry with the dick, and Kenny can attest it feels good.

Shawnetta continues kissing tenderly; leaving lipstick trails down his chest as she to works her way down.

She is missing the taste of his dick in her mouth.

She's stopped at Kenny's nipple line by Arlene's cock-blocking hand.

She starts to pinch and suck them.

*(Kenny never imagined that these two freaks could have him shaking, moaning and calling their names like this)*

He is not sure which cousin is doing what. Hell, he doesn't care. The only thing he is sure of is that he does not want them to stop.

Arlene speeds up her strokes applying more suction causing the giant's ass-cheeks lock; his toes curl.

"Shit! Aww fuck," Says Kenny.

Cheryl never made him feel like this.

Arlene applies still more suction and he has to steady himself as his knees are beginning to buckle.

Oh God he thinks. Shona never rocked me like this.

He is lost in sexual bliss.

Shawnettta knows that Arlene is a selfish; she wants to keep the dick for herself.

Shawnetta presses-on downward as she tries to push Arlene's head away from Kenny's dick with hers. They both pull at the dick.

Arlene pulls in her selfish attempt to keep it to herself while Shawnetta pulls attempting to pry it from her cousin's powerful jaws.

She begs Arlene to share and reluctantly she does; they take turns at sucking Kenny's massive manhood.

They are relentless, stopping only to kiss each other, then the tug of war resumes. Kenny loves this shit! He starts to talk some freaky shit.

"Um. "Dat's right girl, show dat hoe how ta suck a dick.

"Aw fuck, she's gaining on you."

He then fakes as if he is about to cum increasing the tension between the two.

They have turned this into a dick sucking competition.

The prize will be a well earned massive wad of thick nut.

Kenny tries too places a mental bet on which one will win but he is too focused on not cumming; he never wants to cum.

He wants this encounter to last forever.

But he fears he is losing as they are wearing him down.

Shawnetta sucks, Arlene pulls, the dick is free of mouths and it explodes.

The girls press their faces toward it with open mouths fighting to capture sperm like little Mexican children fighting to grab candy from a busted piñata.

Arlene has managed to get a mouth full, so she lets Shawnetta

73

catch the remainder as Kenny is still cuming.

He looks down at Shawnetta's who is still nursing on his dick like a new born baby on its mothers nipple.

His nut is all over them. Arlene is rubbing it about her face, neck and chest.

They all start to laugh as Kenny remarks.

 "Damn ya'll some freaky bitches.

Arlene responds, "Yep." Now can we get that ride?

Kenny gives them a rain check.

The three go to the bathroom where they clean themselves up before exiting the house. They exchange phone numbers as he walks them to their car. They tell Kenny they want to hook up with him again; next time they want to bring another one of their girlfriends. Kenny starts tongue-kissing them both goodbye. But little did he know they were being watched. Buck and three of his boys are sitting in a car across the field. His boys taunting him, "Aww fuck! Ain't dat yo girl Arlene kissin dat nigga dat man-handled you in da club?

 "Hell naw kid", exclaims Buck as he crashes his shoulder to the car door opening it. His boy Lil Pimp grabs his arm pulling it in an attempt to detain him.

 "Get da fuck off me yells Buck", yanking his arm free, he exits the car.

He is not thinking; his jealous heart has the better of him. It leads the way as he rushes across the open field toward the three.

Kenny's back is to him and the girl's view is obstructed as they are still basking in the flavor of this players addictive kisses.

Shawnetta calls out as Buck reaches Kenny.

"Look out!" but her warning comes too late.

Buck's fist is air born. It crashes with the force of an airplane slamming into the side of a mountain to the back of Kenny's skull.

Kenny's night instantly turns to day as the blow triggers sequences of bright orange and white flashes of light inside of Kenny's head: it's a kaleidoscope of colors swirling.

Time slows to a crawl as he falls to the ground; his sense of awareness slips away. The hardened earth provides little comfort as his face comes to rest upon it hard. Kenny tries to clear his head; he is seeing orange stars, blue diamonds and green clovers. If this was a cartoon, he would have little birds flying about his head chirping. However the reality of this event is bought sharply into focus by the force of this nigga Buck's muddy boots.

He is stomping a mud-hole in Kenny's black ass. He is stomping his back and kicking his ribs. It's a symphony of whip-ass as more happy feet join in on the session. Kenny is helpless, all he is able to do his cover his head in an effort to protect it. He thinks to himself, if only they would let up for a second, he could reach his gun which is sandwiched beneath him in the waistband of his pants.

The two girls plead with the mob to stop. Arlene screams out, crying I'm sorry as Buck smacks her cheek. The taste of his backhand sends her sailing to the ground; she joins the once again humbled hustler in the dirt.

Kenny prays, Lord help me as he attempts to muster the strength to go for his gun. But it would seem as if it is too late for that. Buck has the muzzle of his pistol pressed to the back of his head.

He should have done Kenny right then and there but instead he wants to play Hollywood-gangsta. He kicks Kenny hard to his ribcage, rolling him over onto his back. Now standing over Kenny, Buck relishes in the sound of his own voice.

"See kid I told you we don't like strangers around here! I bet you thought you was gonna get away with playing me like that back there!"

Buck squeezes his trigger firing a slug into the ground next to Kenny's head. He then continues grandstanding for his boys.

"Now kid I wanna hear you beg for your life."

He fires again piercing the ground at the other side of Kenny's head.

Kenny tells him, "you better kill me you country bitch, cuz yo ass is as good as dead."

Buck and his boys must have thought that was funny because they all started laughing. They taunt Kenny lightly prodding him with their feet. They dare him to reach for his gun.

"Go head nigga reach for it."

They kick dirt into his face as they continue laughing at him. He is in a bad way. Kenny is all messed up!

Slowly his arms respond to his mind's commands to blast these bitches. His attackers look on in amazement as Kenny struggles to muster the strength to pull his strap.

"Dammed Buck! Diss nigga got mad heart."

FUCK DAT NIGGA snaps Buck making a fatal mistake as he turns his head away from Kenny for a split second to grit on his boyz.

Kenny sees his only chance. It's do or die. His fading brain demands his hand to grasp heat and blast. His body complies. KLACKCOW, KLACKCOW, KLACKCOW, KLACKCOW!

That's the sinister sound of the Giant's gun bearing witness to his rejuvenation and deliverance.

Four copper coated hollow point culprits decimate, disintegrating, the center of a silly bitch named Buck's chest.

A dead man's finger twitches delivering his farewell. BANG!

*(Kenny is hit once in the chest)*

Pappy shuffles from the club holding Old Betsy by her neck. BLAM!

She calls to the crowd surrounding Kenny. She draws their undivided attention as Pappy hollers out.

"Last call fer alcohol!"

The cowardly-clowns break across the field running to their cars as Betsy relieves herself of her second load.

BLAM!! Her second barrel packs an extra explanation point.

Arlene and Shawnetta remain vigilant aiding in getting Kenny to the house. He is heavy in their arms as he has not the strength to carry any of his weight. They place him on the kitchen floor as they are unable to carry him any further. A winded Pappy asks the girls what happened. They tell him that Buck shot him. Pappy is relieved; he sees no blood on Kenny. He knows that Johnny was in the habit of wearing a bullet proof vest. He only hopes it's a habit the cousin's share. He rips Kenny's shirt revealing a large slug embedded in the fibers of the thin vest. The girls undo the straps of the armor removing it. This looks bad thinks Pappy. There is a fist sized black bruise in the center of Kenny's chest. He wheezes as he struggles to breathe. They are all relieved that he was wearing the vest.

Pappy tells Arlene to get a cold glass of water as he opens Kenny's mouth checking for blood.

"Looks pretty good in dare. He'll be justa fine. Just got da wind knocked outa hims all."

Shawnetta continues to encourage Kenny to breath.

Arlene returns with the glass of water and hands it to Pappy who takes it to his mouth drinking it.

The two cousins look at each other, their common thought WHAT THE FUCK! He then reaches into his back pocket lifting a flask of moonshine from it. He opens it and pours some of it into Kenny's mouth.

Kenny coughs, gags, and curses, "Got- dam-it Pappy! Is you trying to kill me?"

Hee hee hec cackles a happy Pappy.

"See dare boy ya just fine. Come on get up off fer diss hern dirty flo."

Kenny cries out in pain as the three help him to his feet.

"ARRGHHH!" The beat-down has taken a toll.

They manage to lug him to Shona's room where they place him on the bed. Kenny's breathing improves and the crushing pressure in his chest eases. His body will need plenty of rest to fully recover. A grateful Kenny thanks Pappy for saving his life as he fades away to sleep. He mumbles God is so good.

## (Pappy's Darker Side)

Arlene and Shawnetta remain vigilant at Kenny's side as he sleeps. Pappy takes a missing, he has worked to do. He takes his heavy work gloves and an old shovel which hangs on a rusted hook in the wall to the left of the back door. He exits the house pulling the door tightly behind him.

Cautiously he makes his way across the field looking for Buck's body: the moonlight accenting his course Negroid features. His coal black complexion and beady sunken eyes refract light. The once cheerful radiant glow of life which once was Pappy has taken a backseat to an ominous specter.

If Kenny did not kill Buck then Pappy will.

Old scratch comes to stands over Mr. Buck Wild. He looks for signs of life. There are none. He sighs in relief as he bends over with a wooden match in his hand. He strikes it lighting it on the bottom of Bucks boot. He lifts the fire to his pipe stoking it; slowly he puffs relishing in the flavor of his favorite tobacco.

He thinks to himself, nice boots. "They looks ta be about ma size."

Pappy reaches down wrapping his hard hands around Bucks ankles. He drags the body across the field deep into the woods behind the large shack. Pappy's speaks to himself in a whisper.

"Dag blam fool! Somebody wuz a bound ta kill ya sum day. Ya been hot-head eary-since you'sa wuz a kid." Lookee at ya now. I member ya use ta steal ma water-mellons out'a diss hern field. I couldn't catch ya den, but I gots ya now. Hee hee heeeeee cackles Pappy.

Never in a million years did he imagine he would have the

honor of burring Clarence and Ema Bell's boy. Pappy continues his private conversation.

"I never much liked ya buck-tooth daddy o ya Fat ass momma. Day always thought day was'a better den crazy old Pappy. Crazy I mights be, buts I'm still'a Kickin.

Pappy finds a clearing in the brush and goes to work. He is a hardened farmhand so digging a hole ain't nothing but a thing to him. Pappy labors long and hard. The dimensions of this hole are custom just for Mr. Big mouth.

Pappy rolls the corpse to the hole lining it up just right. He is about to deliver the final push when he recalls that Buck has something he wants. He shuffles down to Buck's feet to acquire those nice boots. It takes a bit of elbow grease but Pappy gets his new shoes. *(He takes a seat on the ground trying them on)*

"Perfect fit", remarks the grave robber.

Pappy's thieving eye is caught by the sparkle of fake platinum. He makes his way to his knees crawling to the rings on Bucks hands. Another three minutes of pulling and he kneels admiring the sparkle of fake diamonds in the moonlight. He continues his treasure hunt plundering Bucks pockets.

"Whoo Weee! Lookee at diss hern bank-roll, says a happy old man as he stuffs the dead man's proceeds into his big pants pockets. Greed has the better of this scavenger; one final Jewel remains. Pappy's grubby hands are ever busy as he pulls at the large NYC charm around Bucks neck. He can't get it lose. He kneels in ever closer pulling at the chain it's self. He can't get it! He rest for a moment with his hand on Buck's breast bone; it's padded like Kenny's.

A rested Pappy has another go at the chain; suddenly Buck's

supposed- to- be dead hand grasp his wrist. Buck fights pulling Pappy toward him with all the strength he can manage; he knows he's on death's doors step. His weak grip lapses and Pappy falls backward, flat to the ground. Buck is fighting to live; unsuccessfully he attempts to get up. A scared and shocked Pappy rushes to get to his feet, using the handle of the shovel like a crutch. His facial expression is that of a kid caught with his hand in the cookie jar. He lifts the shovel over his head swinging it downward, striking Buck in his forehead. Buck is still once more. Pappy cautiously leans forward placing his foot on Buck's chest while getting a good grip on the chain. He braces his foot and yanks hard. The chain is his. He then kneels down to the ground placing his good ear directly over Bucks mouth. His breathing is faint, sparse, shallow and irregular. Still he is alive.

Pappy thinks to himself, what am I to do? I'm not a killer. Then he thinks about Kenny. His decision has been made. Pappy kicks Buck, pushing him into the hole.

Pappy says. "See dare boy, ya messed up."Pappy then fills the hole with a blanket of dirt. He dances a sinister two step as he packs the grave with his feet. Buck has been buried alive. The tranquilly of woods has been disrupted by the sounds of a disturbed old man cackling.

*(The rooster's crow signifies the start of Pappy's day, his morning chores await him)*

*(It's now 6am)*

*(Elsewhere)*

Danny endures a restless, sleepless night. He dreads the call
he must make to Kenny. In these trying times of conflict, surely
Kenny does not want to casually kick the Willie-bo bo. He wants
something from him. Danny attempts to push these thoughts from his
mind, he seeks comfort. He drapes his arm across his loving wife
Michelle; he seeks comfort and security from the warmth of her soft
body. He wishes she had a dick so he could suck it to awaken her. He
has tried to be a faithful husband to her, but in times of stress, it's the
embrace of a strong man he craves. The smell of Polo cologne and the
coarse feel of a man's hairy chest is what he now desires. The softness
of this beautiful lady lying next to him does not fulfill his needs.
Restlessly he continues in the pursuit of elusive sleep.

*(Back at the farm house Pappy has finished his morning chores)*

He sits at Kenny's bedside holding his hand. Arlene and
Shawnetta have fallen asleep next to him. Pappy gets up to apply a
fresh cold compress to Kenny's chest. He notices one of Shawnetta's
breasts is partially exposed. He can't resist the temptation; he reaches
forward stealing a quick squeeze. Shawnetta opens one eye seeing a
disheveled Pappy standing over her. Pappy is quick of mind. "Justa
checking on ya", says Pappy followed by a low "hee hee hee".
Shawnetta closes her eye and falls fast back to sleep. Shit, thinks
Pappy. Were these girls worth this ass whipping Kenny had taken?
Pappy rubs the top of Kenny's head and says good night turning off
the light. He exits the room leaving the door ajar. He then retreats to
his bed room to get his maximum 5 hours of sleep. He never sleeps
past noon. These are Pappy's golden years and he hates to miss a
second of them.

## (Danny's Dilemma)

Kenny awakens as the sun begins to set. He grabs his ribs in pain as he struggles to sit upright in the bed. Arlene hears him and enters the room to help him.

"What the fuck happened to me", ask Kenny.

His memory of the beating and the shooting is foggy. Arlene fills him in revealing to him the names of his attackers and the location of their chill-spot.

"Fuck! Now I got to deal with these crumb ass niggas, thinks Kenny.

He asks her to hand him the cell phone which rest on the night stand. Johnny's written words play in his head like an old scratched record. Trust Zoe when you need him for a killing. Its Lorenzo number he dials first. He answers on the second ring.

"What it be like K?

" Kenny tells him to get Kee- Kee and Quan and to come to the farmhouse.

Arlene's face shows concern, after all some of the niggas that jumped Kenny are her people. She had no idea how extra special Kenny's shit was when she was running her mouth earlier. She can hear Lorenzo. He is excited. He lives for conflict. One could even say it makes his dick hard. He has come to enjoy conflict and looks forward to killing. He could tell Kenny was fucked up just by the tone of his voice. He tells Kenny they will be there in 2 hours, ending the call. Kenny thinks to himself; I'm lucky to have Zoe.

He then checks his voice mail. There are 3 messages marked urgent, from a worried Danny.

Kenny asks Arlene to leave the room; he does not want anyone to hear the conversation between he and Danny. He calls Danny at home. His wife Michelle answers the phone.

"Hey boo boo, is Dee in? She giggles as she places the phone down to go get him. It takes him a minute to make it to the phone as he was down in the basement lifting weights.

"What up K?"

(*He sounds nervous*)

"I got stupid drama. Ima need yo help to set shit right."

" I'm here. What'chu need?"

"Black's little brother Ricky needs attention. I need you to get close to him."

"What you mean get close? You know I can't get involved with no killing and shit."

" Dee. You know I ain't trying to put you in no real shit. I know you square."

"Solid. So what you mean get close to this dude."

"Danny you know what I mean. I know how you get down."

"Kenny what are you sayin main?"

"Nigga I know you like men!"

"Naw cuz . I don't get down like dat. You know me playa. I'm strictly about the ladies."

"**I** tell you what nigga. I aint got time for no fuckin games! You don't wanna talk straight then put Michelle back on da mother-fuckin phone!"

" OK! OK! Chill nigga. Chill. Ain't no need to go dare. Shit, you want her to divorce my ass? What you need me to do?"

" Dee all I need is for you to make friends with Ricky. Do whatever it takes to earn his trust. Shit nigga, play ball, shoot pool and whatever the fuck eles ya'll niggas do. He hangs at the End Zone down in Shoco Bottom.  He goes there just about every Wednesday around 8pm."

" Dats it? Dats da big favor? Shit I thought cha wanted me to kill somebody or some shit like dat."

"Naw Dee. We just need ta get Ricky alone, to talk to him."

"Did he have Johnny killed."

" Naw. Dat was about some other shit. We took care of dat already. But the word's out his family wants the North Side back. We ain't strong enough to go heads- up with them. They too major league for dat. I wanna work a deal so Poison can still operate here."

"I got you main, I can do diss."

"Dee, One last thing. Don't let him know you down with me or poison. Zoe is going to bring you some money for your trouble next week. Oh and I need you to skip Johnny's funeral."

"Why?"

"Those niggas we dealt with might come back on us at the funeral. We can handle them but I can't risk anything happing to you. If you can't get Ricky's trust poison is history. Feel me?"

"I won't let you down."

(*The conversation ends with Kenny's thanks*)

Danny is relieved and excited. He had seen Ricky at the gym

once or twice with his wife. He wanted to approach him then but he didn't want to blow their covers as they were both with their wives. Danny's mouth starts to water as he thinks of Ricky. He sees Ricky as a fine nigga. He is 6 foot 1, 195 pounds and built like a Mack truck. To him he is the entire package: rock hard abs, biceps, and thick cut chest with a round firm ass to boot. He is always immaculately groomed and smells of Polo cologne even after a hard work out. He has that thug look down to a tee; there is nothing feminine or gay about his appearance.

## (The Broken Heart)

Kenny looks to the vintage alarm clock which sits on the night stand beside his handguns. It's 5:30pm.

He calls to Arlene. There's no answer. He calls out once again.

Arlene enters the room with a tray of breakfast food. It's apparent to him that the cook is lacking in her culinary skills. There are burnt eggs and smoke links on the plate. The toast is singed; it has been scraped with a knife and smothered with butter. The most appealing item on this menu is the tall cold glass of orange juice. Kenny takes it to his nose savoring in its fresh smell before drinking of it. It has pits in it but still it's refreshing to Kenny.

Arlene takes a seat next to him on the bed. She looks into his eyes seeking approval as he lifts a folk full of the eggs to his mouth. He chews them slowly as he cuts a piece of the sausage with the edge of his folk. He looks to Arlene giving her the approval she desperately needs. He is deeply touched that a near stranger could show him such genuine and sincere concern. He eats every morsel, leaving only black toast crumbs on the plate.

Kenny stares at Arlene as she rubs his nearly naked body with muscle rub. Her hands are firm yet tender as she massages his broken body. She has a worried look about her face. Kenny asks her if she is OK and if there is something he can do to repay her for her kindness. He will move heaven and earth to do so. Arlene hands stop moving and come to rest a top his stomach.

She speaks in a meek voice. "Kenny it's not right what they did to you. You didn't deserve that. I feel like what happened to you was my fault. I should have known Buck was going to do something stupid. I hate his ass! He was so mean to me. I wanted to break up with him so bad. But every time I tried he would beat me and put his gun to my head. He was always threatening to kill me. He didn't care who was around or where we were at. I remember this one time, he beat me so bad he almost did kill me.

We were at this cook out at his aunt Mandy's house. He had gotten drunk and started to show off in front of his friends like he always did. I was just talking to my little cousin Jimmy when he threw me to the ground and started kicking me. He said that I had flirted with one of his boys than he accused me of fucking my cousin. He picked me up by my neck choking me and punching me in the face. He wanted to kill me. His eyes, his eyes were so- so cold. Tears start to roll down Arlene's face. She is mentally reliving the ordeal. She struggles to form her words as she continues to speak.

"He told me that I belonged to him and the only way I would ever be free of him was over his dead body. God forgive me Kenny, but when you had that gun in his big mouth I was praying you were going to pull the trigger. People around here are so afraid of his ass; but not you. You made me feel like I could be free again. I thought you had taken his heart. I felt I could be safe with you. I should have known it couldn't be that simple. Buck is crazy.

Kenny reaches forward wiping the tears from Arlene's eyes. She leans her head forward bringing it to rest on his chest. He rubs and pets Arlene on her back telling her she is safe now. Killing Buck

87

has place yet another blemish on his soul, but this is one he proud of. He feels like the noble knight that saved the princess from the evil dragon. It's a good feeling.

Suddenly and unexpectedly Arlene sits upright and starts pleading with Kenny. Her little cousin Jimmy was amongst the mob that had stomped him. She begs Kenny to spare him. She had overheard Lorenzo ranting about killing people during their conversation. Zoe has a big mouth; one does not have to be on the phone to hear what he is saying. You just have to be in the room. Arlene had gotten an ear full. Words like bitch, kill, fuck'em and die seemed to compose the majority of Lorenzo's vocabulary. Arlene is afraid for Jimmy.

"Kenny this is entirely my fault, please don't hurt them. They are all just young and dumb. Buck kept them under his thumb. Please Kenny, please just let it go. Do whatever you want to me." Tears stream from her regret filled eyes as she places her hand into the opening of Kenny's boxers removing his dick. Rapidly she puts it into her mouth sucking it. Kenny's eyes roll to the back of his head from the pleasurable sensations. He thinks to himself, this is some sexy shit! Arlene's crying and begging has him feeling like a King. For a moment he finds himself feeding into the sense of power she is giving him.

## (The Heart Twist)

His hands move to the top of her head pushing it downward. He forgets his pain and hers as he raises his ass from the bed pushing his cock deeper into her accommodating mouth. Kenny thinks to himself, this feels so fucking good, but at the same time he feels bad. Arlene has low self-esteem. Kenny attempts to pull his dick away from her while using both hands to lift her mouth from his happy, pulsating dick. His tone is firm, warm and compassionate as he speaks to her from his heart.

"Stop baby. STOP! You don't have to do this."

Still crying she tells him that she must do this so he won't kill her cousin.

Oh my God, thinks Kenny. What has this nigga Buck done to this girl? Her head is all fucked up. Arlene continues talking crazy.

"Please Kenny let me do this for you. Let me make you feel good. It's Ok if you want to hurt me. I'm a slut, do whatever you want to me."

She presses her head forward while pulling his dick toward her mouth like a hungry dog.

"Please, please Kenny she wines, still crying.

He tries to resist but he is only a man. This shit is turning him the fuck on. This lady is fighting him to suck his dick. She is so sexy.

"You want to fuck me in my ass? I'll lick the shit off of your dick. I'm yours now. I deserve to be treated like the nasty bitch I am. Please don't hurt my cousin Kenny."

Morally he slips; damn-it he can't take it anymore. He forcefully clutches the back of her head ramming the whole of his dick to the back of her throat causing her to choke. He is fueled by the sense of power over her she has willingly given him.

Kenny has been transformed into another type of man; she continues to suck.

He's no better than Buck. Foul words began to surge from his mouth; surely this is not him speaking, he thinks as words form.

" Dat's right you nasty hoe. Suck it. Suck it you lowly bitch! (*He pumps with force*)

"Is this the way you want it. Hun! Is this the way you need it bitch!

Arlene attempts to escape his grasp as he rams her head down forcing his dick even deeper down her throat. She gasps in vain for air.

She has turned him into a monster. Kenny releases the vice like grip he has of her head allowing her to make her retreat. He roars out as his dick explodes releasing his hot lava on to her face as he pull from her mouth.  He spews his juices about her face making sure to squirt some into her eye. His hammer continues to ejaculate jumping jism on to his stomach.

Arlene diligently laps the nut from his navel like a thirsty dog.

Kenny is disturbed by the sight.

She has a look of contentment about her face. This woman wants; no she needs to be treated like shit.

### (Let's Fix Her Heart)

Kenny has returned to his senses. He could never understand why people stayed involved in abusive relationships, but now he has insight. It's the sense of power that comes from a false sense of control some grow to crave. Arlene is addicted to the drama and holds all the power in that she is the one in control. She had made Kenny the villain and herself the victim. She has made Kenny feel dirty; she has made him act in a way which his mother would never approve of. It takes a punk- bitch to abuse a woman. He has been victimized by Arlen yet he feels sorry for her. She is addicted to the verbal and physical abuse.

Kenny must reassert himself as a good man. He tells her, "come here babe", pulling her confused face towards his, he plants a tender kiss on her forehead. With understanding and kindness he speaks to her heart.

"Babe girl we gonna get you right. You're a good person who deserves to be treated with love and respect. You had me caught up in a world of abuse with you for a minute but I promise you it won't happen again. I don't want that type of power over you . Babe you have the control, but first you have to know it in your heart that you have worth. From this day on you don't have to ever worry about a motherfucka disrespecting you or putting his fucking hands on you again.

We gonna get you strong. Im'a put you down with my sure-enough dime- piece Kee Kee. She's gonna school you. Im'a take you to a whole new level; if dats what you want. But babe I can't give you cousin a get outta jail free card. It's just not that simple. I wish you had told me the real deal before I talked to Zoe. Shit! They'll be here soon and I can't be no punk in their eyes. I gotta put a hurting on him, but I promise you I won't kill him.

Kenny sees an opportunity here, one which can benefit Poison. Arlene feels and understands every word Kenny has spoken. She puts her trust in him. This drug dealing killer has opened her eyes to the possibilities of what she can be. She feels she has worth for the first time in twelve years.

The bedroom door slowly opens and Pappy peaks his head in to the room. " Hee hee hee! I sees ya's up an abouts. Kenny is sitting on the edge of the bed and Arlene sits astride his back massaging his shoulders.

Pappy places one foot into the room dangling it in mid air, showcasing his new boots. He then retracts it remaining concealed behind the door. He then places a hand through the door wiggling his fingers showing off his sparkling new rings. Twinkle- twinkle says

Pappy, cackling once more. He withdraws his arm, concealing himself once more.

Suddenly with a quick hop, Pappy lands in the room in full view of his two house guest.

"WHAT THE FUCK", yells Kenny and Arlene in unison? They are in shock.

There stands crazy ass'd Pappy, wrinkled beyond belief. If it were not for Buck's boots and his oversized adult depend he would be buck ass'd naked.

Pappy's visitors struggle to contain themselves, but Pappy ain't making it easy on them. He is now dancing about in a circle like an Indian dancing a ceremonial rain dance.

They can't take it anymore, hysterically they burst out laughing.

Kenny pleads with no avail to Pappy, begging him to go and put some clothes on.

Kenny's bruised rib cage burns with pain; each laugh wrecks his battered body.

Poor Arlen falls flat to the bed covering her face with a pillow in a feeble attempt to block out Pappy's antics. There is no escaping the madness of this crazy old thing unknown as Pappy.

Pappy's Prozac has not kicked in yet, he is unchecked and wide open. His doctor has warned him about mixing his medication and moonshine, but Pappy has to do things his way. He usually calms down about 6 pm and although rather disturbing he is completely harmless.

Pappy starts talking none sense. "See hern boy, whats da

Easter Bunny left under ma pillow last night."

He holds Buck's NYC charm up for Kenny to see. Arlene peaks from beneath the pillow seeing the charm. This angel of an old man has given her closure. If Pappy holds that dammed charm then Buck has to be dead. There is no need to see his dead body.

Suddenly, Pappy hollers out, my bacon and shuffles out of the room. The smell of burnt grits saturates the air.

# *Chapter 4/ Revenge*

K enny regains his composure then makes his way to the bathroom. Arlene accompanies him assisting him in bathing and dressing, the process is slow.  She then helps him to the front porch where he waits for Lorenzo, Kee Kee and Quan.  Hurriedly she kisses Kenny on his forehead as she is rushing off to work, she is late. She promises Kenny she will return later on to take care of him. Arlene is a certified nurse. She digs into her purse handing him a bottle of pain killers then she leaves.

Kenny remains sitting on the swing bench. He ponders how he will deal with Jimmy and Bucks little flunkies. According to Arlene they hang at a dive about four miles down the road. It's a dump called Mandy's Café. Its proprietor is a broken down old maid named Mandy. The café is just a front which her nephew Buck uses to run his crooked crap game and sell his low quality drugs, he operates from the back room there.

Pappy used to trick with her until she stole some money from him. A year ago Pappy had been badly beaten and robbed of the drugs which Johnny had given to him to sell. Arlene had told Kenny that Buck had told her that he had done it at Mandy's request. Pappy had never told Johnny about it. He knew Johnny would have killed Mandy and anybody close to her. Johnny's love for him was that deep.

A dressed Pappy opens the creaking screen door. He's peeps his head out looking for Kenny, and then steps onto the porch, making his way to Kenny. He takes a seat next to him. They both sit leaning forward with their elbows resting on their knees with their hands clasped between their legs. Kenny asks Pappy why he never told Johnny about Mandy having him jacked. This is a soul felt conversation.

*(Pappy answers)*

"Well I didn't wants ta be no bother ta nobody. Mandy's a good gale, she just gots sum problems is all. I didn't much fret bouts da money, and wells as fer da whippen. Well let's say old Pappy is'a just a like a Timemex watch. I takes a licken an'a keeps a rite on'a ticken. Doe I must'a say dat gale hurt ma heart sum'fin bad. Dem dare youngons tooks ma dear Emma's rang." Emma was Pappy's much younger wife of twelve years. She had passed away from breast cancer about three years ago. He wore her wedding ring on a string about his neck to honor her.

Kenny asks Pappy to describe the ring in great detail. He wants to repay him for all of the Kindness he has shown him; if he can get that ring back it would make Pappy so happy. Kenny had yet another reason to straighten shit with Bucks punk assed boys. He stands telling Pappy he loves him.

*(Lorenzo arrives right on time)*

He exits the car to help Kenny. Kenny attempts to put up a front. He does not want Lorenzo to know the severity of the ass whipping he had endured. Surely he would go off on a wild -ass killing tangent.

Kenny tells Zoe that they are just going to talk to these little niggas. He tells Kee Kee and Zoe they are to follow his lead to the letter. They arrive at Mandi's Café with the quickness. They help Kenny to exit the car. Kee kee and Lorenzo await Kenny's instructions with the discipline of seasoned soldiers. They are ready for combat.

"Listen up", says Kenny. "Im'a go in here first an order something to eat. Let's see if these bitches got issues before we do anything. Give me ten minutes then ya'll come in. If any of them nigga's got gun in hand ya'll blast'em! If them bitchs scared and ain't made a move then just be ready to follow what I say do.  Shit be ready ta get medieval in dat bitch." *Kee Kee and Lorenzo have on their body armor and are ready to go.*

Lorenzo readies his street sweeper, making it hot; no safety and finger on the trigger. This is a serious piece of old school hardware, extremely deadly and hard to come by. The government band commercial sells of this gun back in the mid 90's. It placed similar restrictions on the Uzi and A-K47. But make no mistake about it; this is the piece of steel which had police officers cowering in their cars all across the nation. The routine traffic stop had taken on a new meaning; unfortunate was the cop unlucky enough to come up against this monster. He would definitely be having a fucked-up day. A nigga holding a street sweeper holds the power of a small army in his hands.

Kee Kee pops clips into the two Uzi's, which weigh down her decorated, well manicured hands,. She is ready for whatever.

The three embrace in a quick hug saying, "Poison till we die." Kenny slowly makes his way to the door. His walk betrays him. It tells of the effectiveness of the brutal beating he had survived. His walk is not that of The Giant they have come to know. This is the walk of a broken man, his stride unsure, and his steps unsteady. The two Heads fight the urge to run amok killing everybody in the café.

Emotions like compassion and traits like restraint are all too often alien in the game: but revenge and malice wait in the parking lot as ordered.

# (Mandy's Café)

Kenny struggles to opens the heavy door of the café. He enters cautiously making his way directly to the counter where he takes a seat. Mandy is working the counter. She approaches him asking what she can get him. Her attitude is nasty. It's occurs to Kenny that niggas have filled her in on shit. He is correct. Mandy thinks to herself, how dare this nigga , my nephew's killer come in here? How dare he expect me to serve him? He has some gall!

A plan forms in Mandy's air filled head. She's resolve; whatever this nigga orders will be laced with rat poison.

Kenny orders a black coffee with no sugar or cream. Mandy strains her face maintaining a fake smile. She makes small talk as she writes the order onto her pad.

"Say cutie, I have not seen your handsome face around these parts before. What's your name babe? Kenny responds with arrogance, "Kenny, Kenny Nobles. But my friends call me Giant."

"Giant, that's such an odd name for one such as cute as you. Hee hee she giggles, placing her hand over her mouth attempting to cover her teeth(Mandy's grill is all jacked up).

Kenny thinks to himself. I know this skinny, old pale, bucktooth; baldhead bitch ain't trying to holler at me. He is not interested in the least. However what he is interested in is the ring on her finger. It's Pappy's beloved wife Emma's wedding ring. It's also proof positive that Mandy was behind the assault on Pappy. Kenny adds a plate of steak and potatoes to his order. He tells Mandy to be sure to bring him a sharp knife. She giggles and heads to the kitchen area to her rear.

Kenny texts Lorenzo in the parking lot. "Zoe change in plans, Come in the front in five minutes." He then makes his way to a booth off to the side of the café. The view is better from here; he has a clear view of the front door.  He entertains himself by reading the menu. There are a series of short poems printed on its back cover. Kenny thinks to himself, the author of these poems sucks. Every poem is written about the author, there is no range or depth in any of them. He flings the menu to the floor. "Shit! He thinks, I hope this bitch can cook better than she writes. The author is Mandy.

Bored he becomes impatient; his thought, "Where the fuck are these niggas. Just then five young men enter the café, It's them. They take seats at the counter. Mandy rushes to them whispering, she has dropped dime on Kenny. Immediately they approach Kenny at his table standing over him in a grimacing fashion; saying nothing. They have Kenny boxed in.

Kenny smiles; asking them if one of them is Arlen's Cousin Jimmy. Jimmy takes a seat across the table from him in the booth. Kenny tells the others to slowly take out their guns and to place them onto the table. They start laughing.

The biggest of the five has an outburst!

"Shit! Diss dat bitch dat killed Buck!

Four more Heberts approach the table. They think they have Kenny right where they want him.

Kenny places his hands atop the table; he holds a hand-grenade: its pin he casually flicks to the floor at their feet. All are quiet, he has their undivided attention.

"Look lil niggas. It's like this, either I let you clowns get paper with me or I gotta kill ya'll. Either way this town now belongs

to me. He asks who was second to Buck. Jimmy is quick to answer.
He says it's Lil Pimp.

Kenny then asks the group if they are down to make some real money. They all nod their head indicating yes.

"Where is Lil Pimp?" asks Kenny.

They are all silent, they are afraid of him. All with the exception of Jimmy who gestures with a quick cut of his eyes indicating that he is in the kitchen, Kenny smiles. Mandy is approaching the table with his food.

"Solid Lil nigga's, now get da fuck outa my face so I can eat. He tells Jimmy to remain seated.

One of the original five makes his way straight to the kitchen. Kenny smiles again, he anticipated this. Mandy places the order on the table before him *(the live grenade he conceals under the table once more)*. Mandy winks at Kenny telling him that she put her special touch on it just for him.

*She Adds* "I even cut the steak just for you sweetie."

*She crinkles her nose like the little rat she is, then she giggles.*

" Hee hee hee." *Contempt is written all over her face.*

Kenny places the live grenade atop the table releasing hold of it. The countdown has begun. He grabs Mandy's hand holding it to the table. He then takes a hold of the sharp knife slamming it to the table; chopping Mandy's pinky and ring fingers off.

The countdown continues as he grabs the grenade tossing it across the café into the kitchen area behind the counter. KABOOM! So much for Lil Pimp and that telling as nigga.

Jimmy is frozen in admiration, Kenny has mad juice. He

thinks to himself, Shit! This is some action movie type shit! Fuck, Scar face, Nino Brown and the King of New York. The Giant stands tall above all grabbing Mandy by her long neck forcing her to take a seat; his gun caresses her puckered-old cheek enticing her to partake of her own cooking.

Kee Kee and Lorenzo enter the café brandishing their guns.

"AWWW SNAP" exclaims Lorenzo as he rushes over to Kenny.

Kenny tells Lorenzo to chill. This is a personal matter, one which he can handle on his own. Kee Kee remains at the door; ain't nobody leaving unless Kenny says they can. Lorenzo takes position to the other side of the café. They have shit on lock-down. Kenny suggests that all put their hand behind their heads. If they see any movements  Zoe and Kee are going to turn this into a blood bath.

Speaking of blood Mandy is bleeding profusely from her hand. She wraps her apron tightly about her hand in a futile attempt to stop the bleeding. Kenny demands that she start eating. Mandy is distraught, she shakes her head no indicating she will not eat this special meal which she had intended for Kenny. She is crying like a grieving widow at her husband's funeral. Kenny taunts her. "What's da matter Ma? He gives her to the count of five to start eating, threaten he will "blow her fucking head off". He counts backward; at two Mandy begins shoveling food into her mouth. He is not satisfied until she has emptied the plate.  He orders her to get the fuck up and out of his café *(Kenny motions to Kee Kee to let her pass)*. Mandy runs past her crying and gagging, the rat poison is taking its affect.

## *(Niggas Step Up To Get Served)*

Kenny turns his attention to Jimmy. " Lil nigga you had better thank God for your cousin Arlene. It's because of her all ya'll motherfuckers still alive. Now this is how we gonna do it. You gonna work your way around the room and tap every motherfucka who laid a motherfucking hand on me. Kenny calls out to all who are tagged to assemble in an orderly manner in a single line. Everyone else is allowed to leave.

Nine of Buck's boys stand in a line, they look unsure of their future. Kenny is in Giant mode. He reaches deep into his pocket withdrawing and placing a set of heavy brass knuckles on to his hand.

Niggas step up to get served as Kenny averages two to three well placed blows to their faces. He is exhausted as he finishes the ninth nigga off with six vicious punches. There was something about this kids mug he didn't like. He bears a striking resemblance to Dirty Black. The Giant has left a path of broken or bruised noses and jaws, still one remains.

Jimmy had neglected to place himself into the line-up. Kenny turns to him gazing deeply into his eyes. He speaks from his kinder side, he likes this kid.

"Jimmy, I promised yo cousin I would not hurt you, and my word is bond. See dat nigga right dare? Dat's my for sho-nuff-certified, bad assed nigga Zoe."

Lorenzo places his shotgun atop the counter and makes his way to Kenny standing toe to toe with Jimmy. Kenny nods his head upward toward Lorenzo taking two steps back.

 Lorenzo steals Jimmy hard sticking him in his jaw. He's dancing with his guard up. Kenny commands Jimmy to defend himself. He yells to Jimmy to earn his respect. Lorenzo is a skilled boxer and street brawler. Jimmy puts forward the best effort he can muster, but Lorenzo is simply more than he can handle. Lorenzo dances to the left, his right hand circling, switching direction he repeatedly strikes Jimmy with his left hand at will.

He taunts Jimmy. "Say what, say what!" Moving in close he racks the boys ribs like Rocky pounding beef at the slaughterhouse saying, "What you know about dat Lil nigga!"

He continues to circle shifting direction at will serving a barrage of left and right hooks, upper cut and the occasional elbows. Lorenzo is pounding his ass like an African pounds a new drum.

Kenny shouts out! Damn, Jimmy keep yo left up! "

This is brutal, Lorenzo's hardened blackened knuckles are covered with Jimmy's blood; still this kid won't give up. His blooded face starts to swell. Kenny looks on in admiration of Jimmy's courage. He calls his pit-bull off;

"Zoe dats enough!"

"AWW FUCK CUZ! I was just warming up", jokes Lorenzo. He then helps Jimmy to a seat at the counter.

Kenny feels a need to make an abbreviated speech. This is something he had learned from Johnny. It's just as important to have a big voice and words as it is to carry a big stick. The size of his stick is no longer in questioned in Ashland.

"Attention Lil niggas! From this day on ya'll foot soldiers in my organization! We are Black Poison! If one falls then we all fall," he then points to Kee Kee. "Diss sexy, sweet looking lady is my sho- nuff down to ride dime piece Kee kee. She's gonna school ya'll country niggas in how to get big paper; from now on if you doing any business it's though her.

Kenny walks over to Jimmy and places the half of a Key of cocain which he had concealed under his shirt in front of him.

He continues to speak loudly. "Cut it, cook it, sell it! Kee Kee will square up with ya niggas on ya'll cut. If you need legal help Kee Kee gonna see ya'll straight. We got people to handle shit like that. My name is Kenny, my friends call me Giant. But ya'll nigga's don't know me. Ya'll got dat?

They all nod their heads indicating yes; he then walks over to Lorenzo placing his hand on his shoulder.

" This is my second in command. All ya'll need to know about Zoe is dat he's a cold blooded killer. Lorenzo points his street sweeper towards the jukebox and begins unleashing hot buckshot. BLOOM, BLOOM, BLOOM, BLOOM, BLOOM! The sound of his fully automatic shot gun is insanely persuasive, but its his cold eyes steal these niggas loyalty.

Kee speaks softly, I will be back in two weeks, and Jimmy is in charge until then. She blows a kiss at him as the three exits the café as they entered, as friends. The sweet smell of Kee Kee's perfumes lingers behind.

Lorenzo and Kee Kee assist Kenny to the car then they delivering him back to Pappy's care. Kee Kee kisses Kenny on his cheek as Lorenzo lightly pats him on his back. They tell him he needs to get some rest: then they leave for Richmond.

Kenny enters the house and Pappy helps Kenny to the sofa where he can rest once more. Kenny gently grasp Pappy wrist pulling him toward him. He places some real gansta- love into the palm of his hand. It's Emma's wedding ring. The Old man breaks down crying, he does not want to know how Kenny reclaimed it. It does not matter. All he knows is that his Emma's ring is back where it belongs; with him.

Pappy exits the room saying, "thanks God fer ya boy."

Kenny remains deep in thought. He wonders why Quan did not accompany Zoe and Key.

## (Pills and Nutty Bars)

Kenny reaches deep into his pocket pulling out the bottle of pain killers which Arlene had given him, there are not many left. He has been popping them like candy to keep his pain at bay. He shakes three into his hand placing them into his mouth. He is exhausted; thirst and hunger motivates him to take a trip to the kitchen. He opens the refrigerator looking of something, anything to quench his immense thirst. First he reaches in take a carton of milk to his mouth drinking its content. There is only a corner but it's enough to wash the pills down.

Kenny's still thirsty. He reaches in opening an individual personal sized bottle of water drinking it quickly. He opens several more drinking them. His belly is full of water but it still craves food. What he craves is sweets. Surely Pappy has some snacks somewhere. He reaches upward opening the doors of the cabinet above of the refrigerator. Bingo, Pappy's stash of Hostess Cakes, Little Debbie Cakes and various chips. Kenny's arms are long enough to reach but the paining in his ribs is unbearable as he stretches to reach the goodies; they are just outside of his reach. Shit, exclaims Kenny.

Pappy hears him asking is he alright? Kenny continues to put up a front telling Pappy he is fine. He does not want to be a burden to him or place him in harm's way. It's occurs to him that the only way to reach these cakes is to climb. He needs a chair. An aching Kenny maneuvers one of the kitchen chairs over to the refrigerator pushing it snugly against its door. His body's burning with pain as he steps on to the seat standing upright. He grits his teeth not to cry out in pain. The cakes are within his reach. He sees a box of opened nutty bars at the back of the cabinet; they are partially concealed behind a bag of chips. Kenny thinks, that's exactly what I need to curb this hunger.

His mouth waters as he thinks about sweet peanut butter sandwiched in-between wafers and smothered in delicious milk chocolate. Ignoring his pain he strains to reach the box. He mumbles under his breath.

"Almost there. Almost there."

He can't reach, but he is determined. He must have a Nutty bar.

Tipping forward on his toes, reaching, stretching, damn he still can't get them. Kenny inches forward to the edge of the chair still reaching. So much pain! So close! He has them! The chair slips and Kenny loses his balance falling forward. His neck bends as his face slides down the door of the refrigerator crashing to the floor.

Pappy hears the crash and rushes into the Kitchen. Kenny looks bad, he is unconscious. Pappy calls 911; the ambulance is on its way. A worried Pappy stays at his side until the E M S technicians arrive. They tell Pappy that Kenny's vitals are stable. He comes too but he is delirious. He asks Pappy if he will call Johnny for him. Pappy has not the heart to remind him that he is dead. The workers reassure Pappy that he will be alright as they leave for the hospital with Kenny. Pappy remains behind telling himself it's all in God's hands now. He would only get in the way at the hospital.

They arrive at the hospital rushing Kenny into the emergency room where he is seen. The doctor orders a series of X-rays and a battery of test. The results reveal that Kenny has suffered a mild concussion and has three fractured ribs from the beat down, plus he is also dehydrated. He is treated and admitted for 24 hour observation. Kenny asks the doctor if he will call Pappy to tell him he is O.k. This he does for him.

An orderly takes him to his room where a nurse places him on an I V and gives him a strong sedative. He drifts into a deep carefree slumber.

## (How Kenny Be Floss'n)

The nurse's station is a buzz with conversation. Kenny's personal items have been collected and are the subject of discussion. His jewelry and money lay on a plastic tray awaiting inventory.

His watch is heavy in the hands of the head nurse who holds it up to a doctor joking on him. She tells him that if he saves and invest his money wisely maybe one day he can afford a fine time piece like this. The watch is custom made. Its solid Platinum with a fine crystal face, adorned with no fewer than three carats of flawless diamonds. There are twelve diamonds which accent the jade face denoting hours. It's band is a 3" inch wide diamond encrusted intricate mesh of gold and platinum, It's diamond are too numerous to be counted.

There are two large solid platinum rings on the tray. One is a huge pinky ring which sports a single 4 carat black diamond. The other is a simple wedding band; it has no stones but its intricate etched designs are the hallmarks of a fine craftsman. These handmade pieces are far superior to the mass produced pieces found at high end jewelers galleries.

(The young doctor's heart is filled with envy, his eyes covert)

The nurses look on in awe as she lifts Kenny's necklace from the tray displaying it to the group. It's a solid platinum, diamond encrusted thick Figaro chain.

"Oh my God", remarks one of the nurses.

The large gold and platinum charm which is suspended from the chain is a work of art. It has two snakes intertwined about diamond filled script lettering which spells Poison. One snakes head is gold while the others is platinum. They both have rubies for eyes and their bodies' scales alternate in gold and platinum.

The group speculates about the value and weight of this piece. They place it on a scale weighing it. The jealous hearted doctor leans forward reading the scale. "No that can't be right, remarks the spiteful, young, white doctor. They weigh it again using another scale. That's right the chain along with the charm weighs 1 pound and 2 ounces. Its diamonds sparkle like melting ice reflecting off of a shooting star. Like Nicole had said, Kenny is floss'n. The magnitude of how this young- nigga is living is on this plastic tray, for all to see.

Kenny's knot is the final item to be inventoried. This is the grip he had in his pocket when Black attempted to stick him up. It's too much money to be confined in a roll. The nurse holds the money in a fashion similar to that in which a pitcher holds a baseball.

President Cleveland's face adorns the cover of this book. His face reoccurs as she begins the tedious process of counting. Her fingers start to tire as president Franklin makes his value known. Her hands start to cramp as President Grant starts his march at the tips of her tired fingers. She feels a sense of relief as President Adams face starts to repeat. His face is the last she will see as the counting comes to an end. This loaf of bread is 30,000 slices strong.

The blood stained knot of money has a voice of its own, it says; I'm dangerous. It says I have eyes for only you. It says, just maybe I can leave this nigga for you? Many have heard its voice, but those with good sense have known not to listen.

The head-nurse places Kenny's wears into a box than she stores it in the safe under the counter of the nursing station. She closes the safe's heavy steel door, locking it, silencing the sinister voice of that wicked Knot. The crowd disperses; they have sick people to attend.

Three nurses remain at the station, they continue conversing about Kenny. One of them had helped him get undressed. She shares with the other two the details about his pretty fat dick. A forth nurse approaches the station at the tail of the conversation. She thinks to herself. Hmmm. That dick sounds familiar. She takes a seat amongst the others and starts filing charts as the conversation returns to the routine. Mainly they gossip about who is fucking who and which patients get on their nerves the most. She feels as if she has missed out on some good gossip as the others continue in their smiling and giggling.

*(Meanwhile in a different section of the hospital)*

Kenny sleeps deeply as his I.V drip delivering nourishment to his weary, battered body. He's a resident of la la land. It's a wonderful place, here all dreams come true. Here Kenny floats in a fantasy land oblivious to the stresses of his life; he is totally unaware of the impending danger which lies in the bed of the room across the hall (he dreams of better days with Johnny).

Mandy sits upright in her bed tapping her remaining eight fingers on her empty, cramping stomach. The victim of her own food poisoning attempt she rushed here where they pumped her stomach and admitted her; once again Mandy plots on taking Kenny's life. She had seen an orderly roll him past her open door placing him in the room across hall earlier. She speculates that Buck's boys turned the tables on him and his crew. She hopes that they put a terrible hurting on his ass. She thinks all she will have to do is finish what they started. Impatiently she lays in wait.

Back at the nursing station all is calm, the night is winding down. The nurses have left the station to make their rounds. Doctor Lambert makes his way to the station; this is the doctor which the head nurse had joked earlier. The doctor wants something he can't afford. He wants Kenny's watch. He sneaks to the safe opening it. The watch is heavy in his hand but even heavier in his pocket. He thinks it's his. He starts to close the safe and make his getaway but he hears a whisper.

"Psst! Psst! Hey! Yeah you, Yeah you, Doctor Lambert."

The doctor looks around, he sees no one. He thinks to himself maybe his mind is playing tricks on him; perhaps the long hours working his residency are taking affect on him.

He starts to close the safe door once again but there it goes again.

"Psst! Psst! Hey! You! Yeah you Doctor. Lambert."

The sound is coming from inside of the safe.

The doctor opens the safe wide once more. Nothing is in the safe but the box containing Kenny's valuables which he had pilfered.

He hears the sweet phantom voice once again but it's louder. It's coming from inside the box.

He opens the box. Its Kenny's wicked blood speckled Knot talking directly to the young, stupid, white doctor.

It's saying, "I'm not dangerous." It's saying, "take me home with you." It's saying, "I want to leave this nigga for you".

The doctor has succumbed to its spell. He grabs the ball of cash stuffing it into his other pocket.

Finally he closes the safe locking it. He then rushes pass a nurses accidentally bumping into her as he hurriedly exits the hospital. She felt the hardness of the heavy watch and saw the awkward bulge of the knot in his pocket.

Wow, thinks the nurse. She thought the bulge in his pocket was his hard dick. She figured that he was rushing so no one would see him with a stiffy. This is the nurse which had arrived late to the station missing the inventorying of Kenny's wears.

The nurses all returned to the station after completing their rounds. The lights in the hallways have automatically dimmed and most of the patients are asleep.

Mandy decides the time is right to make her move,  silently she slithers from her bed placing her rough feet into the complimentary hospital slippers. She creeps to the door slowly opening it; peeping her head into the hallway, she looks left then right.  The coast is clear.  Like a cat burglar she tip toes across the vacant hall, casually stealing her way into Kenny's room.

There he is thinks Mandy, her nephews killer, the sleeping Giant.  Here lies the man that had mutilated and publically disgraced her mere hours ago. Determination flickers in her eyes and hatred burns in her heart. Mandy holds her pillow in her uninjured hand. She advances taking small steps until her hospital gown lightly touches the guard rail of this demon's bed. She stands over him relishing in the moment. Mandy's pussy is moist from the sense of power which is coursing through her body. With the backside of her injured hand she strokes the left side of Kenny's face. She thinks to herself, he is so handsome, he is so sexy. Her hand she slowly glides down his body stopping it at his groin area. She caresses and pulls at the bulge of Kenny's dick through the thin hospital bedspread, fondling it. She thinks to herself it's so fat, it's so hot, it feels so good. Her pussy drips as she imagines how it would feel inside of her.

She places her pillow between her legs squeezing it tightly between her soft thighs. Sexually aroused her perky hard nipples stand at attention she pinches one as she leans forward placing her lips onto Kenny's. She kisses and pushes her tongue deeply into his non responsive mouth as she gropes her soft, full breast. Rhythmically she moves, kissing, rubbing and groping, all the while squeezing that soft pillow in-between her legs.

She rocks her body harder and faster; her pelvis swiveling, her pussy pulsating, Mandy releases her nut. Multiple orgasms seize control of her body holding it a prisoner until she is exhausted.

Drained she slumps atop Kenny, breathing hard her head she moves downward onto his chest. Her pussy continues to throb as she listens to the beating of his heart, they are in sink. The sense of power which led to her arousal subsides; her hunger for sweet revenge grows once more. Slowly Mandy pulls the cum- soaked pillow from in between her legs. Standing erect she lifts it above her head bringing it down with force, covering Kenny's nose and mouth. She is suffocating him.

The sedated, battered man has no defense. He regains Partial consciousness but is  too weak to mount much of a defense. Mandy is so strong: she is fueled by rage and hatred.

She's giggling, Hee hee hee.

Kenny's fading away fast!

He sees that bright light at the end of the tunnel.

Johnny stands at its far end waving his arms and motioning with his hands for his little cousin to join him.

Kenny's rushes toward him; his body's so very tired, his soul's beyond weary. Mandy presses down with even more force.

The door opens, a shocked nurse rushes in grabbing Mandy attempting to pull her away from Kenny. But the crazed Mandy drapes her body atop the pillow grabbing a hold of the steel bed rails locking onto his face. This leach is sucking the life from Kenny. His arms and legs cease their twitching. Kenny Nobles is dead.

# Chapter 5/ The Deliverance Of The Giant

The nurse's name tag falls to the floor from the struggle as she continues to pull Mandy away from the patient. It reads Nurse Arlene Cambell. She recognizes the crazed woman as Ms. Mandy, Buck's aunt. Thinking back to a conversation overheard about a familiar sounding pretty, fat dick, she deduces that this unfortunate man must be Kenny.

Arlene releases hold of Mandy, to pick-up a heavy, old, metal bed pan which fell from atop the night stand while Mandy's legs flailed wildly. In desperation Arlene repeatedly crashes the bedpan to the back of Mandy's head hoping to force her to release hold of the bed's rails; Mandy goes unconscious.

Frantically Arlene struggles to remove this fiend from atop of Kenny. She's successful, pulling then pushing Mandy's body to the floor. Arlene is quick of action taking Kenny's vitals; he is not breathing and has no pulse. She begins to administer CPR. She breathes into her dead friend's mouth, alternating she compresses his chest. She continues in her effort until she is winded and exhausted.

It's not working, she thinks to herself!

But still she can't give up, she must go on!

Sweat dripping from her forehead, her arms aching, she begins to pray aloud.

"Lord God, please send him back. Please don't take him. I need this man in my life!"

She think to herself there is no use, then collapses in frustration, her head coming to rest on Kenny's chest. She sobs as she fights to understand The Lord's infinite wisdom and his magnificent plan. Still she mumbles.

"Lord please give him back."

A dead silent desends upon the room, so much so that she can hear her own heart beat. Its beats are so strong, yet it is all alone. A sadden Arlene listens to a silent chest and prays. Slowly another sound enters, seizing the room. Deaths veil has been removes as a second heartbeat joins in with hers. At first it's slow and faint, but then it builds momentum, pounding with a life force so strong that surely it must have been commanded by The Lord Jesus Christ himself to return. The sound is that of Kenny's heart. It reverberates, signifying the resurrections of the newly reborn Giant.

Arlene smiles as her head rides the waves of his chest as it rises then falls. She listens to his heart; wiping away her tears she thanks the Lord by commenting that he is so good.

# (Hard decisions)

Arlene turns her attention to Mandy who lies motionless on the cold floor; she's alive. Arlene is unsure which course of action to take next. If she alerts the administration of what has transpired surely they will involve the police. Confronted with an attempted murder charge Mandy will definitely spill her guts about her suspicions of Kenny having killed Buck. Legal terms like accessory after the fact and conspiracy to cover-up murder swirl in her mind. But what is she to do? Ms. Mandy will try to finish what she set out to do. She looks to Kenny. He looks so helpless. Once more she looks to the grim reaper still lying motionless at her feet. Arlene says a prayer aloud.

"Lord father, please forgive me." Mandy's an obstacle in need of removal.

Arlene walks backwards as she exits the room, she must keep her eyes on Mandy. There is a wheelchair just outside of the room's door. She unfolds it and rolls it back into the room parking it along side Mandy. The small framed delicate nurse struggles but with conviction she is able to load the-would be assassin onto the chair's seat. Slowly she rolls the chair into the hallway.

All of the rooms door's are closed with the exception of the one directly across the hall. She deduces that this has to be Mandy's room. Quickly she rolls her into the room closing the door behind them. Arlene places her into the bed then hurriedly she exits the room. Arlene attempts to look calm as she makes her way back to and past the other nurses sitting at the station. She needs her purse which is in the storage room just off to the side of the station. The head nurse speaks to her jokingly.

114

"It's too early for you to be punching out!"

*(The time clock is also located in there)*

Arlene attempts to look amused forcing a smile is her response to the corny comment.

She searches her purse with purpose until she finds what she was looking for. It's a small vile.

Placing it into the pocket of her lab-coat she exits the storage room and takes a seat amongst the gossiping nurses.

Oh damned, exclaims Arlene as she rapidly stands up.

"I forgot to check on Mr. Anderson."

Once more she is on the move, but now she runs; her troubled mind racing, her worried heart pounding.

She has to protect Kenny.

She prays Mandy has not regained consciousness.

The elevator ride to the fourth floor seems to last an eternity but finally the doors open onto the hall, she steps out. Arlene is suffering from tunnel vision; she doesn't recall this hallway ever looking so damned long. She begins to run to Kenny's room at the far end. She's running as fast as she can but it's as if she is moving in slow motion. Eventually she reaches his room, he is as she left him; he is alive. She sighs in relief then she walks over to his bedside and kisses him on his forehead.

She exits the room again closing the door behind her. She takes deep breaths trying to compose her for what she feels she must do. Her heart pounds and the tunnel vision returns as she creeps back into Mandy's room.

Slowly she approaches her bedside.

She whispers, "Ms. Mandy? Ms. Mandy? Are you awake?"

She repeats herself as she gently shakes Mandy's shoulder as if she really wants her to awaken. She remains non responsive. Good, thinks Arlene! She hates Mandy; for the years she stood silent and at time even played a role in helping her nephew Buck to abuse and degrade her.

Arlene reaches into her pocket withdrawing the small vile of liquid and a syringe from it. She inserts the needle into the vile drawing 100cc of the fluid into it. The vile contains Digitoxic; undetectable through routine screening an injection of the substance will bring about instant death by simulating a massive heart attack.

Considering Mandy's age along with her other health risk factors her sudden death should not arouse anyone's suspicions.

Arlene reaches forward lifting Mandy's arm.

She secures it tightly locking it at her waist side.

She does not want to have to struggle with Mandy should she regain consciousness.

Arlene presses her thumb downward on the pump to the syringe shooting a small stream of the poison from the needles tip. This she had done a thousand times to assure she did not inject an air bubble into a patient harming them. She giggles at the irony of her actions; here she is about to take a life but still she is concerned about an air bubble. She holds her head down slowly shaking it side to side as tears start to flow from her eyes.

She's moving the needle closer to Mandy's vain which shows green through her pale skin.

She thinks to herself, but I'm a nurse! I'm supposed to help people?

Her mind is conflicted. I have to protect Kenny; but I'm not a cold-blooded killer. Am I?

God forgive me! I can't do it!

The distraught nurse breaks down crying uncontrollably as she recaps the needle of the poison filled syringe.

*(She fills ashamed as she slides it back in to her coat pocket)*

She exits the room turning out the light and closing the door tightly behind her. She feels she has failed Kenny. Mandy will make another attempt on his life as soon as she regains consciousness.

The hall is dead silent with the exception of a squeaking noise. The sound is being made by one of the smaller wheels on the wheelchair that Arlene is pushing. It does very little to ease her mind and further agitates her already bad nerves.

That is until she stops to listen to what the squeaking is saying to her.

It's saying, "hey bitch, pull yo shit together! With my help you can get this nigga out of this fucking hospital."

## (Arlene's Escape)

It's time for action. Arlene exits Mandy's room closing the door behind her. She pushes the wheel chair which had so recently transported revenge. She makes her way back into Kenny's room parking it alongside his bed. It's to now serve as a chariot on which the Giant can escape Hell's gates.

Arlene removes his I.V and checks his vitals: they are stable ,she will recheck them at her apartment. She lives less than 6 miles from the hospital. She shakes Kenny vigorously in her attempt to awaken him. His eyes open briefly then close once again.

The sedative has a tight hold of him. What is she to do? Kenny is at least 6'0" and weighs no less than 195 pounds; time is of the essence, she must act now.

Placing one hand to the base of his neck and firmly grasping his arm with the other, she attempts to raise him into the sitting position.

Shit! This boy is heavy, thinks Arlene.

(Kenny is dead weight)

She repeats her effort with the same dismal result.

She needs help, but who can she trust?

She speaks aloud. "Think Arlene, think!"

She comes up blank. Kenny's salvation, or rather deliverance is in her hands, nealing forward she resting her elbows on his chest, she clasps her hands in prayer.

"Lord please give me the strength."

Now rested Arlene makes her second attempt at sitting him upright, she pulls with all her might. She pulls as a determined mule dragging a rusty, dull plow into hardened earth. Sweat pours from her brow; her arms, leg and back begin to ache. The aches give way to wracking pain. Lord help me replays in her head, and slowly Kenny's limp body rises into the seated position. An exhausted Arlene embraces him securing him. Her head resting atop his, she kisses his short wave filed head. She rocks him gently, patting his back she whispers to him, "I got you babe." She then tossed the covers back revealing his toned muscular legs.

Supporting his torso she pulls his legs toward the edge of the bed until they dangle freely.

Arlene looks to the wheelchair parked next to the bed. Despair looms in her heart. It may as well be a mile away.

She thinks to herself, how the heck I'm I going to get him into that?

She needs Kenny's assistance.

She shakes him once again. "Come on Kenny. Babe you have to wake up. Please wake up.

Despair turns to frustration causing her to shake him harder and faster. Frustration turns into impatience which gives way to anger.

In anger she panics lashing out smacking the living shit out of Kenny's non-responsive ass. WHACK!!

"Wake your ass up", commands Arlene.

*(His eyes open)*

"What the fuck" he responds in shock.

"Where the fuck Am I?"

Kenny is out of it. Slowly his mind focuses and sharpens, he remembers.

"Yeah, that's right; damned Nutty Bars."

Arlene smiles then briefs him on Mandy's most recent activities as she assists him into the wheeled chair. He wants to deal with her but he is in no condition to seek sweet revenge. He tells himself that will have to wait.

He mumbles "Shit just what I need; more fucking drama. He

fades back into sleep.

Arlene is just happy to hear him speak. She places the blanket from the bed over his lap and they exit the room. She will have to sneak him out of the hospital as he is in no condition to sign himself out. She will have to use the service elevator at the rear of the hospital to avoid detection.

The two take the elevator to the underground parking garage beneath the hospital. She prays as they descend. She hopes no one will see her leaving with him; after all she needs her job. Nervously she bites her nails as the elevator approaches and passes the second than first floors. Finally the slow lift opens into the parking bay. Yes! Success thinks the worried nurse. Her car is less than 100 feet away and with caution she rolls him to it.

Kenny awakens when shaken by Arlene, with her assist he loads himself onto the back seat of her Honda Accord. Arlen covers Kenny with the blanket concealing him on the back seat. Hurriedly she makes her way to the driver's seat; placing her key into the car's ignition, she starts it. Looking into the rearview mirror she tells Kenny to sit tight. He hears her not: he's asleep again. She makes for the exit gate.

Hmm thinks Arlene; there seems to be a delay. Five cars are lined up ahead of them. Patiently she anticipates the departure of each car as the bar raises then falls. Finally it's her turn.

The attendant at the booth seems nervous even jumpy; he appears to be stalling. He tells her they have been having problems with the automated gate and that it may be a minute or so before she can leave. This sound like a crock of shit thinks Arlene; paranoia has a grip of her. Her patience is running short and her heart ponds in her chest like a drum.

She mumbles under her breath. "Come on. Come on."

Just then she notices two security-officers approaching the rear of her car. It's time for action.

She presses her foot hard to the accelerator launching the car forward crashing through the gate, cracking her windshield.

She almost losses control of the car turning its steering wheel sharply to regain control as the car bolts onto the street's wet pavement, it's raining hard.

The cracked windshield and the thick down pour of water make for a deadly combination. Arlene's vision is impaired and she finds it difficult to focus on the road ahead.

Kenny regains consciousness; reaching forward he places his hand on Arlene's shoulder, big mistake. He startles her causing her to lose control of the car (her eye bulged in fear).

The automobile runs off the road; she's on a collision course with the blunt end of a steel guardrail. Arlene struggles with the steering wheel attempting to regain control; Kenny is tossed about the back seat like a rag doll, his limp body moving to gravity's pull.

With a hard sharp turn the cars wheels slam to the coarse edge of the paved road causing a jolting thud. Air bound the car sail toward the center on the highway road. It land hard, destine to meet oncoming traffic. Somewhat relieved she continues in her struggle; certain death at the end of the guard rail had been avoided.

The small car swerves left then right; it's all over the road. Arlene's eyes bulge seeming to leap from her face. She is on an unavoidable collision course with a State Trooper. She prays for salvation, she's not ready to die.

The State trooper's lights are on. He must have been responding to an emergency call. His speed gauge tells the tale of his demise; it reads 95 mph. His reactions quick he slams his foot to the brake turning the wheel away from the impending wreck. Dread fills his heart, his fate has been sealed and he knows it, he loses controle.

His cruiser enters into an uncontrollable spin then violently flips, rolling, tumbling down the roadway. It scars the road surface creating gashes as it moves; chunks to metal, glass, plastic and asphalt mix. It leaves the road flying across a deep trench heading toward a grove of small trees. They snap like twigs when meet by the energy and force of the air born hunk of steel.

An Old Oak tree stand guardian over the forest to its rear. It catches the troopers car wrapping it around its trunk like a belt. The car survives the impact only to be consumed in flames when the bent car explodes into flames. The car, the tree and the trooper have been sacrificed to spare Kenny and Arlene's lives.

Arlene regains control over her battered car and continues on her way. She sobs wiping tears from her guilty eyes as she drives. She tells herself the Trooper has survived the crash, but in her heart she knows it's not likely. Kenny is sleep again.

## (Kenny comes threw)

Once again Kenny regains consciousness. The drugs are wearing off and he is coming too his senses. There are large gaps in his memory and he wants answers. He asks Arlene how he came to be in her car. His last clear memory is of being admitted to the hospital.

Arlene does not answer; she is in shock. She continues to drive, sobbing intensely focused on the road ahead. Kenny senses he has miss out on something, something traumatic. He backs off.

Two minutes pass and Arlene abruptly answers his question. She gives him all the details. She wants to be strong but she breaks down completely as she arrives at her apartment. Her body slums forward, exhausted her head comes to rest on the steering wheel. Now she sobs with even more intensity and at times hyperventilating.

Kenny thinks to himself. What the fuck! I don't have time for this shit!

He then sits upright leaning forward to rub her back. He wants to comfort her.

He tells her it's going to be Ok.

Arlene is babbling something about losing her job, wrecking her car and being a murderer. She is a broken china doll. Kenny wonders if she can be fixed.

Exiting the car Kenny steps into the downpour of hard rain; his only garment the flimsy hospital gown. The cold rainwater runs down the crack of his exposed ass as he attempts to assist Arlene in exiting the car. She has not the desire to move. He pulls at her arm prompting her to get it together; it's no use. He will have to carry her into the building. His wrapped ribs pain him horribly but he knows he has to do this. Arlene had come through for him and he would not let her down in her time of need.

He crouches down slowly extending his muscular arms; he embraces her drawing her near his chest. He lifts her from the car cradling her in his arms like a small child. His head resting aside hers as he turns kicking the car door closed with his foot. He takes his first step; dizzied and in pain he follows her faint voice which instructs him, she directs him toward her building.

Carefully He listens and follows her lead; her meek voice at times drowned and muted by the ferocious sounds of thunder.

Kenny is met by a formidable staircase when they finally approach her building. He asks "what's her apartment number?" She tells him it's 316. Arlene can feel Kenny's knees about to buckle, his body trembles under the strain of their combined weight. She begs him to put her down but Kenny does not listen; this is some symbolic type shit. He must carry her the whole way. He tells himself he can do it.

Kenny attacks the stairs with tenacity; each step is as a mountain beneath his bare feet. Slowly they ascend. Arlene continues to beg Kenny to put her down but he continues to climb.

She sobs "Please; please babe. Put me down. I can make it. Please put me down. I'm hurting you."

He responds. "Baby girl I told you I was going to see you straight. You just relax, I got diss."

He stops to rest his back against a wall as they reach the second floor landing. Arlene kisses his cheek. He rest briefly then he attacks the final flight of stairs with determination. Each step wrecks his body with waves of agonizing pain but he presses on. He feels dizzied, his stomach quizzy , his mouth sourers, he feels as if he is about to vomit. It feels as if some dark force is persuing him. He feels he's being watched as well. He moves faster. His mouth fills with blood as his teeth press ever tighter. He's gritting his jaws. This he does to cope with the pain, this he does not to cry out like a little bitch.

He thinks to himself. *God help me.*

He had been shot on three separate occasions but never had he experience this kind of pain. He wants to cryout. But certified thugs don't cry.

Finally they reach Arlene's apartment. She inserts her key into the lock turning it. Entrance has been gained. The two rain drenched fugitives enter a place that feels safe, It's cozy. Her sweet voice directs him too her bedroom where he places her onto the bed.

An exhausted Kenny undresses Arlene before casting his soaked garment to the floor. He then lays his battered, naked, broken body down aside hers; gently he places his arm around her pulling himself closer to her. Kenny rocks her to sleep whispering sweet nothings in her ear. Now he can rest. His battered naked body he lays next to hers'. He finds comfort within her arms but what or his wife.

*Miles away Cheryl is suddenly awakened; a cold feeling has crept upon her. She feels her husband's pain, she feels insecure; she senses his infidelity. She cries herself back to sleep praying Lord don't let it be*

# Chapter 6/ *The Sun Shines*

Sunlight penetrates the narrower slits of the closed blinds which pretend to conceal the two weary outcasts from the cold, dark reality which awaits them. Arlene is first to stir awakening Kenny with her soft kiss. She smiles then jokingly addresses him.

"Well good morning Mr. Giant. I see you have returned to the land of the living."

Much of the prior night is a blur to him. He squints his eyes as the sun warms his face. His memory improves as he sits upright in the bed. Arlene places her pillow behind his back which rested on the solid Oak headboard of her Victorian style bed.

"Ah", sighs Kenny. *His ribs are relieved.*

He then looks at Arlene, she looks worried, unsure and un-eased. Her hair is all over her head, she looks a mess.

Kenny Ask Arlene "what's the matter?"

*(She snaps with hostile attitude)*

"Well Mr. Man, unlike some of us who don't have to work for a living. I do and I doubt I still got a fucking job!"

Her tone is angry and sarcastic. Kenny does not like it one bit. Bitches don't talk to him like that. He starts to check her ass but he doesn't. He understands her frustration. It brings a smile to his face. It reminds him of how his life was before he got into the life. Always broke and having to put up with stupid ass supervisors and backstabbing, ass-kissing, co-workers. Those jerk- off's that are always smiling in the bosses face trying to look good at everybody else's expense. He tuned Arlen's bitching out reminiscing.

Days ago Kenny had considered leaving the thug life; he smirks, his thought. " What the fuck was I thinking? Johnny should have blasted my bitch ass on the spot for saying I wanted out. I'm a thug for life.

He thinks, *Johnny.*

Remembering his cousin his smile fades fast.

*(Arlene taps Kenny's chest)*

"Are you listening to me at all? Kenny had spaced out for a few seconds.

He responds. Hun? Come again?

*(She grits her teeth)*

"God, why don't you men ever just listen?

*(They both smile)*

Kenny chuckles bring slight pain to himself.

" Come on boo. You know I care, say it again."

127

*(He punches her arm lightly saying)*

"Girl you my niggett. I got you lady."

Arlene repeats herself, this time her tone is more so light-hearted.

"Like I was saying, I seriously doubt I still have my job. It's not like I got caught stealing a few tongue depressor, I stole a patient in the middle of the night."

*(She laughs at her own corny joke)*

She tries to keep a smile on her face but it's not sincere.

She attempts to convince herself there may be a slim chance she still has her job. She is in denial big time.

Arlene leaps to her feet from the bed, shouting I can't take not knowing! I have to call them, after all it's not like I took you against your will or something. "

Kenny just looks at her nodding his head in agreement. He has not the words to comfort her.

Arlene makes her way to the telephone calling the hospital.

She is directed to the head administrator. He seems more concerned about Mr. Noble's whereabouts than with her plight.

He asks if he may "speak with Mr. Nobles." She hands the phone to Kenny.

*( She's tapping her fingers alongside her leg, nervously)*

Kenny explains to him that it was his chose to leave the hospital. He hears relief in the man's voice. Mr. Taylor as administrator is more concerned about possible litigation than he is of punishing an unwise nurse.

Kenny goes on to praise Nurse Campbell for her understanding and compassion.

He pledges a large sum of money to the hospital as reward for her grace.

Mr. Taylor is relieved and excited as he asks Kenny to make the check out to him personally.

*Kenny smiles,* it's always the same; money talks and bullshit runs a marathon.

"Tell you what, says Kenny. Let's do this right. I'll give you cash."

"Why certainly, says Mr. Taylor. Cash would be best."

Kenny enquires about reclaiming his personal effect. Mr. Harrison tells him he just needs to come by the hospital and sign a series of release forms. Kenny tells him it's been a pleasure talking to him and hands the phone back to Arlene. She listens for a brief moment then hangs the phone up. She falls to the bed crying next to Kenny.

They are tears of relief; she has merely been suspended for one month with pay and no formal reprimand; essentially she has earned herself a paid vacation for her good will. She thanks Kenny.

Kenny speaks "Baby I told you I got your back. The job will be there if you still want it but I got some shit in the works with your cousin Jimmy and Bucks boys. I want you to supervise them as I will be going back to Richmond after shit is straight.

*(Arlene looks sad, she does not want him to go)*

"I told you before I was going to put you down with my girl Kee Kee. You can stay with her a month or so until the heat dies

129

down. You know, get yo head straight and shit. Kee can school you on how this shit runs. If you want in that's cool and if not that's cool too. But once you are in then you are in for life; feel me.

*(Kenny's facial expression gets really serious)*

"I like Jimmy but I need somebody I can trust. I trust you. Don't worry about money. I'll break you off a few G's as soon as we get my money back from the hospital. Alright, now get you self together so we can go get my shit.

The two leave the comfort of the bedroom to prepare for the day. They shower together getting in a morning quickie. Arlene exits the shower first as Kenny is partial too long, hot, showers. He is a very particular type of Nigga and getting ready to go out takes him sometime.

Arlene now dressed bangs her hand on the bathroom door joking on him.

"Damned; you are worse than a woman! Open this door! "

Jokingly Kenny tells her to "shut up."

She enters the bathroom with an arm full of Bucks best gear. Kenny smiles thinking to himself. Damn Buck was one country bitch, Wal- Mart all the way. But beggars can't be choosy. Otherwise all he has to wear is the hospital gown.

He put on the clothes. He asks Arlen how he looks, she grins.

"You should wear the gown. That way you can show off that sexy tight ass of yours. *She smacks his butt*.

"Go ahead girl." That shit ain't funny.

Now dressed, the two make their way from the apartment to Arlene's wrecked car in the parking lot.

Awww fuck think the two as they approach it! Her whip is all messed-up!

Well maybe it's for the best thinks Kenny as the car had run a cop off the road. It would not be wise to drive this wreck, surly it would draw unwanted attention.

They reenter the apartment calling for a cab which takes them to Pappy's Farm where Kenny gets his car is.

Pappy sees Kenny from the window and rushes out of the house to meet them. They are about to leave. "Hee Hee Heck Heck cackles a happy old Pappy as he scrambles down the driveway.

" Boy You's sight fer dees hern old eyes. Kenny is happy to see him as well. He gets out of the car and they embrace. He asks Pappy if Old Man Philmore still runs that old junk yard down the road.

"Sure does" answers, Pappy.

"Does he still have that car compactor?

" Sure does", repeats Pappy.

"What ya's needs dat fer ask pappy. "

The less you know the better Pappy."

Pappy sucks at his gums to the left of his nubby teeth saying, "I sees."

"Will you tell him to be on the lookout for me just after sunset?

" Sure will answer the confused looking old man."

Kenny feeds him a small bone.

"We need to make Arlene's car disappear.

131

Pappy gets excited cackling and hopping about.

" aww shucks now! We got some ganster- ganster going on.

*Kenny smiles*, he knows Pappy likes to feel as if he is a part of the thug life.

Poor Arlene just shakes her head. Pappy tells the two young lings to get along; he has more chores to do. Kenny thinks to himself Pappy is something else. He watches him shuffling across the open field until he disappears into the woods behind the large shack. Pappy needs his morning nip.

Arlene's soft, sexy, phat ass sinks deep into the Benz's luxurious, cushioned, soft, leather seat; she makes herself comfortable adjusting the radio controls. She's not use to riding in style. Kenny joins her taking the wheel.

He jokes her saying, "Don't be changing my station to country music either". Off they head for the hospital taking the scenic route.

## (Off to get Kenny's Goodies)

Kenny spies a parcel of land to his right aways down the road, its 3 acres for sale. He thinks to himself Hmmm? Just then he passes a lot of mobile homes for sale to his left. Again he thinks Hmmm?

Kenny has Arlene to write the contact number from the road signs. She looks puzzled. She wonders, could Kenny be thinking about starting a farm?

"That's funny."

She pictures Kenny in a field planting seeds. She smiles.

Kenny speaks. "Check diss. If you gonna be my Queen Bee down here, you gonna need a chill spot with some privacy."

Shit, thinks Arlene: this nigga is serious about getting her into the drug game.

Eventually they arrive to the hospital parking on the street. A few of her co-worker returning from lunch speak to her as they enter the building. Arlene waves saying "Hi."; then she whispers to Kenny saying.

"I hate those phony bitches. Did you see how they were looking at you? Shit if I turned my back on them for a second they would fuck you. Jealous bitches."

Kenny thinks to himself, damned I hope she don't think I'm her man or some shit like dat. I got a wife. He feels guilty as he thinks my wife? How he misses her and the kids. However he is not looking forward to calling her on Sunday, surely by now she has heard about her little brother's (*Baby- Boy*) untimely demise. He wonders will Cheryl blame him for introducing him to the life? Will she blame him for his death? Will she blame him for not breaking silence to tell her? Will she blame him for not being there to hold her? He pushes these thoughts to the back of his mental culprit (the mind). He has more pressing issue at hand.

The two approach the receptionist sitting behind the admittance desk where Kenny enquires about reclaiming his personal effect. Arlene leaves Kenny's side to retrieve her belonging she had left at the nursing station.

The receptionist makes small talk with Kenny as he starts to fill in the assortment of forms she has given him. She flirts with him passing him a slip of torn paper with her phone number scribed on it. Kenny just smiles and places it into his pocket.

Kenny is used to this by now. Women are always coming on to him. It seems he can't ever go into a store without some hoe-assed gold digger leaving her seven digits on the windshield of his ride. He

133

has learned it is best to toss these numbers as these hoes are trouble. He thinks Arlene is different.

The cute receptionist prints a copy of his bill and hands it to him. She tells him there is a side note stating that he has to see the doctor before his discharge can be complete. She then places a call to nursing station three telling them Mr. Nobles will be up to get his personal effect soon.

Kenny makes his way to the nursing station where he is met by The Hospital Administrator Mr. Taylor and the doctor who had seen him on that blurred night. Both the doctor and Mr. Taylor seem happy to see him as they are all smiles. They shake his hand as the head nurse opens the safe to acquire his belonging. She presents him with the plastic tray. Instantly Kenny notices its light.

"Where is my watch?" ask Kenny.

The nurse checks the inventor sheet than looks into the safe once more. She addresses Mr. Taylor saying, it's not here.

Kenny keeps his composure as he asks "Where is my money?"

Again the nurse looks into the safe, its not there.

Mr. Taylor looks over the inventor sheet more thoroughly. His eyes bulge in disbelief as he notes the amount of cash listed. He questions the nurses.

"Is this a mistake? It says Mr. Nobles had 30,000 dollar cash."

" No", she responds. I inventoried his belonging myself."

Mr. Taylor looks into Kenny's eyes and he does not like what he sees. He sees a drug- dealing- killer looking back at him.

Kenny speaks: "So what are you going to do about it?"

"Well Mr. Nobles if you will fill out this form we will submit a claim against our insurance. I'm sure after a short investigation you will be reimbursed." He is nervous the form shakes in his hand as he hands it to Kenny.

Kenny exclaims, "INVESTIGATION!"

Mr. Taylor walks around the desk placing his person behind the circular counter next to the phone. His voice now unease he tells Kenny he will need to have the police come to the hospital to file a report.  Kenny hangs his head in anger his thought; Got damned police! Shit I can't go there just now. This is a loss he may have to suck up. He tells Mr. Taylor not to worry about it. All bystanders are relieved. Kenny removes his remaining wares from the tray placing his jewelry onto his person. He then looks to Mr. Taylor winking his eye he tells him to expect a visitor next Monday. For a brother like Kenny word is bond, he will still give Mr. Taylor his hush money.

Kenny turns to the doctors saying, doc you needed to see me?

"Why yes Mr. Nobles I just need to give you a clean bill of health and schedule a follow up visit for you. Although your concussion was mild I am, however I'm somewhat concerned about those fractured ribs.  We need to be sure we dot all the I's and cross all the T's least you have complications."

The doctor is a good man and Kenny senses it. They go to a small examination room where Kenny is looked over. The two make small talk about their children and what-not.

Kenny asks the doctor if they can speed the examination up as he needs to go shopping for a suite for a funeral tomorrow. "Why sure or course says the doctor", he then opens his wallet removing two business cards placing them into Kenny's hand. One is his and the other is that of his personal tailor. Kenny thanks the doctor shakes his hand before exiting the examination room.

Arlene meets them at the door. The doctor smiles at Arlene and tells Kenny he is in good hands.

"Ms. Cambell is one of our finest nurses and a credit to your race." Kenny and Arlene smile, the doctor meant no harm with his offhand racist remark. Old white men like him tend to live trapped in a time bubble. If someone were to tell him the days of Jim Crow are over he might have a heart attack and die from shock. They allow him to live his illusion.

The two walk away. Kenny fills Arlene in about the theft of his belongings. She is surprised he is taking it so well. Just then her mind flashes back to an encounter she had the night of the escape. She tells Kenny the tale of the young Dr. Lambert and how he had bumped into her on the hall that night. It's a tale of budging pockets and nervous beady eyes.

Their conversation is overheard by another nurse as they all stand at the elevator. The lift arrived and the three entered: The nurse fills the need to share. She tells them that she too had seen young Dr. Lambert that night as he was lurking about the safe to the rear of the nursing station; "he looked suspicious." The elevator reaches the main lobby and they all exit. Kenny is pissed but somewhat relieved. Arlene knows where the doctor lives.

They pass Mandy in the hallway as they exit the hospital. She too has been released. The three cross looks, no love is felt; paths will cross again.

# (Bitch Yo Self Doc)

A short ride and they arrives at the doctor's home. Kenny tells Arlene its best she stays put as he exits the car. He makes his way to the front door ringing the doorbell. No one answers. Kenny gives the doorknob a turn and the door opens; in steps The Giant. Now in Giant mode he explores the lower level of the doctor's home freely. His state of being relaxed. He is ready to do some fucked-up type shit.

He hears running water and singing. It appears the doctor is taking a shower. Kenny smiles as he thinks; white people. "Damned they quick to leave their doors open." If fortune shines upon him, young doctor Lambert may live to regret this.

Kenny enters the kitchen area where he sees his old friend resting on the counter top, chilling. It's the blood speckled knot.

"Over here! Help! Help" cries the Knot.

Kenny snatches it up cramming it into his pocket. Its muffled voice continues to speak.

"I'm so happy to see you. That crooked doctor stole me. I told him I was yours, but he wouldn't listen. I told him he had better return me, but he would not listen."

Kenny knows the knot is a liar but still he listens to it.

"You should kill his white ass for taking me. You should lock his cracker- ass in a closet and burn this bitch down", screams the Knot.

Kenny continues his quest to reclaim his wears. He makes his way upstairs. The doctor's singing get louder as Kenny approaches the top of the staircase. He walks past the partially open bathroom door and enters the master bedroom.

There it sits atop the doctor's dresser. Kenny is relieved. This watch is special to him. Johnny had given it to him when he graduated from college. Kenny lifts the heavy timepiece clasping it to his wrist. Its heavy, it fits like a power bracelet which completes a power Ranger's armor. Kenny is flossing once more and it feels good.

His thoughts now focus on the thieving doctor. Kenny steps into the walk-in closet where he admires the doctor's extensive collection of designer neckties. He soughs through them looking for the perfect strangulation tool. He selects Aunt Cathy's most recent Christmas gift; Strips and flowers, it's a tacky accessory, but will serve alternate purpose well.

*(The singing stops as does the running of water)*

The doctor now hums a tune as he exits the bathroom making his way toward the bed room, clueless of what awaits him.

Kenny prepares the necktie wrapping it tightly about one hand as he hears the good doctor enter the room. Kenny thinks to himself. Ok bitch! You happy and humming and shit, right!

Kenny rushes from the closet charging the wet doctor, punching him on the nose breaking it. The doctor falls to the floors holding his bloody nose. Kenny stands over the doctor yelling.

"SO YOU THOUGHT YOU COULD TAKE MY SHITAND GET AWAY WITH IT?" The doctor crawls like a slug making his way down the hallway leaving a bloody trail on the light colored carpet. The doctor's thoughts are strange and somewhat comical. He's having an inner conversation about how to remove the blood stains from the carpet.

Kenny walks behind him taunting him; he kicks his victim's naked -pink-ass. Mid hallway Kenny drops his knee hard to the doctor's lower back flatting him like a roach. Kenny strides him sitting on his bruised coved back. The necktie he wraps about the thief's throat, leaning forward Kenny presses his chest to the back of the doctor head increasing strangulating force. He's chokes the nude man within an inch of his life before releasing hold of him. Kenny stands and the doctor begins to crawl once more, but now he craws on his belly.

"Dats right, you fucking worm. Crawl! Crawl for your life", shouts Kenny.

He laughs and kicks the vile thief. The doctor is crawling toward the handgun he keeps in the small cabinet in the bathroom. Kenny has an ideal. He grabs the doctor by his ankles and drags him to the top of the stair case. barely conscious the doctor begs for mercy.

"No. No.  Sir please don't do it. I am sorry, please don't. Kenny lifts the doctor to his knees then standing in front of him unzips his pants exposing his massive black dick. "SUCK IT!" commands Kenny.

Dr. Lambert mouth slowly moves forward until it's within a inches of Kenny's tools, it's opened wide.

*(Kenny steps back laughing)*

"YOU NASTY FAGGOT, SUCK THIS!"

Kenny raises his foot thrusting his hard boot heals to the doctor's collar bone.  The doctor's battered body falls backwards tumbling down the staircase, his neck twist and bends as he descends. He lands at the bottom of the steps hard, his head leaving a large dent in the wall. The doctor fights to maintain consciousness, his eyes focus on the blurred dark specter descending upon him. He thinks to himself this is no man. It is a monster, a vile demon released from hell.

Kenny gloats as he stands over the doctor. The doc hears laughter as he fades in and out. Kenny relieves himself soaking him in a stream of hot retaliation. Kenny speaks from his civil side.

"I should kill your cracker-ass, but I'm not, from now on you work for me. You got that?"

*(Dr. Lambert blinks his eyes in concurrence)*

Kenny tells him to have a nice day then exits the house locking the door behind him. He took one of the doctor's business cards which lay on a sidebar just to the left of the front door.

Kenny returns to the car where Arlene waits.

"Well how did it go! Did he give you back your things?"

Kenny smiles, "Yeah I gave him some advice."

"Advice?", responds Arlene.

"Yep I told him to keep his front door locked."

*(Arlene looks puzzled)*

She heard no gun fire, still she wonders if the doctor is still alive. She dare not ask; ignorance is bliss.

## *(Kenny's Things to Do List)*

"Damned I got a lot of shit I need to do, Johnny's funeral is tomorrow", says Kenny. Arlene reassures him saying not to worry things will work out just fine. She then hands him her cell phone saying go ahead and make your calls." Kenny pulls the tailor's business card from his pocket calling him. He tells him that he is a friend of Dr. Stevens and that he's in need of a suite as soon as possible. The tailor tells him that he has several unclaimed suites and invites him to come by his shop to view try them on. He has three blue and two black suits which he could alter for Kenny within an hour's time. Kenny is relieved and tells him to expect him within the hour.

Well that's one less thing to worry about says Kenny as he places his second call to Danny.

"Hey nigga remember what we talked about."

"Yeah", answers Danny.

"Well it's time for action you need to be at the End Zone tomorrow night."

"Solid", replies a happy Danny. Finally he is going to get his chance at that brother Ricky.

Kenny hangs up then places a third call to Chad. He gives him the numbers Arlene had written down to the reality company and to the mobile home lot. He tells him to make it happen and hangs up. His next call goes unanswered, it's a call to Lorenzo. Humph, grunts Kenny thinking about Johnny's advice about Zoe (*Trust him only when you need him for a killing*).

He hands the phone back to Arlene as they have arrived at the Tailors shop. She asks him what's next. Kenny does not answers, instead he hands his money to her asking her to count it. Arlene remains seated as Kenny exits the car. She watches as he disappears into the tailor's shop. She fans herself with the wade of cash. Just watching him makes her hot.

twenty minutes later and Kenny emerges from the store with a black suit folded over his arm. He hangs it in the rear compartment then it's off to the races once more.

"What's next", asked Arlene.

"We all good right about now. First things first, how much money did you count?"

"Its thirty thousand", says Arlene.

"Ok dats good. He didn't have enough time to spend any of it. Take six for yourself and after I recoup from street sales I'll take you to get another car. Start thinking about what you want. But you can flex my Lexus until then. We just need to go get it. Awe fuck! Kenny remembers. Shit that's right, I told Teddy to sell it. Fuck let me think. Ahh, ok alright we can go get Johnny's jeep it should still be out front of the club."

Ever paranoid Johnny had registered it under Kenny's name so driving it won't present any problems. They drive back to Arlene's where they call a tow truck which tows it to old man's Philmore's Junk Yard.

They are met at the gates by a krusty-looking, scraggily, gray bearded old man. He is rather Kantankerist.

"Hey boy! What all ya'll wants around these parts", growls Mr. Philmore.

Kenny drops Pappy's name and he relaxes just a tad.

"Well why didn't you say Charles sent yall." *Charles is Pappy's Christian name.*

"You must be Kenny." Old man Phil opens a gate instructing the tow truck to unhitch the wreck near the car compactor. Arlene stands next to Kenny looking sad. She is attached to her car. Phil calls to his son Buford.

"Boy get yo lazy no good fer nothing ass out here. You got work ta do.

142

Buford slowly exits the rust coved antique trailer which serves as both office and home to the two. He approaches the group scratching his balls with one hand while adjusting his confederate rebel cap with the other. Kenny thinks to himself now this is one crazy looking white boy.

All hell, let's just put it out there, Buford is a redneck for sure. He hates black people and dislikes city folk even more. Kenny has an instant dislike for him too. His Old man commands him to get to work compacting the car. Tears form in Arlene's eyes as her baby is crushed. Its windshield shatters and its metal frame is decimated under the formidable pressure of the car compactor.

"Well that's dat", says old man Philmore.

He smiles; this one was a favor but Kenny laid $300 on him. There business is done.

Buford calls too Kenny as they are about to get into car to leave.

"Hey City boy! "

"What the fuck, is he talking to me" says Kenny.

"I think so", says Arlene. Kenny tells her to wait for him in the car saying to her there is a gun under the seat.

Slowly he Walks toward Buford asking, "What do you want?"

Buford tells him he has some army surplus for sale; Kenny's eyes open wide.

"Show me what you got Bo Duke."

Buford leads Kenny off into a small patch of woods. He approaches a small trap door partially covers in dirt and brush .He lifts the door leading to what appears to be an underground bomb shelter. Buford is one of those crazed survivalist you hear about on the new. He was in the Klan, but they kicked him out when they found out his old man was best friends with a nigger (Pappy). In his younger days Old man Phil was a devout racist. He changed his ways when Pappy saved his life. One night he was heading home drunk as a skunk when he ran his car off of an overpass plummeting into a river. Pappy who was also drunk on the road that night stop risking his own safety to save him. Old man Philmore loves Pappy and there is nothing he won't not do for him. Kenny follows Buford deep into the cellar where he is presented with an assortment of military hardware. Buford has racks of M-16's and grenade launchers. Kenny inspects them asking what else you got. Buford pulls a tarp from atop a opened crate exposing several surface to air rocket launchers.

Now that's what's up says Kenny. "Name you price." Buford says he will sell them for two grand apiece. Kenny unfurls the wicked Knot pealing sx large from it. *He's takes extra care not to spend any of the vintage bills he inherited from Johnny. Ok says Buford, now step this way and I'll show you the rockets they'll cost you extra though. Kenny buys a box of twelve telling him to toss in a crate of hand-grenades in as well. Buford helps Kenny load the goods into the trunk of his Benz and it's off for Richmond they head.*

# Chapter 7/ The Madness

Back in the city Quan is hanging with Paulette at her apartment. He wasted no time in making her acquaintance. She is an attractive, business savvy young lady, but her taste in men is at best pitiful. She met Quan the same night of Poison's meeting and dropped draws too soon. Now this ignorant nigga is in her system. Kenny never understood what Johnny saw in him, as far as he is concerned, Quan is a shastie- nigga. Quan has the same dislike of Kenny.

He runs off at the mouth telling Paulette how Kenny is weak and how one day he will be running shit. She just sits doe eyed staring at this little- dick- bitch-nigga lying naked in her bed. She attracts little dick losers for some reason. Her ideal of a big one is anything just over three inches. Sad to say but Quan would be stretching the truth to claim a solid four. A man of small statue, he also suffers from a little man complex. He over compensates. He drives a Hummer, totes a 357 magnum and is loud and assertive beyond belief. Picture that; a jealous hearted hustler with ambitions of being the man.

His big mouth rings-out louder than the sounds made by the cannon he packs; the 357 Magnum.

"Main check diss; if Kenny don't come correct soon Ima have ta put the pimp hand ta his bitch-ass. You should'a heard dat nigga at the meeting, sitting in Johnny's spot acting like Nino Brown or some shit. Talking about how the cops cut is gonna come outta my operation. Fuck dat nigga. I told'em if dats da way it's gonna be den he had to give me all Johnny's side interest. He was trying ta give them ta Coop but I won't having dat. Dat nigga knows he living on borrowed time. Shit he knows dat I'm da main!"

Paulette sits listening and believing. She had only met Kenny on two occasions and has no clue as to how deeply immersed in the hard-core drug game they were. To her Johnny was just a very nice business man who helped her. Johnny never told her his story and she never asked. She did not know he was a ruthless killer or a Drug King Pin. She was sad to hear of his demise and has no loyalty to Kenny. As far as she is concerned this prank new nigga of her's is the real deal. He is her new Johnny.

The doorbell rings. Quan commands Paulette to answer it, he's expecting company. Paulette puts on her robe and goes to answer the door, it's Lorenzo. She is frighten by him; he is looks so ghetto, and well those eyes, those soul piercing, cold, jet-black killer's eyes. She's Reluctant to invite this demon into her home, but she does.

"Where is Quan", asked Zoe in his cold emotionless manner.

*(Paulette rushes to get him)*

"Quan your friend is here. If you don't mind I'm just going to stay in hear until he leaves. He scares me."

" Ah girl what da fuck It's just Zoe, dat nigga harmless. I got his ass under mind control", says Quan.

146

He then tells her to give him her robe and to "just be the fuck quite." He puts on her over-sized mens terrycloth robe and exits the bedroom. Quan approaches Lorenzo who has taken the liberty of making self to home.  He's more than comfortable. He has the TV's remote, his feet are up on Paulette's coffee table and he is helping himself to the tin of cookies she had placed there.

Munching and dropping crumbs Zoe ask Quan if he has heard from Kenny. Naw, replies Quan. "Well you better be ready to get yo ass chewed out. He won't to happy you didn't show up wit Kee and me. He didn't say nothing but I could tell he was piss, but we handled dat shit. Nigga you should have been there. We mobbed shit for sure. Now we are getting paper in Ashland too.

"Who the fuck is we, says Quan. Kenny ain't sharing shit."

" What the fuck are you saying Quan?"
"Nothing. But you know you should be running shit. Kenny is my main and all but he's weak."

"Weak ", exclaims Zoe as he stands.

Quan is afraid, just maybe his big ass mouth has gotten him into some shit. He thinks. What if Zoe tells Kenny what he just said? In his heart he knows just how treacherous Kenny can be. He attempts to clean it up.

" Naw Zoe, you got me wrong. "I was just saying you know."

" Naw nigga I don't know, say Zoe seated once more.

Quan is sweating bullets.

"I was just saying that if something happens to Kenny then you step up. I would too. Shit you know poison ain't shit without you. Its fear of you dat keeps da money flowing. "

"Look lil nigga. Johnny was my man andhe said to get diss nigga's back and that's just what the fuck I'm gonna do. Feel me."

Naw Zoe "I don't feel you" If Johnny and Kenny was so down with you, why didn't they put you down with their connection?" Zoe remains silent.

Quan shares a secret with him. "You know Johnny was like my fucking pops; he shared shit with me."

"Shit like what nigga", ask Zoe.

"Shit like why he never put you down wit his connection? Dat nigga loved you for real but he didn't trust you. He said if you had yo own connections you might try to ease him out. For real Zoe you know how paranoid he was. He had me keeping an eye on you. I thought dat was some vile-shit: but fuck! What the fuck! Johnny was like my dad and shit. Now Johnny gone who else can I look to. I'm telling you Zoe, now is yo time. Kenny fucked up and Black's people gonna get his ass. It's just a matter of time. Zoe thinks. If what Quan is saying is true then Kenny too conspirers to hold him back. He had asked Kenny and Johnny several times to take him with them to re-up. Neither of them ever did. He then thinks back to the meeting. Kenny failed to say who he would take along with him to re-up when asked by Blue.

"Zoe I know this some hard reality but you know you should be running Poison. I ain't the only Head saying dat shit either."

Word, says Lorenzo. Just that quick shit can change. This little nigga put a bug in a killer's ear and for a moment he is listening. That's all it takes. Lorenzo pulls a fresh bag of weed from his pocket and rolls more blunts.

He utters, "Quan keep going nigga; tell me more," fishing for more information.

*(Elsewhere)*

Kenny and Arlene arrive to Johnny's club. Johnny's Jeep is still park here. Good, thinks Kenny making his way to the front door of the club. Johnny kept a spare set of keys in his desk.

"Come on ma. I got the door key, let's go in says Kenny. We can get a drink too." It's so quite thinks Kenny as they enter. He is not used to it like this, even during the day this night club was always abuzz with activity. It was there private get-away. This is the place where they could all bring their honeys , homies and just chill.

No drug transactions ever took place here. This was their place of relaxation, their sanctuary. It also made good money for Johnny and was a 100% legitimate business. The deed to the place is in Kenny's mother's name as she had given Johnny the initial start up money. She passed shortly after that. Kenny inherited the building, but now that Johnny is gone, he wonders will the club ever be the same.

Tears form in his eyes as he walks toward the white tape outline which must be where Johnny's body came to rest. It is one of many but this one is in front of his office door and fits Johnny's dimensions. Yellow Crime Scene Tape abounds and browning dried blood stains the black and white checkerboard floor; bullet holes are everywhere.

Kenny thinks and speaks aloud. "So this how it all ends, hun cuz?"

Arlene places her arms around his waist, she hugs him from behind squeezing tightly.

She prompts him. "Come babe lets go. Let's just get out of here."

She thinks to herself. Is this the world he is trying to make her apart of? It's so dark and cold.

Kenny walks to the bar area pulling Arlene along by her hand. All the bottles have been shot out and glass is all about the bar top and floor. They head to the office. Only one bottle in the entire place survived, it is the bottle of Barcardi 151 which still sits on Johnny's desk. Kenny takes it to his mouth bucking down the remaining corner his cousin will never get to finish.

He says, 'I finished it for you cuz, and just like dat Im going to handle yo business." Kenny is speaking of the dish best served cold, revenge.

Again Arlene says to him. "Babe let's just go. You don't need to be seeing this, let's just go."

Kenny opens the desk; there they are, Johnny's spare keys.

Picking them up, he tells her." Ok lady lets bounce."

He flips Arlene's cell phone and places a call to Kee Kee as they exit the derelict nightclub. He lets her know they are in town and on their way to her house. Again he tries Zoe, no answer.

*(On the West End)*

Ricky has just returned from his brother's Black's funeral. The house is packed with relatives and friends. They all seem to be sad but those that knew of his long addiction feel a sense of relief. Black was living like an animal: robbing, stealing and killing to get his fix.

Ricky regrets telling him of his plot to take back the North Side. He'd also shared with him his plan to take Johnny and Kenny out. Ricky had the hit planed for the both of them at the club that night; but stupid Black jumped-gun and set out to do the job himself.

He thought he could regain respect by handling it himself. Ricky also regrets introducing him to that simple bitch Chester. If he had known Chester was also strung out he would not have. But now is not the time to cry over spilt milk.

Monster was allowed to attend the funeral and he was not happy at all with the state of things. He loved both Black and Johnny. He had told Ricky to back off and so had their dad; no good could ever come from making a move on Johnny's turf.

*(Ricky thinks, if only I had listened)*

His ambition had killed their brother. He wants to be a bigger man and let it go but he can't. Johnny's funeral is tomorrow and he is going to send him off with a large platter of disrespect. Killing his brother was one thing, but them pissing on his corpse was another.

He starts to plot his revenge. He could have a bomb planted at the church. Naw that ain't personal enough. He could send some young bucks by to spray the church. Naw he thinks. That ain't original enough. Plus security will be tight as hell tomorrow. He sits pondering. Hmm he thinks. It's a biblical thought, an eye for an eye. He will return the favor of disrespect.

He calls two of his cut throat cousins into the room and tells them of his plan. They sit about drinking hard liquor and laughing. They think this is going to be fun.

## *(Arlene and Kenny part company)*

Kenny arrives at Kee Kee's house closely followed by Arlene. Kee Kee meets them at the front door. She is so very happy to see Kenny and she is looking forward to getting to know Arlene.

They enter the split level townhouse. The decor complements Kee to a tee. It's very contemporary and stylish. White is the theme:

white leather, white lace, and white silk. Even the carpet is white.

Arlene's mouth drops in awe of how beautiful this pad is.

Kee Kee speaks. "Girl you make yourself at home. I got one rule and one rule only. Keep my shit clean." She smiles but she's dead serious.

Arlene notices a large pearl-handled handgun sitting on the white marble coffee table aside a large crystal platter. What's on the platter is also white. But it ain't that innocent white.

Three ladies are in this room, Kee Kee, Arlene and Girl. Kee introduces Arlene to Girl. She walks over to the mound of cocain scooping her (girl) under her sculptured pinky nail, quickly she sniffs it up her nostril. Kenny smile.

Kee then says," If you're gonna sell ol' girl, first you have to know her." *She takes a second hit* saying "but you had damned well better know to respect her. Because this bitch will take you to places you never imagined in your worst nightmare. "

"Kenny's tells me you're square so I suggest you never partake of girl's delight."

Kenny nods his head in agreement adding his two cents worth.

"Damned straight! I don't fuck wit girl. Never have and never will. If Kee says the product is good than that's good enough for me. If you know what's best you will do the same. Baby girl I'd hate to see you strung out sucking ten dollar dicks behind this shit. Remember this bitch ain't shit to you but a means to get paper. I hate Girl and her punk assed brother Boy but they pay the bills, feel me?" Arlene shakes her head as if she understands what they are saying. But both Kenny and Kee know she is clueless.

Kee Kee proceeds to shows Arlene to the guest room where

she begins to unpack her things. Kee returns to Kenny and he instructs her.

"Kee take it slow with her. First things first take her shopping for some decent clothes and get her due smoked.

"Yeah she is kinda tore-up", says Kee.

*(Kenny smiles than continues to speak)*

"Teach her how to market the product and school her on how to carry herself as well. And when she is ready introduce her to girl. I hope she can hang but I got to know if she can keep the craving at bay. What say you turn her on to it for about a week than take her cold Turkey. Leave just enough about the crib where she can stumble on to it.

We should know in two weeks or so if she got what it takes. There is mad paper to be made in Ashland."

Kee smiles saying "Baby boy have I ever let you down?"

No Babe, you never have and you know I got big love for you for that reason. You and Johnny always had my back. I'm not talking down on the other heads but I'm just saying."

Kenny stops abruptly as Kee wraps her arms around him holding him tightly. She loves this man. She tells him to be carful. Something about the way she says it the stands out as strange. He does not question her further, he lets it go but it bothers him. Perhaps Johnny had just cause to be so paranoid.

Kenny makes his way to the guest room where he gives Arlene a kiss then tells her goodbye.

He exits the house still wondering what Kee Kee wanted to tell him. He tells himself Naw! Hell naw! shake dat shit off kid. Then he gets into the Jeep and drives away.

## (The Sunsets on Kenny)

Kenny uses Arlene's cell phone to call Zoe. He's riding around with a small arsenal and he needs to offload it. He plans to give Zoe his pick of the litter before he stashes the rest; Lorenzo answers, "What it be like Zoe, where you at?"

He says he's at Paulette's with Quan. Cool says Kenny. "Give me directions there." Kenny wants to see Quan. He also needs to let Paulette know who she owes her loyalty too now that Johnny is gone. He knows how Quan gets down and he don't like it one bit. That Quan elected to disregard a direct order needs to be addressed. Kenny is in Giant mode and with Zoe already at the spot he is sure Quan will get his point. Still Johnny's written words ring in his head. *"Trust Zoe only when you need him to kill."* Kee's words echo in the background. *"Be careful."* He can't shake them.

Is he becoming Johnny; living place to place not trusting anyone? Kenny seeks relief from the poetic words of a fellow hustler's voice booming from the jeep's sound system. Its Pac. Kenny loves this nigga's music. His head bobs as he drives to his destiny. He sings, ya got ta keep yo head up.

Back at Paulette's Quan and Zoe are completely blitzed. Quan is gloating about how he has Paulette under his thumb. These niggaz are disrespecting her house like it was a fucking pig pin. They have empty beer bottles scattered all about the floor and have spilled more on the carpet then they have drunk.

Zoe remarks "Damned, ol girl gonna be piss when she sees this mess."

Quan responds. "Main fuck dat hoe! She knows I'm da man!"

154

He then thumps his chest as if he is King Kong or some shit like that.

He tells Zoe "check diss!"

*(He calls to Paulette)*

"Hey bitch! Get yo stank- ass out here now!"

There's no reply. Zoe looks at him and laughs.

"Awe Lil nigga sit yo ass down, you ain't running shit up in here but yo mouth."

Quans says, "damn-it she gonna recognize."

He then makes his way to Paulette's bedroom door kicking it open.

*(Startled she falls to the bed in shock)*

He grabs her by her ponytail dragging her into the living room where he pushes her atop the coffee table before Zoe. Her head he holds down while lifting her nightgown. Paulette's soft, caramel-colored, smooth ass is so beautiful. Zoe can't help but rub it.

*(Poor Paulette cries out)*

"Why are you doing this to me?"

In anger Quan shouts at her to be the fuck quiet.

Zoe shakes his head. This nigga is tripping.

*(Quan continues in his grandstanding)*

" See diss phat ass? It's mines and she is gonna do what the fuck I say when and how the fuck I say; less she be one dead bitch.

*(Paulette starts crying,She wonders what she has gotten herself into)*

Quan lets her up then takes a seat next to Zoe saying, "Hoe amuse me, Strip! "His large gun sits in his lap. Paulette does as she is told. There she stands, naked- entertainment.

Quan tells her to dance for him, she does. Tears flow from her eyes as she attempts to satisfy this sick niggas command.

"Why ain't you smiling boo", taunts Quan. She forces a smile. She dares not dance; that there is no music has no bearing.

Zoe thinks back to Nicole and how he felt when Kevin was fucking her corpse. The alien feelings from earlier have returned but this time there is a twist. This bitch is alive and sexy as hell.

He stares in Paulette's eyes saying to Qua.

"If you got her under control like dat make her suck my dick."

Paulette weeps louder now; all the while dancing, sobbing and begging.

"No...No... No please don't make me. Please don't do this to me."

(Quan's devilish smirk reveals his inevitable sick response)

"Word Zoe, you ain't said shit! Bitch get down on yo motherfucking knees!"

She hesitates, inciting Quan's wrath. He repeats himself pointing that big gun of his at her.

"Hoe get down now!"

Slowly she does and crawls toward Lorenzo who's unzipping his pants exposing his vile black serpent.

Quan commands her to crawl faster.

156

Paulette reaches her destination. She can't do it. Quan encourages the hysterical girl to open her mouth by firmly pressing cold steel to her temple. Just then the door bell rings, it's Kenny. He rings the doorbell again, and then he enters; another unlocked door.

The Giant crosses the threshold just as Zoe's dick disappears into Paulette's mouth. Kenny likes not what he is seeing. This is not what he intended. Johnny was about helping this young girl, not hurting her. This is classic Quan, but Kenny expects better of Zoe.

He rushes to Paulette lifting her face from Zoe's dick. Zoe's verbal response comes quick.

" Main what the fuck!"

He starts to reach for his gun, but Kenny is faster on the draw. pulling Paulette to his waist. Kenny demands an explanation. Quan drops his gun and starts to explain.

"Damn Kay we was just having some fun wit diss hoe, she was down with it".

Paulette's tears tell another story. Something in her eyes reminds him of his deceased daughter (Kenya).

*(Kenny loses it)*

He begins pistol- whipping Quan unmercifully. Quan whimpers like a puppy as the shaft of Kenny's chrome-plated Beretta turns red and drips blood. It rains down like Thor's Hammer. Silently Zoe looks on, eventually asking Kenny,

"Don't you think dats enough?"

Kenny's response; "FUCK DISS PUNK BITCH!" he shouts as he continues to pound Quan; each blow cutting deeper into his flesh.

When exhausted Kenny takes a seat in a chair across from Lorenzo. A shaken Paulette crawls to him placing her head onto his lap. Still sobbing she thanks Kenny.

Kenny looks at Zoe with disgust.

Zoe stares back at him un-phase, unimpressed and a bit pissed, after all; who the fuck is Kenny to come between him and a free dick suck? Zoe decides to play it cool remaining relaxed. He is studying Kenny.

"Damned, you fucked dat boy up! What you think his brother gonna say about diss?"

He was right. Kenny had lost control and failed to think things through. Blue is not going to be happy about this at all. Kenny had not killed Quan, but this was a major fuck up.

"Aw fuck" exclaims Kenny dropping his blood covered gun to the floor. He then leans back in the chair, his head he holds. Zoe's thought. Quan said diss nigga was weak. Look at him. He ain't strong enough to lead Poison. This nigga is actually worried about Blue. Fuck a Blue! If it was me I would do both of them niggas, Quan and Blue thinks Zoe. Let see if this so called Giant has the balls to finish what he just started.

Kenny tells Zoe to help him get Quan to the bathroom so they can clean him up. Zoe's final thought on the subject; this giant is more like a midget. He helps move Quan to the bathroom. Quan regains consciousness while cold water runs over his head in the bathtub. (He's mumbles)

"You fucked up. You fucked up. Just wait till my brother hears about diss shit, you are done. You fucked up; you weak bitch, you weak."

Kenny pats Quan on his shoulder and says to him.

"You  right Quan Im done. Ya'll can have diss shit. I'm out.

158

He then gets up and exits the bathroom (*Zoe smiles*). The word Weak repeats in Kenny's head. Zoe comforts Quan. "My nigga you was right. It's our time to rise n shine."

Kenny reenters the room, gold tooth exposed, diamond brilliantly shining, gun in hand. He walks over to the tub, placing gun snuggly to the front of Quan's head. He shows him just how weak he is. He pulls the trigger. The overly ambitious kid's blood splatters onto the walls and Zoe's face. An already bloody bathtub deepens in its reddish hue as brains seep from shattered skull.

Kenny looks Zoe squarely in his eyes and calmly comments.

"Zoe, ain't a got-damn thang weak about me. And you remember dat shit my nigga. I'm a killer just like you. Now let's get the fuck outta here we got plans to make."

Zoe smiles saying "My nigga. So you want me to call Kevin or what?"

Kenny's response, "Naw. Let the cops clean this piece of shit up."

They collect the empty beer bottles and wipe the apartment clean of their fingerprints. Kenny tells Zoe to get Quan's money and jewelry." He stops to leave poor Paulette with a cover story before he and Zoe leave. Quan was just another victim of a robbery gone wrong. He should have run his money and jewelry quicker. Surely he will be missed.

## (Spot Check'n)

Kenny and Zoe make their weekly rounds. They both know how important it is to keep up appearances. These are dangerous times but Kenny can't afford to look scared. Zoe's rep is so well known that it's highly unlikely that anyone will make a move on Kenny while he is in Zoe's company. Zoe appears in many a nigga's nightmares. A straight natural born killer, he caught his first body at the tender age of fourteen.

*So many men,*

*so many men,*

*babies, mothers and hustlers,*

*Zoe the killer has sent to their ends.*

This is a little rhyme kids sing around the way. Zoe has survived so many hits that it seems as if he is immune to death, he's Satan's spawn.

Zoe follows Kenny in his car as he makes his appearance at each of Poison's Get Big Money Spots. The Money is flowing, business is good. He will need to make a trip out of town soon; they are all running low on product. Kenny continues in making the rounds closely followed by Zoe in his car. He calls Zoe on his cell saying they have one more stop.

Kenny heads to North Avenue. He wants to make a firsthand assessment as to whether this spot is dead or not. Those kids getting shot by the playground had all but shut it down. He talks to Zoe as they ride down the strip slow.

" Zoe you see any of our people?"

"Naw dog I thought I saw Rock a block back, but it won't him".

"Is that Gerald to my left."

"Yeah dats dat nigga", says Zoe.

Kenny ends the call then circles the block; he pulls up next to Gerald who is standing on the corner next to the North Avenue Food mart.

"What it be like Big-K ask the corner knot clocker giving Kenny dap followed by pound.

"It's all good says Kenny. Me and Zoe just check'n shit the whole nine yards and all. What's the word; You getting paper or what?"

Gerald looks to the ground, shaking his head he answers.

" Main niggas don't know what's up. The cops sweating every nigga dat stops to tie his shoe. Mike and dem workin da alley behind the Laundromat but fiends ain't online like they should be. Kay it's rough out here."

"Alright hold shit down says Kenny motioning to Zoe to follow him. Just as they are leaving the strip Lorenzo gets a call from Tony Boy.

"Zoe you seen Kenny? Zoe is slow to answer.

"Yeah I'm shadowing him now. Why what's up." Tony Boy sounds worried, but more so agitated.

" Zoe, Quan is dead! Blue just called me. Main he all fucked-up; dat boy on tilt. They saying some niggas jacked Quan at some bitche's crib. But I ain't buying dat shit. I think its Ricky and them. We need to act on diss shit! I ain't trying to see Poison go out like some bunch of bitches! You tell Kenny he better step up! People talking; People saying he weak!"

Zoe interrupts his ranting.

"Who is People?"

Tony Boy goes silent. Zoe asks if he is one of the people. Tony slows his roll.

" Hey nigga I was just saying. People talking."

"I'll give K the message", says Zoe before ending the call.

Just then Kee-Kee checks in. She seems shaken and concerned for Kenny. Zoe baits her; he is curious if she is People.

"Calm down Ma. I gave Kenny the word on Quan and he says we gonna ride for Poison. We gonna ride for all our fallen soldiers."

He listens for her response. He listens for her loyalty. Kee says "Dat's what the fuck's up! Dat nigga Ricky don't know who he fucking wit! You tell Kenny I'm down for him however he wanna handle diss. You have Kenny call me when he can. Ok sweetie? I'm worried about him. Anybody touch my nigga and day gonna answer to me."

Well I guess she ain't people thinks Zoe as they end the call.

He calls Kenny saying they found Quan.

*(Kenny's snappy response)*

"Fuck Quan!" Let's go chill at your house. I need to smoke some shit."

*(Zoe starts laughing)*

" My nigga dat's what's up. Let's get lit."

*(Kenny lets Zoe take the lead as they drive to Zoe's)*

He calls Chad then Teddy. Chad tells him that he can have the club up and running in about a week and that he has purchased the land in Ashland as instructed.

Teddy informs him that he sold the Lexus and lit the house as instructed. He wired Cheryl the money from the car and told her to get in touch with the police so she can file the insurance claim. Kenny is happy with the news.

Teddy and Chad have also heard about misfortunate Quan. They too suspect that Ricky set it up; first Johnny then Chief and now

162

Quan. That Nicole is thought missing furthers suspicion that Ricky is busy making big power moves against Poison.

Kenny wonders what would be the outcome should the others discover that it is he and Zoe who are responsible for the majority of the killings being blamed on Ricky. Surely it would destroy Poison. Kenny won't let this happen.

He is not worried about Zoe but Paulette is a concern. He calls and she answers. He can hear the police in the background. He asks her if she is good. She says to him

"Yeah mama I'm ok. I'm just shook up. My friend was robbed and killed but they did not hurt me. I'll call you when the police are done with me. She then says "mama don't cry I'm fine. I will be just fine. She ends the call.

Kenny is impressed; he knows that if Johnny handpicked her she will hold water. The cops could give a fuck less about a looser like Quan. They will however fake the funk and put on their mock investigation as they always do when a baller reaches the end of his rope. After all, where would they even start? Quan had so many enemies. His own mama even hates him.

## (Two killers feel Each Other Out)

It's now dark outside as Kenny and his second in command arrive at his home. For all the money Zoe has made, one would think he would have a better spot to call home. Zoe stays in the Whitcomb Court Public Housing Complex with his main chicken head. This bitch is so fucked up she is not even worth a mentioning. But for the sake of telling the tale let's just say she is at best trifling.

Zoe enters the apartment lighting an incense. Little good it does as the place still reeks of weed, cigarettes smoke and old cooking grease. The roaches greet them at the door. It must be the first of the

163

month as Kenny swears one of them hands Zoe rent money.

"Damned Zoe why the fuck don't you get diss bitch exterminated", jokes Kenny. Zoe laughs saying, "it ain't dat bad."

He's stomps one of his tenants then heads over to the ragged, clothing covered couch pushing his girl's things to the floor. He tells Kenny to make himself at home. Kenny sits but can't get comfortable. He keeps feeling as if something is crawling on him. Zoe plugs up the Play Station and they start to play Maden.

*(Zoe calls to his stank-hoe)*

"Bitch roll us some blunts."

Fifteen minutes later she swanks into the room bringing them a full platter of phat- ones.

Zoe smacks her flat butt saying, "dat's why daddy loves you. Now bring us some 40's and some of dat left-over Chinese Food." She does. They take turns passing blunts and bucking 40s. Kenny passes on the food. Zoe on the other hand has the munchies and is tearing into the egg- noodle like it's his last meal.

Kenny shakes his head as he watches Zoe eat. He's dropping food everywhere and it bothers him not. The roaches are well fed here for sure. Stuffing foods into his mouth Zoe ask Kenny when he is going to re-up. Kenny changes the subject. He starts talking about Ricky instead. Zoe lets it slide for now.

Kenny tells Zoe it's been good rolling with him the past few days than bluntly ask who he will side with if one of the heads challenge him. Zoe falls back to his previous question but this time he comes straight at Kenny.

"Look K, I need to know what the fuck is up wit us. If we cool and I'm second in command when you gonna take me wit you to meet yo people. I ain't wishing bad on you but what if something happens to you. Poison is fucked. We all fucked. Somebody needs to be down wit yo connection."

Kenny looks at Zoe agreeing he says. "Well that's kind of like insurance for me Hun?"

Zoe is pissed. But what the fuck can he say. If he was in Kenny's place he would carry shit the same way. Kenny is the golden goose and without him they are sincerely fucked.

(Sensing Zoe's frustration Kenny tosses him a bone)

"Look Zoe, we crew and I'm not gonna leave ya'll out in the cold. You got it!"

*(Zoe shows rare emotion)*

"I got it! For real you gonna put me down? Aww main, fuck, my nigga! K you won't regret it. Nigga, on my life I'll die before I let anything happen to you."

Kenny extends his hand to Zoe shaking his he says.

"On yo life?"

Zoe yells to his project hoe again saying. "Tameka breaks out da good shit, we celebrating n shit.

She brings a bottle of cheap champagne. Kenny smiles to himself then Zoe pops the cork spilling bubbly all over the floor. Two hustlers on the same page passing drink and taking long, hard pull from blunts. Now the true riding begins. These two gangsters are fitting to wreck shit, and shit's name is Ricky.

Zoe then tells Kenny about all the crazy mess Quan was talking about him being weak. He also mentions that Tony Boy's loyalty may be in question. Quan was expendable but this lil nigga

165

Tony Boy is Poison's major earner. If they take him out, Kee, Butter, Chad and Teddy won't be happy at all. They all love this crunchy black nigga. For now he has a pass, but Kenny will keep a close eye on him. Nobody will challenge him and live.

"K we just need to show everybody that the sleeping giant is awake and crushing everybody and everything. From now on it's me and you; on my life Kenny, on my life. The two hug cementing their new pack with the placement of hard thug's hands on backs.

## (West Side Katz at Kenny's North Avenue Spot)

Zoe's phone rings. It's Gerald with some dire news. Some West End Katz have set up shop in a rooming house across from the old Gun Laundromat on North Avenue; they slanging big rocks and monster eggs. They even got police protection, but these two criminals ain't sweating that shit. Zoe tells Gerald he and Kenny will be back on the set in twenty minutes. Zoe is excited. It's been too long since he last lavished in the exhilarating passion we Americans call homicide.

*Genocide, infanticide,*

*Bloody Zoe don't give a fuck,*

*he's down to ride.*

*Run bad children, under mother's beds, scared thugs hide.*

That's the second verse of the nursery Rhyme the kids sing about Zoe if memory serves correct.

Tonight Zoe vowels he will bathe in a river of thug nigga's blood.

Kenny sits watching Lorenzo as he rushes to get his Street-Sweeper. It's unnatural and disturbing the way Zoe response to the call to kill. He is wide eyed like a kid on Christmas day. He can't wait

166

to hit the streets. This nigga has no fear of death, he worships it.

Kenny however approaches the situation as a consequence of doing business. He is calm and calculating, he checks to make sure the straps are tight on his once plugged bullet proof vest. He asks Zoe if he is going to pad his chest. Zoe looks at Kenny smiling he tells him.

"Nigga sometimes more is less." Kenny thinks to himself diss motherfucker is crazy. Not only is he thrilled by killing it also seems if he has a death wish. Zoe puts on his two shoulder holsters jamming desert Eagles into them he says.

"Come on Kay it's time for sweet homicide."

Kenny tells him he needs to slow down, he's moving at light speed, and haste makes waste of Niggas like that. He tells him to breathe slowly.

Zoe exclaims, "Nigga I'm breathing and so are them West End Katz at yo money spot. Da quicker we get there the soon dem niggas stop breathing. Fuck Kenny, dem niggas breathing our fuckin air." *He stops all movement and says.* "Shh. Quiet. Shh. You hear dat?"

"Hear what", says a now grinning Kenny.

"Listen. Shhh. Dem niggas just took another sniff of yo air." Zoe starts laughing. Kenny smiles saying.

"Nigga I see why the kids call yo ass Bloody Zoe, You just a natural born killer. Let's go my nigga, you driving."

*(They arrive on North Avenue parking on a side street three blocks away from the rooming house)*

Kenny tells Zoe he has a present for him. The two make their way to the rear of the Jeep where Kenny reaches in moving a tarp to the side showing Zoe the crate of rocket launchers.

"Aww shit, exclaims a wide eyed Zoe; weapons excite him. If he knew Kenny was packing like this he would have left his gauge at home. Kenny takes one rocket launcher from the crate and handing it to his partner. He then helps himself to one stuffing two rockets under his coat.

Zoe tosses his shotgun into the jeep's cargo bay and the two make their way to the rooming house via the alleyway. They conceal themselves beside a storage shed just out of sight of the target. Kenny tells Zoe to get ready as he is loading his rocket launcher. Zoe is about to do the same when he says.

"K we got the drop on these fools from here but I like to do my dirt up close and personal. That's it Kenny knows for sure now. Zoe is crazy.

There are the five thugs guarding the rear of the house and at least three on the front. Zoe wants the maximum body count and the best way to get that is to get all them niggaz into the house. They want front page and Morning News. Ricky needs to know Poison ain't to be fucked with. A plan forms in Zoe's mind.

He sits his launcher on the ground and tells Kenny to follow his lead. He tells Kenny to stay put, and to be ready to light the house when he says too. Kenny wonders what the hell this fool is planning. A curious Kenny watches as Lorenzo makes his way to the front of the house.

These boys don't know it but they are about to make Bloody Zoe's acquaintance.

He makes his way along the sidewalk then opens the wire gate headed to the front door. Immediately the three thugs surround him saying they don't know him and that he would want to be step'n. Zoe laughs at them, his response.

"So I guess you, niggas really don't know me."

He introduces himself, "I'm Zoe. The word on da street is dat ya'll pranksters setting up shop on my boy's Turf."

One of the thugs does that old school nigga whistle. If you are from the hood, you know that's a sound you don't want to hear when in the company of unfamiliar niggas and outnumbered.

They close- in asking Zoe "who the fuck is his Boy?"

The six at the rear of the house join the group. They all crowd Zoe pulling heat.

Kenny looks on wondering. Does Zoe really have a death wish?

*(Zoe answers the mob)*

"Johnny was my boy but it seems like a bitch made faggot named Ricky saw fit to close his eyes. Now my boy Giant sent me to serve ya'll niggas wit eviction notice. Ya'll in violation. Diss his spot, so if you bitches kindly vacate the premise, he instructed me to let ya'll faggots live."

One of the mob enters the house and the young buck in charge emerges. He can't be older than 19 years old.

He walks to Zoe and stands nose to nose with him saying.

"Fuck Kenny Nobel! And yeah Ricky did his bitch cousin."

*(They then relieve Zoe of his guns and take him into the house at gunpoint)*

Well thinks Kenny, Zoe got all of them into the house, now how the fuck is he going to get out in one piece?

Ten minutes pass and the house is silent. Kenny thinks maybe he should call in some back up. Suddenly all hell breaks out. It sounds like a war zone erupts inside of the house.  A loud mixture of small and large caliber handguns' fires fills the air. Zoe's Desert Eagle's screams loudest.

A lower floor window shatters when met by the force of a body crashing through it. Kenny is seeing this madness unfold in what seems to be slow motion right before his eyes.

It's crazy assed Bloody- Zoe. He's sailing through the air; his two guns' drawn and blazing. Bloom! Bloom! Bloom Bloom! His Bullets re-tracing his path as he descends.

Niggas are catching wicked slugs.  It's like some Matrix type shit.

He shouts to Kenny. "NOW!!" as his backside comes to rest meeting the ground.

Kenny doe not hesitate. He pulls trigger sending propelled rocket through now broken window. KABLAAAAMM!

The house explodes, erupting into flames: thick, dark, smoke funnels from every orifice of the house which is now on the verge of collapse. Its wooden frame cracks and shifts as its roof fold inward and down. Not one of those West End Kats survives.


Kenny bolts to Zoe, helping him to his feet. The two killers make a hasty retreat back up the alley, returning to the Jeep. The sounds of sirens abound as the colleagues in crime escape the North Side. They head to Kee's house where they will stash their new hardware. Kee can also make Zoe's Desert Eagles disappear.

(Elsewhere)

# (Wolves in Sheep's Clothing)

Danny needs to get out of the house. Michelle is on the rag and she has plucked his last nerve, bitching and moaning about his spending too much time playing video games and sports with his boyz. He needs to get out of the house for some fresh air. But where will he go. He decides to just drive.

He thinks of Ricky as he rides. He can't wait until tomorrow. He wants Ricky so very badly. He finds himself drifts toward the downtown Shoco Slip District. He circles the block scooping out The End Zone, then he parks. He's curious and thirsty. He thinks, surely it can't do any harm if he just goes in for a quick drink.

He exits his car then goes in the building. He feels relaxed as takes a seat at the bar. The bar is packed with a large variety of fine gents. His mouth starts to water as he sits sipping a beer and looking at firm man ass.

Ten minutes in and he's approached by an older gentleman who invites him to join he and his friends at their table. He's not really feeling this brother. He looks like a businessman, and Danny prefers thugs. Danny says what the hell why not. He joins them; they are regulars here. They sit watching a boxing match on the large screen TV while engaging in lively conversation. Mainly they share sports trivia and gossip about others they know.

Thirty minutes pass and Danny is up to speed on this new set. He knows who the major players are and has the dirt on all the wolves' scrubs and queens. Down Low Brothers are kinda funny to watch; most look like real men so one never knows who is pitching and who is catching. Danny is a pitcher. And oddly enough so are all the other dudes at this table. No love connections are apparent here. These brothers have deep pockets so empty beer pitchers accumulate rather fast.

Danny doesn't know it but they are hoping to get him drunk. He's sitting with a pack of wolves in sheep's clothing. They get off on flipping brothers. It's like a game to them. It's kind of like when straight nigga's try to flip dikes, It's kind of like when little- dick dogs seek tight virgin pussy. It's the thrill of conquest they all seek. Danny is not to be pitted.; he too plots on pile driving virgin ass-hole. He encourages his new boys to drink up.

He wants Ricky but the small framed man sitting next to him will do for tonight. They have been playing footsy with each other under the table for some time by now. Nature calls and the two of them go to the head to answer. The bathroom is empty.

Danny places the lock on the doors and they start to kiss. It's a power struggle, both try to dominate and assume the male stance. It's a tug of war of tongues. They take turns pulling the other's hands from their asses to their dicks. Danny will not break.

He pushes the smaller male downward. He wants a dick suck. Danny has more testosterone then the small framed male who breaks. He drops to his knees sucking Danny as if he were his wife. He sucks Danny's dick like a dike eats pussy. He thinks he is still in the aggressive position. He's rough and teasing Danny, halfway sucking a dick. Danny tells him he wants to tap dat ass.

The man's response, "well I might let you if you let me go first."

Danny is hip to this game. He tells the man. "Bet but I ain't loose enough yet. Just keep sucking me till I loosen up."

He allows this guy to play with his asshole as he sucks. The man is so wrapped up in the thrill of fingering Danny; he's so turned on that he forgets he's supposed to be holding back.

He's caught up in the moment. He fails to realize that Danny has become more aggressive and is now fucking him in his mouth.

Danny has flipped this so called wolf and he doesn't even know it.

Danny talks down to him. "Yeah dat's how I like it. You want this tight asshole don't you nigga."

 The man incorporates his response into his dick sucking, his head he shakes yes. He removes his finger from Danny's asshole smelling it. The scent heightens his excitement. He sucks with more intensity.

Danny continues to run game; swirling his hips he fakes as if he is trying to pull his dick from the man's mouth saying.

"No not like this. Nigga don't you want me? I want you up in me. I'm almost ready for you. He pulls the man's hands placing them back to his ass. But now he pumps with even more force.

He says, "Do dat shit nigga. Aww yeah, nigga make my asshole hot. Suck diss dick if you want diss tight chocolate ass hole. Suck it red nigga!"

Danny gives no indication he's about to cum but cum he does. He bust hot, thick, creamy nut all in this man's mouth.

Danny then pulls his dick away from the man's face. The man looks up to Danny asking if he can have some ass now?

Re-packing his pistol in his pants Danny says. "Maybe later." and exits the restroom leaving the so called wolf on his knees. Before he closes the door he says, "game recognize game dog." Danny knows he could have dug this nigga out but he is saving the dick for Ricky. He's infatuated with him.

He goes back to his seat at the table. The others ask him where is Maurice? Danny asks 'who?" They repeat Maurice. The guy you went to the head with?

"Oh that's his name, Maurice." Danny smiles saying, "Oh him. I think he's taking a dump." They all go back to acting like ordinary men talking about sports, car and other guy stuff. Danny's feeling this Fudge Packer bar.

*(It's now 10:15pm)*

Kenny and Zoe have visited Kee and are now back at Zoe's filthy crib. Ricky and his cousins are on the streets and on the prowl.

They have heard of Kenny's and Zoe's recent visit to their newest drug spot. They are not concerned. They will deal with them later. They have other plans for this night. They are on their way to the church where Johnny's remains rest. They want to pay their final respects to Mr. Superstar.

# (The Bliss of Standing over a Dead Enemy)

A black sedan slowly creeps down the alley which runs behind the Third Street Baptist Church. It parks at the side of the building.

Inside the car are three grimmy black males snorting cocaine , drinking beers and loading handguns. Should they be interrupted by anyone the silence of the night will be replaced by gunfire.

They exit the car making their way to its trunk where they remove a medium sized yellow plastic carrying case, vinyl coveralls and a crowbar.

They casually chatting as they head to the door at the rear of the church. They force it open. They are here to pay their final disrespect to a one Mr. Jonathan R. Harris; People called him Superstar.

They look about the church as they walk down the aisle headed to a grand casket which sits just below the pulpit. Paintings of Jesus Christ and his disciples adorn the walls and ceiling. Just behind the Pulpit is a eight foot high wooden statue of Jesus on the cross.

Ricky and his cousins claim to be Christian's but the act they are about to commit, will forever defile this sacred place of worship.

They reach the coffin dropping the carrying case atop it. Ricky curses as he starts to open it.

"God damn it! I can't get this fucking latch open."

His cousin Chris gives it a try.

He too curses. "Mother- fuck! Shit did somebody glue diss bitch shut." His brother Frank tells him to step aside and, he gives it a shot. It opens.

175

Ricky tosses the carrying case to the red carpet and says.

"Dat's what the fuck I'm talking about. Now we can put in some work."

He holds a small gas powered chain saw in his hand. He rips this bitches cord and she buzzes like a million busy Honey Bees.

Frank opens the upper lid of the silver with gold trimmed casket. There he lays, Mr. Pee Body himself. Chris makes his way to the other side of the casket taking a firm grip of its lower rail, he lifts hard toppling it from its petal stool. It crashes hard to the floor hard.

Ricky stands ready holding his razor tooth friend. He shouts orders.

"Get his bitch ass out of the box!" The two brothers are more than willing to oblige him. Here lies a former man of power and prestige.

Ricky says, "Let's get this party jumping." The two brothers unzip their pants and start to urinate all about Johnny's corpse. They piss long and steady; Robert Kelly would be proud of them both. Feeling left out, Ricky turns the saw off and joins them.

He plays pilot to bombardier. His piss is the ammunition and Johnny's make-up covered face is the target. He jokes as he prepares to relieve himself. He talks like they use to in those old World War 2 movies where the pilot is just about to deliver his payload of bombs over Berlin.

Frank and Chris make airplane engines noises with their mouths as if they are old B-14 bombers.

Ricky says in a vintage movie voice. "We are over target".

He makes a static sound as if he is talking over an old long-

176

range radio.

"Clitk! We have visual confirmation of target. Clitk! Clitk! Red Rooster Can you confirm orders to lay the egg? Clitk, Clitk!"

Frank joins in the fun, talking in a similar fashion, he says.

"Worm Wrangler you're breaking up! Can you repeat; Copy can you repeat?" Ricky repeats and Frank responses,

"Clitk! That's an affirmative Clitk! Deliver the payload" "Clitk! That's affirmative."

Ricky makes a whistling sound mimicking bombs dropping, he's unloading his payload pissing directly onto Johnny's make-up covered face *(They all burst into laughter).*

*(Ricky talks to Johnny's corpse )*

"Look at you now Big Shot! So you thought pissing on my brother was funny, hun bitch! Well look at you now."

He takes out his gun and starts filling Johnny's corpse with red hot, hollow-point lead bullets.

BLAM! BLAM! BLAM! BLAMM echoes though the temple.

Chris jokes his brother Frank saying. "You said worm wrangler." He laughs aloudly.

The violators pack there six shooters back into their pants then step into their coveralls; they continue rejoicing.

*(Back at Zoe's pad)*

Kenny and Zoe are winding down for the night; they sit smoking Mary Jan and reminiscing about Johnny. Zoe tells Kenny he is about to crash saying to him he is more than welcome to sleep on the couch. Kenny thanks him but declines the offer. He plans to stay at Butter's House. He knows he is always welcomed there.

Zoe sees him to the door telling him he will see him at the funeral in the morning. Kenny has a question he's dying to ask Zoe. He ask him how did he manage to get away from them West Side Katz when he was in the rooming house. He believes in luck and in God's grace but for the world he just can't understand how Zoe pulled that shit off.

Lorenzo smiles and says. "K, I just closed my eyes and prayed on it."

Kenny looks deep into his eyes; his final thought. Is Zoe serious?

He leaves for Butter's Crib.

*(At the church)*

Ricky stands behind a bible which he has placed on the floor. It serves as home plate. There he stands like Babe Ruth tapping the bottom of his shoe with his mighty bat. Chris now stands on top of the church's organ. It serves as a pitcher's mound. He winds his arm preparing to throw Ricky a Five Fingered Knuckle ball. Chris holds a collection basket which he's using as a catcher's mitten. He stands to the rear of Ricky calling to Frank.

He say's "come on boy sock one in her." Frank throws the improvised ball. Ricky swings and misses.

Chris says, "Strike two" then tosses the ball back to his brother the pitcher. Rick argues with the catcher saying that was a fowl ball. He then prepares himself for the next pitch. Once more tapping his improvised bat to the heal of his shoe; Ricky's eyes are intensely focused on the ball. Frank pitches his famous fast ball. Ricky swings and misses.

"Strike three and you out ", shouts the catcher. Ricky slings his bat saying", Fuck diss I need another bat that one was crooked. Conversation turns into a heated debate. They start to argue about which one of them was the better ball player in high school. Ricky was All- American, so he insist there is no way a third string pitcher like Frank could strike him out. He tells them to give him a better bat and he will prove his point. Chris tells him to get it himself.  He will. He starts his trusty chain saw and cuts Johnny's one remaining stiff leg off. Frank tells him to get another ball then tosses Johnny's left hand into center field (the pews).

Ricky says damned, is this all he got left, as he holds Johnny's stiffened leg up. He is right. Bits and pieces of Johnny are strewn all about the church. Johnny's torso is all that remains; it resembles ravished Thanks Giving Turkey caucus.

Ricky Says. "Fuck! We can't play without a ball. He drops Johnny's leg. They have paid their final respects and now it's time to split. He kicks the torso then the three exits as they entered: wicked, godless heathens.

# (Midnight Rondavue)

Kenny arrives at Butter's house parking in the visitors section; he makes his way to her condo.

*(Butter opens the door)*

She is not surprised to see its Kenny. He and Johnny were known for showing up unexpected. Butter's girlfriend never approved of the practice but Butter encourages it. She knows it pisses her girl Jazzy off. They never argue in front of Kenny but when he leaves it's always on.

Jazzy is forever accusing Butter of fucking with that poison. Poison, that's what some dykes consider men. Jazzy is asleep and

Kenny knows not to wake her. He is quite as he moves about the house. Butter tells him he does not have to tip toe about. Kenny is like a big brother and as far as she is concern this is his home as well. Still Kenny knows Jazzy from back in the day. She is one of those loud bitches that like to get in niggas' faces.

His boy Sean used to fuck with her back when she played straight. Many a night he sat with his nigga nursing many a black eye. She's a quick to throw shit at a nigga's head type chick. Kenny tries to stay on her good side because he knows his temper and he would put that hoe in a coma if she ever tries him. Butter loves this hoe so he tries to keep the peace. For real he can't stand her ass. He feels Butter can do better.

Butter shows Kenny to a spare bedroom than goes to prepare him a warm glass of milk. She knows him almost as well as his wife. Milk relaxes him. She returns sitting next to Kenny who's undressing aside the bed. He pulls his shirt off and she sees the bandages around his ribs. She asks him what happened. But he does not answer; instead he just looks down shaking his head. He tells her. I'm ok Lil mama. She kisses his forehead then dims the light as she leaves the room. He tells her goodnight.

So many thoughts swirl in Kenny's head as he lies staring at the ceiling. He thinks of relatives that have passed and family and friends that are still alive. He wonders who all will be at the funeral. He takes out the book from Johnny's traveling bag and silently recites a poem by Roe Jay the poet before fading off into an uneasy sleep. Kenny loves this nigga's work, *His words comfort him.*

# Mad man's prayer / Kane's curse

So many forgotten dreams

as I the sinner cast my head atop a rock

seeking a restful night's sleep,

But For fear I'd bare the label weak,

would if I could bare the burden but weep,

I the Old Lion, who would lay with sheep,

all the while the fanged-viper in me speaks,

Shackling the minister, who'd prefer to speak,

the weak and weary sap my strength like the common leech,

while the gullible dead, for my life they reach,

the difference between shark and whale, is

minimal, when both are stranded on a beach,

Is cheery plumb, is apple peach?

Do nightmares dare, to touch saint's sleep,

In slumber's care, where babies peep?

it's black as crow at eagles peaks,

vultures pick at old bones that have Sun-bleached,

it's from my sub-consciousness,

this poisonous venom seeps,

I am the tiger,

I crave fresh meat,

*Lord bless the bold,*

*and protect the meek,*

*As I the sinner lay my*

*demons down too sleep,*

*Erase Kane's mark,*

*Dear Father,*

*I do beseech.*

*Roejay the poet*

*(Back at the End Zone)*

Danny is enjoying himself to the fullest. He sits with his new friends talking and drinking.

They have an Arm Wrestling Contest going on and Danny is winning. It would seem all of that time he spends hiding from his wife in his basement weight room is finally paying off. These men act as if they are really into the competitive spirit of matching strength, but truth be told it's probably just an excuse for them to hold hands.

It's hard to cut brothers on the Down Low slack. After all who knows what motivates them. They have girlfriends, yet they want dick? They look like men, but they kiss men? What the fuck! One could go crazy trying to figure those brothers out.

Danny's new friend Maurice is now a stalker. Every chance he gets he makes goo-goo eyes at Danny. Danny is carrying this Nigga like he never met him. It's like their bathroom encounter never happened. But Maurice knows not to shadow him too closely. The last thing he wants is for Danny to pull his bitch card in front of his

182

fellow wolves.

For real he knows he's a bottom bitch and these so call friends of his would all but rape his little gay ass. They don't know it but he spent a year in jail. He was passed around and traded so much that he had to be removed from the general population. The guards mainly look the other way but the prisoner's abuse of him escalated to a point where it was so sever they feared for his life.

Maurice wants to be a wolf because he was prey for so long. He wants Danny. He sits smelling his unwashed hand fantasizing about penetrating Danny's tight, virgin, asshole. He declines offers to arm wrestle. The obsessed punk sits drooling, fantasizing and sniffing the scent of dried ass-juice from his fingers.

Danny sits with his back to the door. He's unaware the building occupancy has increased by one. He's locked in a battle of strength with a rather buff gentleman. Sweat pours from his brow as a large blood vessel in his arm pulsates. He wonders if he has met his match.

Money is on the table and fresh bets are being place by the crowd surrounding the table. It's loud and noisy in the smoke-filled bar. Danny bears down grasping the edge of the table with his free hand. His thought, so much pain. Anguish fills the face of his worthy advisory as he too is taxed to his physical limit. It's just a matter which one of them will break first. Hands locked they feel the others power: bets grow. Who wants it more? Danny gives it his all, releasing a deep groan from the pits of his nut sacks taking this man's pride as he sends his hand crashing to the solid oak table.

The crowd cheers. Some have made money, some have lost. But it's all in fun. Shaking the loser's hand and wiggling his fingers Danny says, "Whose next." The blood flow returns to his hand and he's ready to take on the next rival. A familiar scent catches his attention, it smells so good; Its Polo cologne.

Danny sits attempting to bait yet another patsy. He's talking mad shit. He shouts at the top of his voices repeating himself.

"Who's next? Who else wants to give me their money?"

The scent of Polo cologne becomes even more noticeable. He sniffs left then right; it seems to be coming from behind him. Still there is something familiar about it. Good cologne mixes with its wearers body-oils giving each person a distinct aroma. Whoever it is, he wears it well.

Danny's geared up for the next round as fresh-meat takes a seat across the table from him. Danny says, "Lets up the stakes." He puts all of his winning up against anyone willing to match the pot. Three- hundred dollars of winning are on the line. The brother across the table says that's too rich for his blood then he stands leaving the table.

*(A voice comes from the crowd to his rear)*

"I'll take your bet." The crowd parts and a gentleman makes his way through the crowd taking the vacant seat. He introduces himself, but it's not needed. This is the man on Danny's dreams. It's Ricky.

Ricky reach in his pocket pulling out a conservative money clip and loosens Three Franklins, arrogantly tossing them atop the table. Someone yells the pot is now $600.

Danny's heart is racing. It's too soon; this is not how he wanted to meet Ricky. If he beats him, will he harbor harsh feeling toward him?

Ricky rolls up his sleeve then places his elbow on the table and says. "Damned has anybody ever told you that you look just like a model?"

Danny blushes showing those perfect, pretty, pearl- white teeth of his and answers. "Yeah all the time but it ain't so bad."

His elbow meets the table and the two lock grips; they stair right into each other's eyes as they await the countdown. Danny's thinks, his hands are so soft. Ricky's thought, I wonder if he is a top or bottom.

The countdown reaches one and "GO" is shouted!

It's all Ricky as he powers Danny's weary arm mid way of defeat.

Danny grits his teeth as the veins in his forehead bulge . Something is not right. The pain is unbearable. Has he pulled a muscle or sprained something?

*Ricky continues to apply steady force and Danny's arm starts to give way. One centimeter at a time he is losing, but his pride won't let him just toss in the towel. He sucks the pain up; he gives it his all and slowly his arm start to ascend. Big bets are now being placed by all.*

Ricky starts to show signs of fatigue as Danny rocks his world powering his arm back to the center position. The two are where they started, even in the middle, but now it's not polite thoughts and compliments. Its all sweat and balls, it's time to man the fuck up. Some cheer for Danny but the majority of support is for Ricky. After all he is a regular here and Danny is a newcomer.

Maurice stands at Danny's side patting him on the back he yells, Go Danny you can take him! This distracts him causing a mental lapse which could lead to his defeat. Ricky has a brief thought about Kenny and Zoe's recent visit to North Avenue. It enrages him.

He transfers that rage from his heart to his arm, and that's it. Wham! Danny's arm crashes to the table hard. He screams in pain His winning streak is over; even worst his arm may be broken..

The crowd disperses but Ricky remains at the table with Danny and the wolf pack. Ricky summons a waiter and has him to go get a bucket of ice along with some towels for Danny's arm. He likes Danny, so he feels bad that he is hurt.

Ricky sits wrapping ice into a large bar rage making a cold-compress giveing it to Danny. They hold hands in the transfer as Danny accepts the offer of kindness. There is a definite attraction here and all at the table are aware of it. A jealous Maurice attempts to cock block. He interjects himself into what should be private conversation between the two. The other men at the table see that the two want to be left alone so they all come up with cool excuses and depart the table; all except Maurice.

Danny and Ricky continue with their meet and greet conversation until it is apparent that Maurice is getting in the way. They have to shake this scrub. They leave the club together.

*(It's now 4:50am)*

# Chapter 8/ Grief

*K*enny is sound asleep. He's trapped in a nightmare. It's the type of dream where you try to wake up and you can't. *Its cast of familiar phantoms appears at random. They are those he and Johnny killed in the line of conducting business. He relives executions; all mindless acts of genocide. Nicole's niece acts as his guide as he revisits bloody crime scenes. Her face is blooded and her brains seep from her left eye just as they had the night Johnny ended her life. She repeats herself saying. I was going to pay him. Kenny tries his best to explain to her that it was not personal. He asks for her forgiveness, but his voice is muted. She can't hear him. Johnny's* face appears as a huge, gray thunder cloud which follows them. Lightning surges from Johnny rapidly striking his victims as if he is attempting to kill them again. Words repeat in the fury of his thunder. Vengeance is mines say'th the Lord. Kenny's sweat soaks the beds sheets. He is aware of his body but he is paralyzed. He can hear the water which runs in the fish tank beside the bed, but he can't awaken. He is a hostage to terror; there is no reprieve from this nightmare.

Three small children appear on a playground jumping rope. They are dressed in white. The sound of their laughter gives Kenny a faint sense of relief. Nicole's niece haunts him saying look what you did. The scene changes and the children which were dressed in white are now wrapped like mummies in yellow crime scene tape. Kenny's wife Cheryl appears dressed in black. She's crying, her screams those of a dying Raven. She screeches the names of their children: Darren, William and James. Ricky appears as the Grim reaper dressed in a money-green colored cloak. He's feeding the children ice cream, but it's not vanilla or chocolate. It's a mixture of crack-cocaine and assorted body parts. Kenny shouts to them not to eat, but their father's voice they can't hear. The three brothers kneel in a row lapping the disgusting treat from gold with diamond encrusted dog bowls. Ricky laughs as he separates the boy's heads from their bodies according to their birth order. Darren is first. Kenny is powerless to stop him as a sea of ghouls pull at him holing him a prisoners. Kenny roars so hard that blood surges from his vocal cords turning the sky blood-red. His mother appears and he is no *longer a man held by demons but a baby being rocked in her arms. She looks down on him; her head she shakes in shame as she rocks him. She looks so sad, she looks so disappointed. She's weeping. All the while the thunder cloud Johnny roars lighting the crimson sky. Kenny is trapped in a hell he can't escape. Scarlet flames erupt from the ground beneath his mother's feet then acid rain pours down on them. He's not a Giant. He's a helpless baby. He's trapped in this Nightmare, this stick-up; a tale where life's desires intersect with lust, corruption and vice. Black sought to take his riches and he and his friends waged war sticking up others for the ultimate possession; their lives. They are all guilty. Kenny prays this Stick up will end soon. He prays the nightmare will cease.*

*Kenny hears the telephone ringing, but he can't break free of his nightmare to answer. He prays someone will shake him, awakening him. He begs for forgiveness in his prays. Butter answers the phone than rushes too Kenny shaking him hard. It's an urgent call. She shakes him harder and faster. But he awakens not. In the dream he feels a tugging at the blanket which his mother holds him in. He embraces her tightly seeking security in her loving arms. As much as he wants this dream to end he does not want to leave his moms arms; he misses her so very much. She speaks to him saying. "Son I have faith in you. Put your trust in the Lord and the Sun will shine on you. She then places him on the ground where he is transformed to a man once more.* The dream is over. Kenny awakens to a horrified Butter. She's shaking, her voice trembles as she tells him it's his aunt Mattie on the phone; something awful has happened.

# (The phone call)

Aunt Mattie is hysterical; she sobs and gasps for air as she tries to speak. "My poor baby; Oh lord my baby!" She drops the phone then falls to her knees. She claws at the carpeted floor like a rabbit dog trapped in a cage, her head she shakes in solace. "Why?" She repeats and murmurs. What had her poor boy done to deserve this?

*The church attendants have discovered Johnny's violated corpse. No funeral will happen on this grim day. The church is now a crime scene and the Superstar's remains evidence.*

Alarmed Kenny shouts in to the phone's receiver.

"Aunt Mattie! What's wrong! Aunt Mattie!" He is met with silence then more sobbing. He wants to console her but she sounds so far away. She seems so-so very distant. He starts to panic. His Aunt was a strong woman and it would take a horrific tragedy to bring her to her knees. He wonders if something has happened to his uncle Herb.

Just then Uncle Herb picks up the phone. Kenny is relieved.

" Unc! What's the matter! Tell me what's going on!"

He is again met with more silence. Uncle Herb sighs then he set about the business of telling Kenny of Johnny's final ordeal. He breaks down crying midway of the story, and then somehow he manages to regain his composure to finish.

*(He has final words to Kenny)*

"Son you be careful. Lord knows it's hard but you just got to let it go. Just give it to God." A better man than Kenny, he ends the call, sobbing.

He has more urgent affairs to attend now. He has questions for the police and needs to make alternate arrangement for the disposal of what remains of his beloved son. Cremation seems to be the best option now. Johnny was a proud man who commanded respect in life, and in respect of his memory he ask Kenny not to tell others what has happened at the church. He makes Kenny promise and reluctantly he does so.

## (The Irreconcilable Indifference of Revenge When Felt)

Kenny sits on the side of the bed, his head hangs low, a Newport burns to its filter, and its searing heat bothers him not. It burns to its filter only to be extinguished by the seared flesh of a once proud and confident gangster's left hand. He's ashamed. His cousin has been disrespected in death. His tears flow like rivers of molten lava burning his cheeks; a volcano of emotions is about to erupt, but for now there is silence.

Butter stands in the door way gazing in disbelief. She has never seen Kenny like this. He looks broken, weak, diminished. He looks like a man who has not the will to go on. She is concerned for him but her loyalty is to Poison first. Someone needs to step up and handle their business. She does not know what was said to Kenny but she knows it's connected to the series of shit Ricky has been putting down.

She closes the door leaving Kenny to his thoughts. Kenny saw betrayal in her eyes, her footsteps pat as soft as Judas's last kiss; she makes her way back to her lover's arms. John B's *They Don't Know* plays low on the CD changer. Kenny thinks about the life he use to have and the new life he wants. After hearing what was done to his cousin's corpse things will never go back to how they were; his future looks bleak.

He thinks of his family, just maybe he can take them and run away. But he was taught a man doesn't run from his problems. He has no choice but to meet them head on. He Calls Zoe's phone but there is no answer. Butter is placing calls as well. Things are in motion; damned Kenny Nobles and his weakness, she whispers. Loyalties are about to be broken.

Angela Winbush's _Smile_ now plays in the background. Kenny hears hear the songstress soothing voice and he smiles. He smiles for all their fallen soldiers that can't. His head rocks slow to the beat. He decides to write his last wishes in a letter to his wife Cheryl. Cheryl Pepsis Riley's thanks for my child plays as he scribes his devotion to her and the kids. Come sunrises either he or Ricky will be dead. Tact in dealing with the situation now seems un- acceptable. He is going to do Ricky at his home and anybody standing in the way is as good as dead. Fuck his kids, wife and any other bystanders.

He calls Kee telling her he is heading back to her house. He needs the weapons he had stashed there earlier. He dresses for his fate. No vest, no cares, no tomorrow; only sorrow and a hollow, hard, heart will accompany him in this endeavor through madness's maze.

He drives slowly as not to attract unwanted attention as he stops at Kee's then heads for Ricky's home. He arrives and park atop a hill overlooking the gated complex. It's almost sunrise and he can see the children preparing for school through a window with his binoculars. He spies other windows as well. He sees Ricky's wife. He thinks about Cheryl and his kids, he take a deep breath than hefts the rocket launcher atop his broad shoulder. It's loaded and ready to commit infanticide.

The metal trigger feels so cold beneath his finger; this is wrong plays to the back of his mind: the madness wrecking his soul; Aww, what the FUCK, thinks Kenny. This is revenge and its sights are locked. Slowly he rises, the paining of his bruised ribs remind him just how harsh reality can be.

The distant sound of a familiar ring-tone finds its way through the complex web of confusion and, hate that has become Kenny's thought process. Should he answer before or after the foul deed his quagmire? Yeah A nigga said quagmire. That's a situation from which extrication is very difficult.

What the hell thinks the soon to be baby killer. He pulls the trigger but nothing happens; he's somewhat relieved. The rocket is a dud. He Shucks it to the ground and heads to the Jeep to get another. The phone continues to ring so he answers.

Of all people, it's Lorenzo.

" K ?" Danny hooked up with dat bitch Ricky; they at a motel on Chamberlyn Avenue. This bass head nigga I know works the front desk there. He just called me saying he saw Danny creeping with some bald-head Kat. It got to be Ricky."

"What?" responds a relieved but excited Kenny.

"Give me the address I'll meet you there." Kenny thinks long and hard as he drives to the motel. He wonders why Danny jumped the gun. He hooks up with Ricky ahead of schedule and didn't even let him know. He hears the distant ghost of his mom's voice whisper into his hear from the past. "Boy never look a gift horse in the mouth she'd occasionally say.

He smiles, diving deeper into though he thinks God must be at work. He was seconds from committing the most unthinkable atrocity and just like that the rocket misfired and Zoe called. There has to be a God, and if God is real then so is heaven, hell and the Devil. He was never one to waste much time thinking of such things, but this was an epiphany. Sometimes he felt bad about being in the game: the dirty deeds he and his friend did but never did he consider their actions of evil origin. Should he reconsider what he feels he has to do? Will this be the deed that condemns his soul to Hell for sure?

"Naw fuck that weak right vs. wrong, good vs. evil Judo-Christian bull shit. Im'a do this slimy nigga for me, my cousin, and Poison." He's decided. If he be hell bound then the damning deed will be horrific on a scale so monumental Satan himself will be appalled.

*(At the motel)*

Danny awakens from a heated night of steamy sex. He looks upon Ricky's naked hard body thinking. This could be the man I been seeking. Ricky had turned him out: flipped his ass. He remembers how good this man felt tenderly taking his manhood. Once a wolf he's now a sheep. He rubs his hand about Ricky's chest playing with his hair; gently shaking him to awaken. Ricky is a hard sleeper but Danny has a trick. It always worked for his wife. Slowly he pulls back the covers and places Ricky's soft dick into his mouth. He gives a little suction as he takes the whole of a chocolate sensation deep into the back of his mouth. The rawness of their sexual smell saturates the air. He inhales it, embracing the scent of combined testosterone, his nipple he pinches while playing with Ricky's nipple ring with his free hand. A groggy half sleep Ricky responds with a slight moan.

Danny is not satisfied with his meager response. He applies more suction and Ricky's rod begins to rise. Slowly his ass he moves up and down as he awakens. What he feels for Danny has grown beyond a simple lust in but a night's time. He loves this man. This man he had allowed to take his manhood has taken his heart as well. Two dicks had been seasoned the prior night. There is no longer the conflict of dominance; only two men with sincere admiration, respect and love of each another. They both share a similar vision. It's a simple one; that they could be together, forever. But for the moment what they share will due.

Ricky's body tingle with delight as his pulsating cock explodes filling Danny's mouth till white cream runs from its corners. He is new to sucking dick yet he tries to handle the situation like a pro. He continues sucking while pulling firmly at the base of Ricky's pole which he now squeezes and strokes. He wants every drop this killer has to offer. He suck until there is no more. Ricky says to him. "Let me do you next, and he does. He likes the taste as well. They are addicted to one another.

Exhausted the two lie still as calm waters embracing one another; they share a common thought. What's next? Should they abandon their false lives? The down low is played. Maybe they could start over as a couple. Could they escape to paradise un-explored? To be openly gay, to be free: perhaps they could relocate to a more understanding locality, maybe some place like San Francisco.

*(RAW DOG)*

Kenny sits in his Jeep parked around the corner on a side street just shy of the motels parking lot entrance; he's waiting for his man, his partner in crime , his new found road dog, Zoe. What the fucks taking this nigga so long, he mumbles. Just then a motorcycle's head lights beam through his rear window. Through his rear view mirror he sees its Lorenzo. He remains inside the car and Zoe approaches from the rear coming too stand aside the door of the Jeep. He's got that cold killer look he always has but this early in the morning it three times intense.

"Damned nigga why the fuck you looking so crazy", ask Kenny.

"Shit who the fuck wants to be up this damned early" says Zoe.

"True dat, true dat", replies Kenny. Rubbing his eyes he exits the Jeep. He stretches his arm out and upward as he releases a long yawn. He asks Zoe what he's packing. Lorenzo lifts his shirt to show his wears.

"Naw dog that ain't gonna get it" says Kenny reaching into the Jeep, he pulls a sawed-off shotgun off its floorboard. He pumps that bitch stock and says to his second.

"Nigga you my dog so we gonna give it to this bitch raw. Zoe shakes his head giving his unconditional approval. He thinks to himself; maybe, just maybe Kenny ain't to be messed with. That cold, distant stare Kenny has reminds him of someone. But whom, he can't put his finger on it.

He looks deeper into Kenny's eyes searching for a clue as Kenny barks.

" Come on Zoe! Come with me to Hell! Darkness lives in this man's heart, there is no longer a Kenny Nobles merely the Giant; a nasty motherfucker with a jet black disposition. Just then its strikes Zoe fast, Kenny has inherited his Cousin Johnny's cold, vacant heart. For the first time Zoe sees Kenny as a killer to be respected. Zoe would never admit it but he too feared Johnny.

The two proceed to the check-in office where Zoe's contact gives them the key to Ricky and Danny's love nest.

(In *the room Ricky and Danny ready themselves for round two. They can't get enough of one another*)

Up the green painted cement stair, left at the rusted iron rail and 22 steps and the two malice thugs come too stand at the door of room 209. Zoe slowly inserts the large key into the lock gently turning it he is careful not to make a sound. Kenny stands close to his back as they quietly enter the room.

The shadow they cast is busy. The screen is disturbing; two

men going at it. Huffing, puffing, moaning and groaning. Danny's in the driver's seat and Ricky's car is up on the rack getting a lube job. By the sounds Danny's making he's about to inject Ricky with a quart or two of pure petro. He shakes violently as shivers overtake his body.

His words "God! Nigga I think I love you." He releases then slums over his chest resting on Ricky's back.

*The room is dead silent* then Kenny speaks after pumping the slide of his 12 gauge shoot gun.

"Don't move!!!"

They dare not. Kenny's voice is distinct and both Ricky and Danny fear the trail has come to an end. Zoe's footsteps are heavy as he walks to the head of the sweat drench bed placing a small caliber handgun to Ricky's temple.

"Shit it stinks in here", grunts Zoe.

"Yeah this some nasty shit we walked in on Zoe. Ricky finds himself in the awkward position of trying to bargain for his life with a limp dick in his ass. Danny starts to explain himself.

" K. I, I, I was going to call you", he stammers.

"Awright Dee I got you, now get your shit and go home to your wife."

He is slow to move pulling soft dick out of the man he has come to love in but such a brief moment.

In the back of his mind there is hope that he will see him again. After all Kenny did say Poison wanted to work a deal with him. But the look in Kenny's eyes and the twisted smile on Lorenzo face dashes that hope. He hops as he scrambles to put on his pants tripping and falling to the floor. Zoe laughs then says.

"Damn Dee, diss nigga got you weak at da knees like dat?"

Danny regains his footing collects his gear he exits quickly not looking back. Ricky's thought. Fuck! This nigga set me up! If he gets out of this predicament, he vowels too kill Danny. But now is not the time for that: he has a more pressing concern (*talking Kenny into letting him live*)

He can tell by Kenny's facial expression the Johnny's desecrated corps has been discovered. Kenny walks to the bed smacking Ricky hard on the ass as if he was a phat stripper. The nose of his shotgun he presses to the base of the king-pen's neck. Slowly he slides it downward pausing briefly in-between Ricky's sweat-beaded shoulder blades.

"Jack dat ass up bitch!", he commands.

Ricky's start to whimper saying, "Man I'm sorry ..... Kenny cuts him off. "Bitch shut the fuck up. Now jack that yellow ass up higher." Rick does as he is told. Kenny's shoot gun continues on its path down Ricky's back traverses the slight curve which is Ricky's butt (cold barrel meets swollen asshole). Ricky makes un- natural sounds as he trembles and cries quietly.

"After what you did to my cousin", Kenny abruptly stops mid sentence and looks to Zoe. " Naw dog, it ain't gonna be dat clean."

Zoe looks puzzled. He thinks damned! What could be colder then shooting a nigga in the asshole with a shotgun?

"Bitch stay still, commands Kenny, placing the shotgun on the bed next to Ricky. He unzips his pants and motions as if he is about to pull out his dick. Zoe looks on in disgust; he's like what the fuck!

Kenny re-zips his pants, kicks his head back to one side and

198

let's lose with a wicked laugh. " Psyc ! We Poison and we don't get down like dat. Get your gay ass up!" Zoe's facial expression is one of relief. Kenny may not have always had his total respect but dammed, he never took him as being gay. Still he thinks to himself that was some gay ass shit. He wonders would Kenny have greased this nigga if he was not there. Ricky stands before two pissed off killers; buck ass'd naked.

## (Sending Ricky home)

It's strange the thoughts that can grip one when place in life or death predicaments. Kenny's thinks about Pastor John and the serum he preached about forgiveness. Jesus would turn the other cheek and let Ricky go home to his wife and children.

Lorenzo thinks about the half eaten sandwich he left sitting on the table at Tameka's house. He wants to do Ricky quickly so he can get back to eat it.

Ricky should be thinking about making peace with his maker but instead he can't stop thinking about Danny. He can't fathom that this night they had shared was just sex and a set up. Here he is standing at the brink of his demise and his wife and kids don't even enter his mind.

Kenny Picks the shotgun up once again pointing it at Ricky's privates.

"So you like men. Zoe what say we give this faggot a sex change right here and now?", *Zoe nodes giving his approval. His thought on the matter.*

"Yeah I guess that would be colder than hot buck shot in the ass. At least that would promise a quick death. After all to live as a Unix is every mans worst nightmare.

Kenny asks Lorenzo "what would Jesus do?

" Zoe's hastily responses "How the fuck would I know! Blast diss bitch so I can go finish my got damned sandwich."

" Naw Zoe, showing mercy is the worst I can do him now. Look at him sniveling like the cowardly bitch he is. I think he gets the point. We won't have any more problems out of you, will we? Will we bitch?"

Ricky is fast to answer "No." He grovels at their feet thanking them for sparing his life. His thought they must don't know about what he and his sick cousins did to Johnny's corpse. He continues to give thanks but in his mind he starts to plot the next step in bringing Kenny and Poison to an ending.

Lorenzo has an outburst. "FUCK THAT! WE ARE GONNA DO HIS ASS RIGHT NOW!!!

Kenny checks him with the quickness raising the barrel of his gun pointing it at him. He commands him to drop his gun and Zoe does, tossing it onto the bed. Big mistake Kenny may have signed his own death warrant with this move. No one ever pulled strap on Zoe and live to tell the tale. Kenny tells Ricky to gather his things and releases him to go home.

Ricky collects his things and starts to get dressed but Kenny interrupts him.

"Naw dog don't get dressed; just get the fuck out!"

Ricky bundles his clothing in his arms and leaves in a rush. Zoe and Kenny remain in the hotel room, tensions run high. Zoe has caught feelings. He looks to his gun on the bed asking Kenny, So now what?"

(His though)

If this motherfucker let me get that gun he is dead. Kenny starts to count back from ten slowly. At four he starts to walk toward the door; gun still pointing at Zoe.

He reaches one then turns the door knob quickly flinging the door open.

He yells to Zoe "Come on Nigga get you shit he aint getting away that easily.

He runs outside closely followed by Lorenzo.

Ricky is now at his car fumbling to find his car keys in the bundle of clothing still clutched in his arms. Kenny approach with the speed of a centipede pushing the barrel of the shot gun to the small of Ricky's back.

BLAAM!!!!!

Dude, didn't even have time to turn around. The force of the shotgun blast violently pushes him forward pressing him to the car before he falls backward landing face up to the heavens.

Kenny stands over Ricky. Zoe stands at his back looking over his shoulder. They look down on him.

"Damn. He ain't dead yet says Zoe , puzzled?

"Naw, dog. He just real fucked up", chuckles Kenny.

Help me get his ass in his car. Zoe pops the truck and in goes Ricky.

Kenny drives the car two miles or so to an abandoned housing complex closely followed by Lorenzo in Johnny's jeep. They park just shy of a thicket of woods at the rear or the complex. It's a desolate secluded spot long neglected. Kenny and Zoe sit on the hood of Ricky's Mercedes; both have lit cigarettes in their mouths. Lorenzo looks to Zoe asking what's next. He looks at him looking down he shakes his head then smiles. It's not a happy smile more like the expression of a sick release of tension. Kenny answers saying, "Just enjoy your smoke. I got diss."

He walks to the Jeep pulling a  gas can from its rear. He soaks the car's interior with the majority of the gasoline but save just enough to coat the exterior. They can hear Ricky moaning and moving in the trunk. He's kicking but the thuds are weak, he's fading fast. Kenny is at peace with his thoughts. His thought.  It's a wrap. No turning back.

He plucks his lit cigarette through the car's open window; a quick flash and the car burn out of control. They drive away. Ricky's ghostly screams for help go unanswered. Smoke rises to the sky taking with them the soul of a once power hungry drug lord.

# Chapter 9 *Broken Angel*

*Cheryl sleeps comfortably in her childhood bedroom. The same pink flowered patterned comforter which kept her warm as a child now provides warmth, comfort security for she and her three sons which she nestled closely too her bosom.*

A phone rings in a typical middle class suburban neighborhood home in Northern Virginia. It's not answered immediately as the inhabitant of this typical dwelling where the phone resides is slow to respond. An older woman of 65, she rushes as best she can. Eight rings and counting, she stubs her toe on the leg of an early American coffee table which stands in the front room.

"Jesus! Lord have mercy", she sighs and continues to scurry toward the phone.

Her early morning Coffee routine has been interrupted. She's off balanced spilling hot liquid from a large mug .She now limps as she scuttles along.

"Who in the heck is calling here at 5am in the morning she mumbles.

She's a God fearing Christian woman And her home reflects her
beliefs. The walls are adorned with a slew of religious portraits and plaques. Various nick- knacks expressing similar themes are scattered about.

Her favorite piece is a porcelain figurine of a black angel praying now lies on the floor cracked and broken in many pieces. For some twenty plus years it has adorned and protected her home. If was given a voice it would tell the story of a loving and devoted wife and nurturing mother. It would speak about warm Christmas gathering, Birth Days and many other festive occasions witnesses in this quaint home. A gift given by the woman's mother its sentimental value far surpasses that of even a ship full of Spanish gold doubloon and jeweled treasures. The woman scrambls to answer the ringing phone ,failing to notice the folly of her blunder: somewhat feeble of mind she ignores the fallen angel. e phone.

*(She reaches then answers the phone)*

"Hello?"

*(It's Kenny)*

"Oh. Hey baby! I was just thinking about you the other day. Cheryl and the babies been missing you some awful." She rambles on about her aliments and routine daily events uneventful as they may be.  Kenny is pleased to listen. He loves Ms Charlene, and she he. To her he is simply a wonderful man; a loving and diligent husband. She has no idea he is a ruthless drug dealer and killer. Cheryl had always been carful and secretive in discussion his occupation with her. As far as she knows he's in real-estate and owns a few small businesses. Eventually Ms. Charlene tires of talking and goes to summon Cheryl to the phone.

Cheryl asks "Why are you limping mama,?"

"Oh it's nothing to concern you with baby. I'm just fine. Kenny is on the phone for you."

Cheryl is excited and relieved as she starts to converse with her beloved husband.

"BABE!!! I miss you so much!"

She goes on to talk about the kids and her unwanted retreat to her mother's home. Kenny listens occasionally giving a calm chuckle as she talks about the funny little things her mother does to pluck her nerves. Kenny assures her she will be able to return home soon. He tells her he is well and that unresolved business has been handled. Soon they can rebuild their life. She is disturbed by a number of the events he shares with her.

She has doubts about returning to Richmond and suggests that maybe they should relocate elsewhere. But Kenny is the head of this family and she will do as he says. More troubling to her are these phantom feelings and suspicions of his infidelity. She's been losing sleep with worry. Troubling dreams haunt her nightly. A beautiful woman this ordeal is taking a toll on her appearance. She now has small, dark circles beneath her eyes, her hair pulled back in a pony tail, manicured nail go unkempt; she looks weathered. Kind of like the old wooden framed screen door on Pappy's front porch; chipping paint and splintering cracks. It's seen better days as has Cheryl.

She does not share her troubling thoughts with Kenny. Instead she reassures them both saying.

"Things will be just fine and that she misses and love him very much. She ends the conversation. Kenny feels guilty. He was not completely honest with her. The Ricky issue may never go away. He lights A Newport taking slow pulls he enters into deep thought. The bottle of Grey Goose he holds is almost gone.

Pappy enters the room, wild eyed, hyped and cackling. "I see ya's dealt wit dat situation." Kenny blinks two or three times, leans his head slowly, tilting it to the left. I look of curiosity moves over his face like an ocean wave meeting the shoreline. It's like Pappy is psyic or something. Ricky's body is probably still smothering and undiscovered. The early morning new broad cast made no mention. He wonders how Pappy knows. It's simple his face tells of the dirty deed. It betrays him. Killer is etched on his soul and manifested on his face. He asks Pappy. How can you tell? Pappy looks down grins, pauses, wipes a tear from his eyes and says " Boy us'a knowed dat I loved Johnny? Johnny had dat sickness, He was'a killer just'a like dat other'n ya calls Zoe. Boy us'a a good man but today ya looks moe like them other'ns than yoself. Slowly he backs out of the room leaving Kenny to his thoughts. He ponders what was said. He knows it's true. He's killed before but a premeditated murder always comes with a distinctly different feel. He thinks about the death penalty just then he catches glimpse of movement in a shadowy corner of the room from the corner of his eye. A cold chill runs down his spine. He looks; there's nothing there. He silently reads a poem from the book he got from Johnny's traveling bag.

# Restless Nights

*Restless nights abound*

*Noise filled silence is an eerie sound.*

*A chill like thrill hints of paranoia in the air.*

*Like that of a peeping tom caught gazing*

*into his neighbors bedroom window.*

*For tonight I am the victim of an unearthly midnight voyeur.*

*What is this presents which fills the air?*

*I know I'm alone in this room.*

*Yet of something run afoul I'm aware.*

*The bed moves as if a small child has taken a seat.*

*What is this movement so subtle down by my feet?*

*Frozen;*

*Am I afraid to take a momentary stare?*

*My paranoia now heightened with fear there will be someone*

*or even worst , some ghastly, ghostly creature there.*

*I dare not look.*

*Instead my head I cover with the sheets.*

*I tell myself my mind is playing tricks on me.*

*Or could this be a deceased relative attempting to visit me?*

*Restless nights abound.*

*As I resume the pursuit of a peaceful night's sleep.*

*Still ever elusive somber escapes me.*

*As I concentrate on counting sheep.*

*Restless nights abound; Noise filled silence is an eerie sound;*

*a phantom breeze Wisk past my ear.*

*Like a blow swung but missed creating the slightest movement of air.*

*Mentally am I tripping, I know I am home alone?*

*Paranoid and pissed I dare to take a momentary stare.*

*Almost to my surprise there is nothing; No one is there,*

*damned these restless nights.*

*With all my might I rebuke these feelings of fright,*

*As I toss and turn trying to deny these strange events  this night.*

*I search for that perfect sleep position,*

*But try as I may I just can't seem to get it right.*

*What's this sound, Did someone or something whisper my*

name?

*I shrug it off but there it goes again.*

*Now way passed paranoid or afraid, my mind is racing my heart.*

*Am I about to be punished for my past sins?*

*I'm haunted by Visions of faces, So many men;*

*that I the Executioner have sent to their end.*

*Restless nights abound.*

*Roejay*

*(He lies down praying he can get a few hour of peaceful sleep)*

*(It's now 6pm)*

Kenny is up once again and on the move. By 8pm he is back in Richmond. His intent is to meet with each member of Poison individually. He makes the all too routine rounds getting briefed on product flow. He informs them that unresolved business has been handled. They don't need detail. He conveys that image. He's about business and not to be crossed. He feels for descent in the ranks as well.

Zoe will be the last he meets with but first he need to go by Kee's to check on Arlene. He had spoke with her earlier and the report he got about her was not good. Her use of complementary cocaine has increased at an alarming rate. If she can't keep craving in check there is no way she will be able to manage Poison's new interest in Ashland.

The taste of Girl that Kenny had instructed Kee Kee to give her has developed into a full blown habit. The Days spent at Kee's has been a virtual all you can eat Buffett to her. Kee has done as Kenny asked; leaving small amounts of powdered cocaine about the house where Arlene could happen upon it. At first she was polite asking Kee if she could partake of said powdery, white, goodies happened upon. Kee Kee the ever gracious hostess would say like a trained parakeet ,

"Girl you don't have to ask. Help yourself." Arlene's response was the same each time; a casual smile, a giggle and up her nose disappeared ol Girl like dirt sucked up by a hungry Hoover Vacuum cleaner. Rapid was the progression of the disease of drug addiction for unwitting Arlene. She is in the honey moon stage . Now would be the best time to kick it. But Kee Kee has taken her mandate from Kenny to another level. Increasingly she talks down on Arlene and what was free now has a price. In a matter of days Arlene has relinquished more than half of the cash Kenny had given her.

Kenny arrives at Kee's home a little past eleven o' clock. An eager Arlene greets him at the door, wide eyed and coked up. She's excitable and full of energy like a dog welcoming its master after returning from a long vacation. She rushes him pawing at his pockets patting them asking for money.

Kee stands leaning against a door frame, she looks content as she says to Kenny. "I guess this bitch ain't the one." She then leaves the room switching her phat ass hard.

The house phone rings and Arlene runs to it answering it. It's Zoe, He tells Kenny his baby brother is being released in the morning and that he won't be able to meet with him as planned. He is going to rent a hotel near the prison so he can pick him up bright and early. It's been six years since he last saw him; He has just pulled seven on multiple conspiracy to commit murder charges.

Zoe's little brother Geronimo AKA Clearance White is a contract hit-man; one of the best in the country. Mainly he works abroad but occasionally he does domestic work. He got caught up messing with the Italians as the mafia attempted to restructure in the wake of a rat infestation. Geronimo joined the U.S marines after graduating high school. He later went on to become special ops navy seal and later a CIA associated mercenary working in the Middles East.

Kenny never feared Zoe but there was a darkness about his little brother which always unsettled him. Johnny he and Zoe have all killed but some thing seems evil in Geronimo. Johnny killed to protect what he perceived as belonging to him. Kenny killed out of necessity and Zoe from lack of impulse control disorder.

# *Chapter 10* / *A New Frontier*

**R**oaches crawl about in filth and clutter as an annoying cell phone's ringtone is ignored. On a stained sofa a weekend couch potatoes watches The Life Time Channel. The movie shown is a classic. Its Farrah Fawcett's <u>The Burning Bed.</u> Its sole audience member sits on edge anticipating dark drama. This is a story of love gone wrong, love turned unhealthy from spousal abuse. It's a story of street justice served suburban style: He can relate to the heroine on so many levels.

Zoe curses his maker, The movies at its climax and that damned phone is ruining the moment for him. He sounds off with his course voice howling.

"BITCH GET THE PHONE"!

A less than angelic female voices screams back in response.

"FUCK U NIGGA, YOU GET IT!"

"Dammed Tameka. What the hell are you good for? A nigga can't even watch a movie in peace.

He rises up from the couch making his way to the bedroom where the phone was last seen. He trips over toys, shoes, clothing and an assortment of clutter on his trek. Stepping on small Lego blocks makes his mood ever less pleasant.

*He answers the phone gruffly,*

"WHAT!

*(A relaxed caller responds with a light chuckle)*

" Damned Man, was you that deep into that Life Time?

The  angry hoodlum stats to chuckles as well, this Kat knows him too well, he relaxes.

Damned K, what the word Giant?

Walking to the window Lorenzo looks out of the closed blind peeping through a slit onto the front of the building. He sees Kenny walking up the cement pathway toward the apartment. This is classic Kenny , popping in on people un-announced. He likes to catch people off guard. That way he can see who they really are. Johnny had taught him this. And he had used this tactic to weed out many a perpetrator, phony and fake.

But a Killer like Zoe is seldom caught off-guard, especially in the projects. It' here his killer instincts are at their sharpest. Poverty breeds resentment and young dudes are always on the come up.

Lorenzo opens the  heavy steel door just as Kenny raises his fist to pound on it. He's  greeted with dap, pound and a hug but Kenny declines Zoe's invite to enter;  instead he gives orders. He motions with his head for Zoe to follow him.

"Today's the day."

"Day for what", ask Zoe?"

"The day I put you on nigga."

He then hands Lorenzo three  Department store shopping bags filled with two dress casual outfit and matching dress shoes.

Favoring one bags he says, put these on and meet me at the car."

*(He returns to the car leaving Zoe looking confused)*

He dresses and stops to admire his refection in the mirror. He thinks to himself, it's not a bad look.

He call to Tameka  before leaving the apartment Saying,

" Hey bitch; clean up while I'm gone."

Her response come fast,

" Fuck you nigga. I ain't cleaning shit! And where the fuck you gonna be at?"

His response, " Bitch I'll be where I'm at"!

Tameka is at best trifling , but Zoe loves her.

*(Zoe rocks his head to the beat of the music coming from Kenny's car as he walks there. The track playing is Ice Cubes' Today Was A Good Day)*

He gets into the car asking Kenny what the clothes are for. Kenny smiles catching sunlight with that diamond adorned tooth of his handing him a pair of plane tickets. Florida is the destination but oddly enough it's a one way fair.  Kenny's response is swift and deliberate.

"We have to dress for success or Chucky wont fuck with us."

Oh shit, says a happy Zoe brimming with excitement and holding one hand about his mouth. He's  moves his legs up and down patting his

214

feet in excitement.

"My nigga".

Kenny turns the volume of the  cars system way down to ensure Lorenzo hear what he says next. He tells him they won't be carrying any guns on this trip. Zoe responds,

" Nigga are you crazy! You mean we going to a drug deal in another state with a known homicidal psycho with no heat?

Kenny nodes just once not even looking in his direction. He is focused on the road and what lies ahead of them. He's in Giant mode. Johnny's words from the past repeat in his head. "It's important to have a big stick to back-up big word." Fucking with chucky is Chess, not Checkers. He offers no further explanation .

The phone rings at that moment, It's Teddy and he has an urgent message. Mr. Nelson wants to meet with Kenny and from the tone conveyed he has harsh words and terms for him. Kenny is clear telling Teddy there will be no meeting. Teddy is not pleased with this, Kenny's decision seems foolish. Mr. Nelson is reaching out to them and Kenny is smacking his hand way. He was a friend to Johnny and his family so he wants to make peace,  otherwise retribution for Ricky's murder would have been set in motion by now.

Teddy ends the call not sharing his disapproval or concerns, now he wonders how the other heads will feel about this potential opportunity missed. After all the heroine Poison distributes comes from Mr. Nelsons stores via Blue. He's aware there are whispers or mutiny amongst the heads and wonders if Kenny is adding fuel to the fire?

Kenny explains to Zoe that from now on all routine business calls from the Heads will go through him first since he is now second in command , it was that way for he and Johnny and so it shall be with them.

"Zoe you my main man now, so Teddy and the rest of them got to respect that. Now    call Teddy back and get Mr. nelsons number from him. We might have to meet with him when we get back. But right now I need you focused on this meeting with Chucky. Zoe you have to meet this man's approval or it's a good chance we won't be coming home."

*(Kenny decided to give Zoe the entire score)*

"Zoe I bought you the clothing because Chucky takes his business dealings very seriously. He won't deal with niggas who look thug. He's Jamaican and you know they think they better than us anyway. Zoe no matter what this man says I need you to stay calm. You though Johnny was paranoid? Well magnify that ten times and there you have Chucky."

He found religion ans is now known by his dispels as Minister- Father Chucky the Almighty Servant of God. The Feds are on him more than ever before. His following is diverse, large and he is now a political power house, a force to be reckoned with. All of his associations are closely scrutinized. Chucky is known to make associates disappear on a paranoid whim. Beyond Johnny and his closet associated Sly and Butter bean he trust nobody. A solid trust between  he and Johnny was the cornerstone for many years of successful  business.

"Zoe I have to win his complete trust and he has to accept you as my second. We have to assure him this organization is in capable hands or simplest stated. He's going to literally have us feed to the alligators.

*(Zoe looks confused)*

He blurts out, "And we not packing no heat?"

"Zoe just be calm no matter what".

*(They ride in silence the remainder of the way to the airport)*

Zoe's thought, today is a good day. Unknown to Kenny he is packing a very special type of hand gun made completely of composite plastic. It's about 4 inched long and completely cylindrical. It conceals in his underwear alongside his dick. It shoots one 40 caliber round. Air port security's metal detectors will be easily evaded. Kenny's thought these may be their last living days on Earth.

Kenny phones Chad while waiting to board the plane: he ask him if he has made arrangement for the buy money to be shipped to the suite of the 4 star hotel they have reserved in Florida. He has but there is a pressing issues with a large debt they need collection on. It's the new kid they fronted two keys to hustle in Jackson Ward. He's a disrespectful punk introduced to Poison through Zoe's younger brother Geronimo. He's in desperate need of an attitude adjustment. Kenny hands the phone to Zoe telling him , " deal with it".

Zoe places a call to his little brother with very specific instructions. He is to go to Zoe's crib to get the jewelry he and Kenny took from Quan and deliver the chain to the young kid, La'Quan as a gift. The script-lettered-charm which hangs on the chain spells Quan in gold and diamonds. He's also called Quan so he'll assume the chain is a custom made gift for him.

*(Their flight arrives and they board the plane)*

The flight to Florida is an uneventful one. Teddy has a rental car reserved for them at the airport. From their they go directly to the hotel. Kenny lays claim to the King sized bed leaving Zoe to the pull out sofa sleeper. They play video games late into the evening then go out to score some weed and later liquor from the ABC store.

Upon their return to the hotel Zoe goes to into the bathroom to make a private call , he calls Blue.

" What up big Big Blue?"

" What You want nigga?"

" Damned cuz you don't have to be so hostile all the time."

Everybody knows Blue don't fuck with Zoe like that. He has never like Zoe and that goes back too many years to count. He Johnny and Zoe were all kids together and schoolyard buddies until Blues pet dog Rex was found hung by his leash from a tree at the old run down vacant lot they all played at. It was never proved but Blue felt Zoe did it.

" Blue I got the  run down on who killed Quan.  That new kid we been fucking with LaQuan did it over that college Chick Paulette.

*(Blue ask Lorenzo how he happened upon the information)*

" look,  you wanted to know, so I'm giving you the 411. What you do with it is on you. He won't my brother. Zoe abruptly ends the call as Kenny's knocking on the door.

"Come out of there Zoe I got to go", he yells.

## (My home town)

Back in Richmond Blue is left alone with his thoughts and emotions; he flips through old photo albums reminiscing. He stares at page after page of happy moments capture in time of he and his much younger brother. He was more like a son then a little brother. One picture in particular catches his attention and he breaks down sobbing. It's a Kodak instant picture of him holding the then newborn baby Quan. As of late he's been drowning his sorrows in distilled spirits. A large bottle of vodka sits on the table in front of him. *Blue is wasted.* So much of who he is was connected to being Quan's Big brother, Blue. *Without him he is lost.*

He collects himself as best he can then makes his way to his S.U. V parked outside.

*(less than a mile away near Virginia Union University)*

Paulette is restless at her apartment. She has felt haunted since that night Quan was murdered; she's uncomfortable in her own home. Everything reminds her of that night, she relives the ordeal in her mind continually. She has requested another apartment, she want to move to another complex but as she is not willing to break her lease. Management has replaced the blood ruined carpet but Quan's blood saturated the carpet and sank in to the sub floor. Paulette is bothered knowing Quans DNA stains remain beneath her feet . She's unable to bring herself to enter the bathroom where he was killer and is making frequent trips to her next door neighbors to use theirs. Her bed room is the only place that feels un marked by the murder.

She lays on her bed engaging in her favorite pass time. Paulette is a compulsive masturbator. Her nightstand drawers boast a large assortment of toys both electronic and manual. Tonight she craves her old friend Mr. Blackie. He is a huge strap on variety black rubber dildo measuring just over eight niches. Paulette rubs her clit and plunges Mr. blacks large synthetic head into the opening of her sweet creamy pussy. She is moving it in around and about looking for that perfect rhythmical groove. She searching but it eludes her. She strokes faster, harder than slower and gentle." She's found it. Her pretty vanilla face tell the tell of ecstasy as her soft pink lips quiver in anticipation of her gushing. She takes as much of Mr. Blackie into her as she can handle. She allows her mind to wander, she slips deep into an erotica fantasy. She recalls the touch of Kenny's cock as her face rested on his lap that tragic yet magnificent night. It was big just like Mr. Blackie but hot like a homemade butter milk bisque fresh out of the oven. She recounts how safe she felt kneeling at his sides. She's been missing that feeling and thinking of Kenny constantly since. She wants to know him in the biblical since of the word. She want to fuck him.

In and out she thrust her friend all the while envisioning her new savior. The cold impersonal fell of hardened rubber is replaced by the tingling sensation a woman can only receive from the real thing. Squeezing her firm yet soft breast and rubbing her soft stomach she moves her hand down her picture perfect body rubbing her phat-ass. She begins to smack it hard. She talks to herself

" Oh yes Kenny. Love me, Fuck me daddy! Make me feel whole. Yes  fuck me daddy, harder , faster, She moans"

She releases her nut, squirting; soaking the bed drenching the sheets. She curls into the fetal position and, reaches for the business-card on her nightstand picking it up. She holds it close to her heart as she falls fast asleep. Kenny's new cell number is written on its back.


*(elsewhere in the city)*

Deep in the heart  of the city in  Jackson Ward's Gilpin Court Housing Project Blue sits parked on a busy side street. Its busy with that night time pedestrian traffic; mainly dope heads , crack whore ,teens and bad ass'd little kids mixed with the occasional drunk . He studies the scene, business is good, the drug traffic flow is constant. It doesn't take him long to identify the major player on this set. He's interest in one person in particular, he seeks revenge. He's here to act on Zoe's tip. He's scanning the set for LaQuan. He spots him making the  rounds managing this drug spots. He and two of his boys notice Blue parked sitting in his Lincoln Navigator.

They approach him to see why he is there. He recognizes Blue as a member of Poison. Unknowing LaQuan  is walking to his own demise, he has on the chain given him by Geronimo. The same one Blue had given Quan as a birthday gift. Blues eyes widen, this is proof positive, this is his brothers killer. He extended his massive arm pulling the  young hustler toward his window; up comes a razor blade slashing LaQuan's jugular vein. He falls to the ground bleeding out, his boys run away abandoning him. Blues drives away drinking on a 40 oz bottle of malt Liquor, content.

*(in another section of the city)*

Not far away in the Ginter Park section of the City a man sits in a dark blue min van. On the passenger seat sits a brand new roll of duck tape and a box cutter. He thinks to himself the time is almost right. He has been staking-out a two level colonial house. Through its large bay window he can see its inhabitants going about their evening routine. It's a typical family scene, dinner, family time and story time for the little one. The sight sickens him, he feels cheated , he's being left out. His insides burn with hatred and jealousy. His heart completely filled with an unhealthy longing. He mumbles to himself in a low tone of voice.

" I will have my turn."

The disturbed man turned stalker is Maurice. He had followed Ricky and Danny when they left the sports bar that night. His stalking of Danny started that horrible night at the hotel. He followed Danny home that early morning as he fled leaving Ricky to his fate. Since then he has been a shadow learning Danny's daily routine. He wants to be with him but there is an obstacle which he must remove, Danny's wife Michelle.

His plane is a twisted one. He will be reunited with Danny at her funeral. Maurice thinks it will be a minor adjustment but Danny small daughter will call him uncle Maurice once he  moves in. He fantasizes about how he will console the grieving widower and guide him in moving pass his loss. He relishes in thoughts of sharing his bed as well as his life. He dare to anticipate how sweet taking him will be. Danny's last words to him repeat in his head. " *Game recognize game dog."*

Maurice finds himself getting restless. He decides to engage in some minor mischief. He lurks about the parking lot a short while then vandalizes Michelle's car. He lets the air out of all of her tires and pours a bottle filled with a corrosive chemical into her gas tank. Just to add insult to injury he keys the driver's door scratching the *words die whore:* before leaving.

*(Far away in Florida)*

*Kenny and Zoe chill late into the evening and early into the morning hours getting blitzed. They pass out around 3am ; the meeting with Chucky is set for 3pm this evening.*

# *(Meeting with the Rev)*

*(it's now 2:00pm)*

Kenny and Zoe are up dressed and ready to leave for the meeting with the reverend formerly known as Chucky at just a little past 2pm. Both are slightly hung-over but they look fresh in their new dress clothing. Kenny wears a two –piece, light fabric, powder blue suite with a collared tan dress shirt with a unassuming necktie . He has on matching tan leather shoes. He has toned down his jewelry game and simply wears his diamond encrusted chain without it's serpent medallion. He has no watch or rings on. A vintage simple leather brief case finishes the look.

Zoe compliments him saying, "Dang bro you look almost as sharp as me."

The outfit Kenny put together for him makes him look like a

businessman, Zoe cleans up nicely. It's a traditional light gray with thin pen strips, light cotton blend jacket with matching pants. Beneath his jacked he sports a white collarless shirt and a lighter grey vest. The shoes are square toed black patent leather with subtle buckles. He sparkles in the sunlight adorned with his new Rolex and diamond studded cross and white gold chain combination. The two discuss etiquette as they stand in front of the hotel waiting the car chucky has sent to bring them to him.

Zoe listens as Kenny goes over a vast list of do's and don'ts. Kenny explains that he is to maintain eye contact with Chucky as much as possible. He is a creature of extremes, just as staring him in his eyes could have dire consequences 10 years ago' likewise today a perceived slight such as looking down while he is speaking can have fatal results. Zoe is confused; So much so he has to interrupt Kenny for some clarification.

" Wait K, I'm lost. Didn't you tell me this nut almost chopped your head off for looking him in his eyes when Johnny first put you on with him?"

"Yeah Zoe but that was then , since then he's had some major life changes which inspired him to move past such petty insecurities.

" Damned! What happened to him K?"

Zoe I was getting to that. About six years ago He and his crew tortured and killed an undercover D.E.A agent by the name of Christian Slate. He was a dirty cop on the take who attempted to shake Chuckey down. His body was never found so no charges were ever bough against chucky. The powers that be knew he was on the take, so distanced themselves and stayed clear. But his fellow crooked cop friends knew what had happened all too well. They decided to erect a little justice of their own. They set out to teach him a biblical lesson *(An eye for an eye)*. They conducted their own private sting

223

operation with one goal; kill Chucky. But they wanted to make him suffer first for the manner in which he dispatched of their co- worker. Word on the street was that Chucky had perpetrated unthinkable deed which left the agent welcoming death. Chucky had the body dismembered, grounded like beef than fed it to his two pet Lions. The detective final state of existence was as a pile of steaming Lion poop.

The agents raided Chucky's mansion and abducted him taking him to an abandoned warehouse. They beat and tortured him within an inch of his life. They went to work on him with a rusty crowbar, vice grip pliers and a blow torch; they poured acid over his face and cut one of his hands off as well. As Chucky lay dying he had a near death experience. He traveled to the light. Chucky says he touch the face of God and he was commanded to return to spread the Lord's message.

Chucky was save when his henchmen showed up spoiling their sick party. He lost a hand and an eye but gained a third eye. A third eye which he claims can see beyond the physical world and into the past and future. Since he has become known as a clairvoyant. His accurately prediction of three major world changing event, one of which being the attack on the World Trade Center, Two being of the second Attack with the foretelling of the collapse of the twin towers and three being the resulting war on Islam. He has since established a church that has a growing cult-like following. Chucky also consults with the heads of several States on world political matter and for the most part is allowed to continue his criminal empire un- hindered. He has dirt on some important people. He's hailed the world over for his generous monetary contributions to charities. He now lives in a small self-contained City of his own making called The Garden. It's has its own bank, grocery stores and several large farms. They produce organic crops for sell to the public . They have major distribution centers and stored along the East Coast.

They house and feed the poor, while providing educational and job training . His mandate from God is to uplift people. The drugs he sell are now a means to giving the masses a vessel to spiritual enlightenment. He prophecies that the world will end soon and that a chosen few will be spared and taken to another planet to began anew. This civilization will be based on the true laws of God and its citizens will walk and talk with God just as Adam and Abraham had. He' says all will know the goodness of the God. He claims to be the savior who will lead them in this age of enlightenment. Currently he has a following of roughly six thousand followers and membership in his church is rapidly growing daily.

## (Going to church)

A black Lincoln town car  pulls along-side the curb stopping and Kenny and Zoe get in; they are driven to a gated complex *(The Garden City)*. The road inside of the gate is covered with a metallic yellow surface making the streets look as if they are actually paved in gold. Lorenzo  looks to Kenny who returns a gaze of inquisitiveness. They wonder could it be the streets are as they seem. They drive up to a huge white building with large glass panels windows. They are met with even more audacity as the side walk and walk paths leading to the huge door are covered in what appears to be real gold. Unlike the road the hue of gold has a deep richness only associated with the real thing. Armed guards stand vigilant to the left and right of the door.

Kenny and Zoe are given the once over with metal detector wands  before being allowed to pass. Four ushers approach leading them into the inner sanctuary of this mega church. The place is pack with worshipers. They are gathered to hear the words of the Reverend Almighty Chucky. He's spiting fire and brimstone from and elaborate wooden pulpit. He speaks of the wickedness of Satan and of the secret societies that seek to build a new world order in his names. The Holy Ghost is  in the house, apparent by the scores of people shouting, flailing their arms about and collapsing as they catch The Ghost; some even speak in tongues. Kenny and Zoe are impressed, this is a pretty good racket Chuckey has going here, or so they think. This is the perfect front for a large drug operation. Lucrative in and of its self and ideal for money laundering. The two take the sermon as entertainment.

The service concludes and the two are lead to  a room behind the stage. It was a good show but this is what they are here for. Chucky enters greeting them. He is closely follow by a little black midget with dreads. He embraces Kenny  hugging him. The midget pat about Kenny's waist and ankles searching for weapons.

"Calm now Molie. E'm Ok now. "

He looks into Kenny's eyes then glances over his shoulder to Zoe. Saying.

"So em' da one ya talk about?"

Kenny nodes, indication yes.

He walk over to Zoe placing his hand and hook on his shoulder, he gazes deeply into his eyes. He then take a few steps back looking him over.  He quickly turn to Kenny saying, "E'm one sharp  man. E'm family Now. E'm alright.

*His eyes fixate on the large diamond cross Zoe has on.* He chuckles deeply from his gut saying. E'm gud."

It's that simple. He has met Chuckey's approval and from this day on he is down. He claps his hands and his men bring four large bags placing them on the table. Kenny places his brief case on the table overturning it; clumps of hard cash fall onto the table.

Chucky smiles then thanks him for such a generous donation to his church. He then writes him a receipt handing it to him; This concludes business. Chucky ask Kenny if he needs any help calming things with old man Nelson offering him the assistant of his enforcer Lil Molie. Kenny declines the offer. He knows Chucky well, he's always wanted a foot hold in Richmond, but his offering the services of Mollie is vexing. Mollie is his ace up the sleeve, he goes nowhere without him. Kenny briefly ponders the angle before shaking these thoughts . Chucky takes the two out to dinner then to the airport. Kenny gives Chucky man his rental car key so he can return it. Soon after they board the plan home bound. Today was a good day.

*(The flight home is uneventful with the exception of some turbulence. Zoe and Kenny are both reclined in their seats and quite content enjoying first class accommodations. They reflect on this excursion.)*

Lorenzo thinks of how this was as easy as cake. Now he has the connect, he is less anxious about  Poison's future. No longer will they be dependent on Kenny as the sole means to get work. Still he remain a bit apprehension of Chucky but for now he allows himself to day dream about how things could be with him ascending to head Poison's.

Kenny thinks about moving past recent event. He day dreams of the days to come enjoying quality time with his family, reunited. He sees himself nestled close to his wife's' breast suckling on her. He closes his eyes imagining her sweet smell, he whispers her name  and closes his eyes to rest. This stick-up has affected their marriage in the worst way. He need to get back to his wife and children.

The drugs are in transit via Chuckey's distribution network. He uses the same distribution channels he uses to ship his farm produce along the East Coast. The drugs go to his Fredericksburg processing center where Butter's picks them up and transport them back to Richmond. She's accompanied by six cars loaded with soldiers. Nothing will stop this convoy not even the State Troopers. The cars form a buffer around her as she makes her way back. Johnny used to meet her a few miles away from The Spot where he and Kenny determine what went to which Spot. Kenny has to decide what role Lorenzo will play on this end.

## (Breaking news)

*(Kenny and Zoe are at Johnny's penthouse apartment at the Marriott, chilling. Kenny has decided this will be his new residency, it's a great place to crash)*

"Zoe?

" What up K?"

"Order us sum food, I'm about to take a shower"

"Aw'rite, what you want,pizza or chiness?"

"Whatever you get is good with me, I don't care. I'm just hungry."

Kenny leaves the room and Zoe makes himself comfortable with the TV's remote. He flips channels surfing for something to watch. An action movie would be good right about now. He flips past news channels until he catches a glimpse of a local breaking new story.

" Oh shit! Oh Shit! come here, quick man quick! You got to see this! AWWW FUCK!!!!

Kenny rushes back into the room with only a towel wrapped about his waist. What he sees and hears blows his mind.

The scene on the TV's screen is courtroom footage. In the defendant chair sits Theodore Quincy Nelson, AKA Monster. The judge is ruling on an appeal.

*(Zoe turns the volume of the TV up as they listen)*

They watch per recorded court room footage of the judge ruling

" Mr. Nelson has been the victim of a great miscarriage of justice one which we can never repay the debt for the years of incarceration he has unjustly suffered. The preponderance of evidence of police misconduct will no longer be overlooked.  This court orders the hasty release of Mr. Nelson.

*Behind the scenes Old man Nelson has made a more than generous contribution to the Judges retirement fund. 2.5 million was the cost of this acquittal.*

Kenny looks too Zoe, shaking his head in disapproval before departing the room. He's not going to let this news spoil his shower. The sound of running water and sight of steam seeping from under the bathroom door beckons him.

He call to Zoe, "later for that shit."

*(Zoe calls ordering Pizza)*

Kenny steps into the shower, it's  very hot; it's steam opens his nasal passage revealing sinus congestion. His head placed under the large round showerhead, water drenches his wave filled hair than runs down his neck traveling down his back delivering relief. All his body aches disappear if just for this moment. The shower is like a liquid massage, all of his stressful thoughts seem to wash away down the drain at his feet. Sometimes it's the small things in life that remind you just how good you really have it. His though, "I can handle Monster, after all he's been out of the game for years. He's old and rusty. Just as he turns the water off he's alarmed by Zoe calling to him like a mad man.

"K, hurry up! Come here main! HURRY-UP!

Kenny damned near slips rushing to Zoe, hurriedly wrapping a towel about his waist.

"DANMED ZOE, WHAT'S UP!"

*(Zoe points to the TV)*

"What the Fuck" , exclaims Kenny.

He sees big Blue being lead in cuffs and leg irons. He's being arrested and charged with homicide for the murder of the youngster LaQuan. They both appear surprised. Kenny more so then Lorenzo. The seed he planted took roots and sprouted. He hides his satisfaction pretending as if he is upset. Zoe's sympathy raises a red flag with Kenny; the two never got along. He has little time to think on it as the next story breaks blowing his mind.

*(The news cut to live footage)*

The background scenery if familiar to them. It's Kevin's house and there he is being lead hand-cuffed to a Pattie wagon. The reported speaks

*Police responded to multiple complaint from neighbors reports of putrid smells around the property behind me. When police arrived on scene to investigate what they found both horrified and disgusted them. Inside the residence they arrested local mortician Kevin Jerrod Henson. At this point the remains of four unidentified women have been discovered in a macabre scene straight out of a Hollywood horror movie. A spokesman for the department says that the women's corpses were found position about a formal dining table inside the home. Preliminary investigation of the scene suggest that this may be a case of necrophilia. The reporter goes on to*

*interview several of the neighbors. They all basically say the same of him.*
*He was a strange guy who kept to himself.*

*(Kenny and Zoe stand speechless for a minute)*

" Damned, and to think you was tight with this mother fucker. With all the years you been knowing him, how didn't know he was serial killing and shit?

"Naw for real K, aside from his having a cold streak, Kevin was cool as fuck. But now dat I think about it he did kinda change when he found out he had Aids.

"Changed? I mean How? You mean it was like one day he was normal then all of a sudden he just had a urge to be killing bitches and fucking  their dead bodies?"

" I'm not saying that K, I just mean he got cold over night and started withdrawing from people. Aside from a few of the morticians he work with I'm the only regular person he hung with after getting that news."

Kenny is having difficulty processing this conversation. Zoe referring to himself as normal or as regular people. What the fuck! And him saying Kevin was like the coldest motherfucker he's ever meet. That's saying a lot when you consider Zoe's a Killer who can run with the worst of the lot of murderers. Kenny's interest is peaked, he has to know, what could Kevin have done to make Zoe see him as the coldest person he has ever met. Kenny goes there.

"Nigga how the fuck you saying this crazy- ass nigga was colder than you or Johnny or your little brother Moe?"

A humbled Zoe shakes his head and say, "I'm telling you K, he was . Check this, I'm gon'a tell you about something he did and I guarantee you'll say this nigga is the most heartless nigga you ever heard of."

Kenny smile  shakes his head he say's "shoot nigga I'm
listening."

Aw'rite  K, do you remember that summer the Whole East
Coat was hit with that massive Heat Wave and drought with daily
temperature  over 100 degrees and shit? Ok, well me and him was
riding past Midlothian Village  Apartments and decided to pick up
this fine lil honey who was  waiting at the bus stop in front of
George Wythe High School. She couldn't have been more than
nineteen or twenty years old. Kevin was riding his old school 98
Oldsmobile and had the A/C pumping. I mean it was like a fucking
winter wonder land in that bitch.  It had to be about 103 degrees out
there when I got out to let her get on the passenger side. I hopped
into the  back and stretched out cool'n drinking my 40 oz.  Kev was
drinking a extra large Slurpee.  She asked if she could have some to
help cool her down and he handed it to her. Shit the rapid change in
temperature coupled with the brain rush from the Slurpee must
have  fucked with this chicks  brain or something because she went
into convulsions, having a seizure or some shit. I ain't going ta lie,
that shit had me freaking out. I was like what the fuck pull over so
we can help this bitch.  We was just crossing the overpass where
the traffic mergers from Belt blvd onto Midlothian Turn Pike when
this nigga reached across this wiggling lil hoe, opening the door, he
pushed her ass out while the car was still moving. I was like what
the fuck! I shut the door, hopped over the seat and and he just kept
going. I asked dat nigg why he did dat shit. Man that nigga looked
me right in the face calm as a bitch and said in a Snoop Dog voice, "
We don't love dem hoes". K , I'm like this nigga cold as fuck, but
from that day on me and him was like joined at the hip. Regardless
what they got him on, he still my nigga. I'm going to make sure he
keep money on his canteen. He's always been down for me
whenever I needed him.

Kenny's thoughts switch to Nichol; he wonders if her corpse is amongst those now being removed by the corners. He's feeling bad, but crying is for the weepy woeful type. He must move past it and he does.

" Ok Zoe let get down to business. What do we have on our plate right now?

*(He is slow in his response)*

" Well , I talked with Teddy and according to Detective Howard the cops taking this Quan homicide more serious than usual. Now that Blue is locked down it don't look like we going be expanding out heroin distribution."

"Do you think La Quan's people going to ride for him?"

That's for certain K. Them Jackson Ward Kid's ; they are born with guns in their hands. But I'll send my lil brother through to calm shit down. We drop some free Keys on them niggas and they might calm the fuck down. Shit either they can get money or die, it's up to them.

"Do you think Kevin will rat us out. He put in a lot of work with us over the years."

" Naw K, Kevin ain't no rat, he won't snitch. Besides he is a certified crazy mother fucker ,having sex with dead bodies and shit; he ain't creditable as a witness. How is the Ashland operation doing. I was thinking we shouldn't trust no local with it."

" Look Zoe, I told you I trust Arlene with that."

" Yeah I heard you K, but I'm thinking we need to send a Head down there to handle it personally. Geronimo can go to assure nobody fucks with them. I think Kee should be there until we know what's up for sure. K I'm just saying you don't know that Arlene

233

chic that much. *Kenny changes the subject reverting to earlier issues.*

" Zoe put in a call to D-Mac in P town, he owes me a favor. Ask him to front us some bundles until I can find a more permanent heroin connect. We need to fill Blues spot while he's locked down, who do you think should come up?

Zoe does'nt have an answer, he's the type of Kat who never likes to see anyone move ahead. And Kenny knows this.

"Zoe I got a headache you got any Aspirin?"

"I saw some in the medicine cabinet in the bathroom."

Kenny leaves the room to look for them. Bingo he finds them, he pops a few. He and Zoe chill for awhile watching movies, then he calls Paulette. Shes excited to hear from him. He asks her if the police have been back to question her further about Quan's murder. They have not.

Paulette takes this opportunity to get to know him better asking numerous personal questions, she wants to know more about him. She goes into telling him how bothered she is having to stay in the apartment where Quan died. Kenny wants to appease her; he shows sympathy and understanding by extending his hospitality to her. He invits her to stay with him at Johnny's penthouse until she can find somewhere else to stay. Paulette jumps at what she sees as an golden opportunity, she repeatedly thanks him. She is eager asking, "what's the best time to come over". Kenny tells her to give him two hours to tidy up the place a bit.

# (Monster's return home)

Monster stands at the Nelson's family plot with his elderly father, Nelson senior. His father's stance steadied by his hand around a loving son's waist and the other clutching a curved handle Kane. He's in bad health; he coughs frequently and trembles terribly. Monster's thought. dad has seen better days. This is a dismal scene. They had hoped their reunion would be a time of celebration; lively and festive. But the Oak grove cemetery is not a place of smiles; it is one for mourning.

The two are assembled here to pay their respects to treasured, loved ones passed. The consecrated ground beneath their feet houses two sons and brothers. Monsters sibling now rest in peace beside their mother in the family plot.

Heads bowed, eyes closed they reflect upon recent events and better days. What has brought the brothers to this end? Tears streams down each mans' cheeks, racing and diving to their shirts like scored lovers plummeting from a cliffs. They have been robbed. Death has stolen the senior Nelsons pallbearer; no parent should outlive their seeds. It brings a pain unlike anything imaginable.

Mr. Nelson's partially opens his eyes and speaks to the soul of his youngest son, Ricky.

"Boy I tried to keep you from becoming like us."

His eyes shift toward Black's grave glaring and grimacing all of a sudden, his facial expression changes to one of ambivalence. It lives and grows in his heart even more in death for his middle son because he has dragged his little brother down into the cold, unforgiving grave with him. In his drug addiction he had taken him through changes, lying, stealing and violating the family's trust but this he may not be able to forgive. He speaks to Blacks spirit.

" Why couldn't you stay away from Ricky. Everything you touch withers then dies."

He blames Black for his wife's passing as well. He says she died from a broken heart brought about by worry . This may have some validity; she died of heart failure many years ago at a relatively young age. He has an emotional outburst.

"It's all because of you Boy!"

The old man breaks down crying, he struggles to keep his balance transferring all of his body weight onto Monster's arm. He's strong enough to hold the weight and he's resolved that he will be the rock his father needs him to be.

"Easy now pops. I got you.

(His massive frame and tree trunk like arms steady him)

He has the words to comfort him as well

"They are all together now. One day we will be with them again".

"Yeah son that's right. I got you back here with me now, everything is going to be just fine."

His time on death rows has thought him the value of life and to appreciate the ones you love regardless of their short comings. His years at the top of the drug game have given him a different set of skills as well. Now back on the street he will have to reinvent himself. In the past he was ridged in his thinking, cleaver of mind and heartless in his actions. When he was at a loss for words a deadly silence most- often insured, followed by the eruption of gunfire. He was a master of terror and vice. He schooled Johnny well, teaching him all of the in's and out's of being a criminal. He was the master and Johnny was his most prized student. In his absence Johnny had build an empire almost on a par with the one he had in the past.

He sees himself in Kenny's recent actions, it's obvious that Johnny has past many of his teaching onto Kenny. Likewise he can see Blacks twisted influence on his brothers lives. He wishes things were not as they are.  But these young Katz have lost sight of some key values necessary to stay alive in the game. Respect has become an alien concept to them, they have no boundaries or morals. It sickens him the way they have conducted themselves. In his day disrespect was not to be tolerated. Kenny's refusal to meet with his dad will be addressed; if need be in the harshest fashion.

But for now they have another mission. It's out of respect the two travels to the North Side where they visit Johnny at his final resting place, his parent's home.  There his ashes rest in peace in an urn on the mantel place. They are welcome with open arms and visit for hours with Johnny's mom and dad.

# Chapter 11 / Touching

## Shadows

Paulette crosses the threshold to Johnny's penthouse placing her suitcase and traveling bag neatly aside the wall; she steps toward Kenny extending her arms wide. Her thought; he seems stand offish. She asks him if she may have a big hug. He complies but pulls away as she attempts to embrace him squeezing too tightly.

He picks her bags up telling her to follow him, they proceed to the guest bedroom. He hand her the TV's remote from atop the dresser saying to her "make yourself comfortable. He adds, "I am relaxing in my room if you need me for anything. I'm kinda tired and may turn in early." Paulette smiles saying, "Ok."

Kenny goes directly to his room closing the door behind himself. He selects several of his favorite jazz CD's to listen to. He then lights several incense sticks placing them about the room he dims the lights. He settles down lying across his bed smoking a cigarette while rolling blunts (*he takes strong pulls savoring the flavor of menthol*). A large glass filled to the rim with rum and coke on the rocks sits on the table adjacent to the bed. It's a cool vibe he has going on. Now's a good time to check in on Arlene; it's been a minute since he last spoke with her. He dials her number but gets no response. He then calls Kee Kee's house, she promptly answers.

She's exceptionally bubbly and extra happy for some reason.

"Oh, Hey Kenny. what do u want? I know you want something because it seems those are the only times you call me; when you need something."

" Kee stop tripping and let me talk to Arlene."

"She's not here. I thought that bitch was with you. Let me tell you something Kenny that's one stupid chic. She gave me all the money you gave her and sniffed up damned near an eight ball every day. You're going have to bring me some personal to replace what she used. Baby boy I usual try to go along with you but u pick wrong this time.

"Damned Kee I don't need this sermon right now, where is she at?"

"I just told you I don't know, she been gone about two days now. She didn't take no clothing or nothing, she just got in Johnny's Jeep and left in a hurry late at night."

*(Kee Kee is putting off major attitude)*

"Ok, thanks Kee. Call me when she comes in. I'm going to makes some call and see if I can find her."

*(They end the call)*

He tries to think of someone, anyone who knows where she may be; just then it hits Kenny like a ton of bricks. He knows nothing about this chic. But he's not going to let her mess up this evening for him, he continues to enjoy himself smoking and drinking all alone. He's content, Kenny G and Boney James's music never sounded so good; Still he's a bit stressed he has a thought. *A warm bath would be great about now.*

He makes his way into the large master bathroom making his way directly to the large marble, sunken tub with turbo jets. He fills it with just the right combination of hot warm water and bubble bath. He uses Mr. Bubble. It reminds him of those Saturday night baths his mother gave him as a kid. It's special the way something as simple as a bath can spark wonderful feeling of nostalgia. In the comfort of the tub he reminisces about his mom and of how he misses her. Tonight he's not a powerful drug dealer he's simply Mrs. Noble's treasures son, Kenny.

Kenny exits the tub, dries, lotions applies powers then jumps into the King sized bed; clean and refreshed, he fades into sleep. His last thought. I think I will call Mr. Nelson in the morning.

*(On the West End)*

Tragedy has struck the Nelson's house hold; Old man nelson is dead.  The victim of a hit and run he was struck by a car on Broad Street while walking to his car after leaving the Bingo hall late this afternoon. It' official Monster is once again the man. He is broken hearted but resolved to handle his father's empire as he did. His first order of business will be addressing Kenny's disrespect of his now late father by his declining to meet with him. Detective Howard has been assigned the hit and run homicide case and the pressure is on. The ex-governor has made a personal appeal to the chief of police to solve this tragic crime. The detective will not let this case grow cold there were multiple witness and physical evidence left behind of the car that struck him. Witness report the car was a jeep.

# (Making love)

Kenny is awakened from a sound sleep. He opens his eyes to the flickering of candles light's reflections dancing about the walls. The soft solo sounds of saxophone from a jazzy CD pleases his ears, His awareness increases. He's not alone. Brief fear creeps upon him until he realizes it's a softer touch which awaked him. It's Paulette, she crawled into his bed and nestled herself close to his body spooning him. The softness and heat of her more than ample breast gives him movement down below. her soft voice blends in with the jazz music now subdued in the background. She speaks and it's like music to his ears. She places her small delicate hand about his shoulders and starts to knead his flesh as if he were made of doe. Kenny feels himself melting in her touch.

He asks her "what's she doing?" Her response a simple one "I want you in me" She begins kissing and sucking his neck. He ask her if she sure she want to go there with him. She has no words for him instead she rolls him onto his back and crawls atop him, her long legs straddling his back. She sits massaging his back, her hips moving back and forth then up and down at times making swiveling motions. Her pussy is hot, moisten and swollen in anticipation of Kenny entering her. Paulette wants this man who had shown her compassion and protected her. She thinks to self than pushes soft air from her mouth making soft huffing sound. Kenny listens it's a sexy scene and he digging it.

"Damned babe let me roll over to look into your beautiful face", says Kenny.

She rises up stopping for a split second to allow him to turn over. Her soft butt plants just above his rock hard hammer. She continues in her rhythmical, erotic moving, her huffing and puffing give way to sweet moans as she; leans forward placing her nipple into his open mouth. He bits down gently holding her nipple a

241

hostage between his K-9 teeth. He tantalizes her with movements of his lips and soft tongue; His right hand caressing the pronounced curve of her arched lower back. His left hand grips her, cupping her round plump ass pulling her toward him. His touch is firmly yet gently. He releases her letting her retreat then pulls her back with masculine force. Both fantasize about the feel of the others kiss. Neither of them wants to rush that special moment they both plot on ways of delaying that ever so precious first kiss.

They continue in therefore play adding pillow talk they whisper sweet nothings to the other. Paulette sinks her teeth into the flesh of Kenny's neck sucking. She wants to leave her mark of passion. He squirms and ties to pull his neck away from her mouth. Her hands clasp his and she hold his hand flat to the mattress to the sides of his head. Paulette releases grasp and move down kissing his chest. Kenny moves a hand to nipple pinching it. She moans loudly then says to him, "Harder Daddy."

Kenny obliges her. He wants to see just how far this car has been driven. He inserts the tip of one finger into her pussy then another into her tight ass hole. She sucks and bits her lips now feeling herself she squeezes her breast.

Dry humping Kenny, her sweet juices run down onto him soaking his lower stomach region. He wants to be inside of her and is ready to make that a reality. His hands he place about her waist firmly holding her; he guides her as she moves back and forth. The moment is right; he plots on timing this just right. She pulls back and he lifts her then rapidly drives her toward him. His penis aligned just right penetrated her love canal. AWWWWW fuck, they think. They feel so good to each other. They lose themselves and become as two wild animals; grunting, panting and sweating. They abandon the missionary position; he turns her entering her from behind,their lust is unbridled. Kenny thinks about one of the more juvenile poems from Roe Jay's book of poetry while he's tearing Paulette's ass up.

## _Doggie Style_

So you say you like the rawness.

Come here.

Closer... Closer girl.

Jack dat phat- ass up in da air.

I see doubt in your eyes.

Ain't no need for acting scared.

So you like it deep and hard form the rear?

Do you mind if I take this dare?

Let's do dat nasty- nasty shit.

Shit, I'll take you anywhere.

We can do it on the floor

Or perhaps you prefer the comfort of the bed.

If you're lazy in your skills,

Lean dat ass over a chair.

I live for pussy!

Pussy I live for!

I ain't dat on looker how would rather sit and stare.

Reach around like a pro,

Hoe insert this stiff dick in there.

Let a nigga know right now

If you're funny about your hair,

Like the lever is used for leverage this pussy I'm about to tear.

All the neighbors gonna here is.

BANG! BANG! BANG! BANG! BANG!

Damn Papa!

Call 911, he's fucking a

bitch to death over there.

Through the walls the culprits voice they here.

So crystal clear,

"STOP SQUIRMING BITCH!

YOU AIN"T GOING NOWHERE!!!!!

I DON'T CARE IF WE BREAK THIS MOTHER-FUCKING CHAIR!

BITCH!

TAKE DISS DICK SINCE YOU THOUGHT A NIGGA WAS SCARED!!!"

Smiling and smacking ass while pulling hair.

"Mama you think she wanted it doggie style?"

Forceful rhythms all up in guts,

Lady screaming.

"PLEASE- PLEASE!

BUST YO NUT!!!"

A nigga hollering, WHAT'S MY NAME?"

U giving- up"

Lady sreaming.

"I HAD ENOUGH!!!

you trying ta kill my ass?"

"BITCH DAT'S WHAT'S UP!"

Lady asking,

"WHY YOU FUCKING ME LIKE A SLUT?"

Dat's it daddy!

I likes it rough!

I'm yo bitch .I'll be yo slut!

Please.. Please.. Please.. release yo nut......

Damned

Doggie style...... it's coming up.

Pussy squeezing,

Sucking up;

Holding back,

I can't hold diss nut.

We scream in pleasure.

She receives this nut.

Doggie style.

All in her guts.

WHAT THE FUCK!

My dick's covered in shit..... That was her butt

*Heee hee hee*

*Roejay the poet*

# (The morning after)

Kenny and Paulette awaken. Paulette stares at him, the conversation is not typical chit chat and turns weird; borderline bazaar.

"Kenny last night was so wonderful. I knew we were meant to be together. Our baby will be so beautiful. After I have the baby we can move to New Orleans, to be closer to my family. They can watch the baby while we work and when we need down time for just us. My mom and dad will love you."

Kenny says nothing. He's shakes his head while trying recall the night before clearly. He smiles, it was great sex. But he can't recall weather he came in her or pulled out. Paulette fills in all the blank as if she was reading his mind.

"My goodness, you came so hard in me it's almost like I can still feel you pulsating in me right now. She goes on thinking up and pronouncing potential names for the baby both male and female. She stares dazed looking at the ceiling daydreaming. *Oh snap thinks Kenny, he has a bonafide crazy laying beside him ;time for action.*

He gets up, tosses on some sweats and rushes out to run a quick errand. He's going to the drug store to buy some morning after pills. He plans on making and serving her breakfast in bed, with a little something extra added to her pancakes. He gets the pill and a large box of condoms. He's not going to get caught out like this again taking chances by going raw.

*(he leaves the drug store)*

Heading back to the hotel is slow going, stoplights take longer changing this early in the morning. While sitting at a red light his attention drifts to the car beside his.

What in the hell, is the sentiment that bum-rushes his mind like a tornado. That's Johnny's Jeep, but who is this nigga driving it, and Where is Arlene? The jeep takes off speeding, Kenny trails making sure to hang back far enough to stay out of sight. He follows this guy to the end of Broad Street down into a large apartment complex in Fulton Bottom. He sees a woman standing on the balcony of a second story apartment, it looks like Arlene but he's not sure; she looks a mess. He parks and goes on stakeout. He observes the flow of foot traffic in and out of the building; this pattern is all too familiar to him. This early in the morning it's obvious there is a crack house in the building. Many fiend hurries in and out.

Kenny gets impatient; he decides he will go investigate closer. As he walks across the parking lot toward the building where he sees the man who drove Johnny's jeep there. The man has a pull out car radio in his hand. He approaches Kenny.

"Man checks diss out. I got diss bad ass Alpine radio for sale. It the top of the line. Give me $20 dollars for it." They are standing next to the jeep. Kenny looks inside and the radio is missing. Picture that, this nigga is trying to sell him his own shit. Kenny punches this dirty nigga directly in his throat, hard; dropping him to his knees. He clutches his neck as he gags and wheezes trying to catch his breath.

"Where you get this car?"

"I don't know. My boy rented it from some chic for a few grams of powder.

"Where is she now, calmly ask Kenny"

"She's inside there", he points to an apartment building.

"Which apartment?."

"205".

"Give me those keys nigga"

*(Kenny snatches them from him then tell him to)*

" get the fuck up from around me!"

*(The junky rushes off disappearing behind a dumpster)*

Kenny goes to the apartment. Its door ajar, he enters. It's like as if he has walked directly into a scene from the movie *New Jack City*. It's a real life Carter, men and women lay about the floor some sleeping, some passed out others squabble over drugs. He calls out, Arlene!

Arlene! Where are you?

*(A couple of fiends point toward the back of the apartment)*

Kenny flips his switch and into Giant mode he transforms. He's like Optimus Prime he's on a mission looking for Deceptacons. The power is off in the apartment so there are no light,but he can vaguely make out movement ahead in the dark hallway. He can make out shady figures at its far end.

There is a short line of three or so men is assembled standing to one side of the hallway. They stand outside a closed door with another guy. He appears to be collecting money. The door opens, money is exchanged and the line advances as one man enters the room, closing the door tightly behind him. Five or so minutes pass and the man reappears from the room. The next two go and Kenny is next. The line behind him is growing. He's curious like George. What's the racket? He asks the guy at the door, " what's the admission price. The dude tells him $20.

Kenny plays the role of a crack haggling he says, " I only got $15. Hook me up." The doorman tell him he will let him slide this once since this is his first time here. He takes Kenny's money. The wait is longer this time; ten minutes elapses and finally the door opens. A man exits and Kenny moves forward entering the room.

The room is for the most part empty, beyond modest. They have the windows covered in heavy black plastic, duck tape to the walls virtually no light  seeps in from the outside where the courtyard is populated with large post lamps; one shines directly outside of the window. The only focal point is a small worn , tattered lumpy mattress laying on the floor in the center of the room; next to it sits and old splintering, wooden fruit crate, it serves as a night stand. On it sits a small oil lantern. The light it makes is weak ;like a sick old man it tries to recapture its youthful shin. It has momentary burst of flames which making the details of a dim reality more visible for a millisecond  before shrinking as a wilting flower only to repeat in cycle.

Kenny can vaguely see some personal effects scattered about in clutter around the bed and makeshift table, clothing, shoes mixed with fast food wrappers and crumpled paper bags.

He ventures in further. He's confused, puzzled. Cautiously he checks out the walk- in closet to the rear of the room. The smell pushes him back. There is a large bucket in the corner which serves as a toilet, there is also a small sink with working water. Kenny backs out of the  closet covering his nose and mouth with both hands. This appears to be a dead end and a waste of fifteen bucks, Arlene is not here.

He turns to exit the room. As he approaches the door to leave he catches a glimpse of movement, it comes from a dark corner to the left of the door. It's a small figure, huddled in a ball. Kenny whispers, " Arlene.

Then again more inquisitively," Arlene, is that you?"

He rushes to the window ripping away the plastic covering from the window. pale light enters.

The light reveals Arlene; naked, dirty and broken spirited. She's hysterical, rocking back and forth crouched in the fetal position. She mumbles " I'll go home soon. I just need one more hit. In her hand she clutches a small metal rod, she's been using as a crack pipe; in the other she hold a dead lighter. She flicks it repeatedly but it will not give light.

This is a sad scene thinks Kenny. He ask her who has done this to her, but he does not expect an answer. He knows he is the culprit.  He should have not left her to Kee's care. Unlike those other men who paid a fee to have her fulfill their lustful needs; he spends his ten minutes comforting her.

He kneel down blanketing her in his arms. She bathes in the warmth he gives off. She listens to his heart just as she had that night in the hospital. It gives her comfort, purpose and sanity. Like they say "Karma is a bitch" what she gains Kenny loses.

There is an attack on his perception. The air in the room suddenly changes, a dark dampness descend along which the feel that he is being watched. He feel as if some unnatural, ungodly presence is pressing in upon him. A sweet, foul odor saturates the room;it's as if someone lite a blood soaked Jasmine incense. It's a sickening scent' making his  stomach cramp, and his hairs stand on ends as if caught in an electrical field.

His sense heightened. He hears his name whispered so faith he is unsure it was uttered at all, it sound as if a snake hissed his name. He quickly turns his head catching a brief glance at something or perhaps somebody. His reasoning tells him it's more of a nobody. A shadow without a host; a Shadow Man. This is not the first time he has felt this presence.  The night of the escape from the hospital he felt this same presence while carrying Arlen up the stair to her apartment. Johnny spoke of their existence but Kenny wrote it off as him being dramatic.

It's time to leave this sick place. Kenny picks Arlen up cradling her in his arms. He  drapes her covering her in a thin blanket from the bed. He opens the door stepping into the hallway, Wrong move, there is a line of horny men waiting their turn to have sex with Arlene, eagerly they stand clutch  money tightly in hands. Kenny is stopped in his tracks by the door man.

" Naw dog this ain't no take out joint. She staying here till she work off her debt. She smoked over five hundred dollars of our shit on credit. She belongs to me now. This nigga don't know it but this is his lucky day. Kenny digs in his pocket pulling out a small stack, dropping it on the floor at the crack pimps feet.

"That's two stacks, consider your business with her done.

*(The man picks up the money and steps to one side allowing Kenny to past with Arlene)*

Kenny calls Dr. Lambert  from the car as he leaves the complex. He barks orders. He is to meet them at Pappy's farm. He does and they spend the morning doctoring Arlene. He pumps her with antibiotics and Pappy feed her nourishing meals. Kenny comforts her reading her poems from his now favorite book of poetry. Arlene fades in and out of sleep. She is exhausted there's no telling how little sleep she has had while on her crack binge.

Kenny get to know Dr. Lambert during this down time. He apologizes for brutalizing and disgracing him at his home. Kenny gives the Dr. a special gift. It's a gold Rolex which he originally bought to replace the  one Zoe cracked  when Pappy shot at them. Kenny figures it will mean more to him then to Zoe who can easily afford to buy many more. The Dr. happily accepts it and offer his apology for stealing from him. They are now cool.

"Doc, I need you to get her checked into a rehabilitation center and keep a check of her. She's important to me. I have to go back to Richmond for an important meeting in a few. "

*Teddy has arrange the meeting with Monster at his request in two hours time. Kenny's unaware they are being watched from outside the window man lurks in the bushes.*

## (The dreaded meeting)

Kenny meets Monster at a local gardening center. A less likely location there never was. The two gangsters walk about browsing seedling and mulch piles. They discuss difference , air grievances and review mutual interest. The scene is less than extraordinary but the conversation is mind blowing. Monster want to tax Kenny; he demands an unforgiving thirty-five percent operating fee to allow Poison to continue its North side operations. The term is ridiculous and they both know it. Monster wants war and he wants the North side back under his sole control. Secretly he has increased the bounty Ricky had placed on Kenny to a quarter of a million dollars. He's placed additional contracts on Zoe, and his brother Geronimo. The other members he will allow to live if they agree to work under his banner. There will be no more Poison Clan. He hopes the large bounties will inspire mutiny; surely a Head will step-up to chop the head off of this two head serpent. The chain around Kenny's neck will be the claim check for a huge pay day for someone. Zoe and his brother are to be considered collateral damage.

## (Kenny takes a missing)

Days elapse after the meeting with Monster and no one see or hears from Kenny. The Heads are concerned; their weekly meeting comes and goes and there is no word of or from their leader. Zoe steps up taking the helm. The word on the street is that the Giant is worth more dead than alive. Sunday passes and Kenny's promise to call Cheryl and the kids is broken; he misses his weekly check in. Alert levels reach critical when Pappy calls Kee Kee asking of his whereabouts. The question on everyone's mind is whether someone has cashed in on the two million dollar contract. Has someone made the giant small; is Kenny Nobles dead?

*The looming threat of urban war prompts Lorenzo to reaches out for help; they don't have the man power to survive a drawn out conflict with Monster. He reaches out to his newest ally for help and his call is answered in person.*

THE STICK-UP CONTINUES

# SOUL RIPPER

The boatman navigates the river of discontentment which
run through the sinner's mind.
Murky waters conceal sharp and jagged rocks,
the stumbling blocks, which repeated in time.
Inflict Gashes to the haul of the boat, stranding the
average man within a putrid mind.
Memories grow old as both acts of love and hatred fade
with time.
The unrepentant sinner is at peace in a place of shadows,
entangled by withered- thorny vines.
He questions what it means to be an abomination, fearing
his existence is a crime.
The steward of peace is missing; the Good Sheppard is left
for dead, sacrificed for being kind.
The final hour breaks like the surf upon the beach,
even Armageddon has design.
Laughter is heard before the hour glass shatters,
the last bells are poised to chime.
The river of discontentment sailed by the boatman,
runs through the sinner's troubled mind.
Deviant are the though and urges that rob the once
innocent of moral mind.
A soul ripper in our mist, still there may be time.
Guard your soul carefully.

*Roejay the poet*

# ABOUT THE AUTHOR

## I Am

*What I am describes the combination*

*of the inner essence and the outer shell*

*which is me.*

*What Am I ask the question of others of*

*my essence and bodies, what do they perceive.*

*I find knowledge of self in who I am.*

*There is unawareness of self in who Am I.*

*Knowing who, what and from where I came*

*empowers me,*

*Accepting what you say I Am makes a poor*

*servant of me.*

*We all have chose in who we choose to be.*

*Many a path to lead us astray but only one*

*which sets us free.*

Either define who you are or become that

confused random person that the world of the all

knowing THEY would have you to be.

**Alone in a crowd I stood as this realization**

**subdued me.**

**Understanding of the I Am's had long alluded me.**

**So concerned about others that myself I could not**

**clearly see.**

My sealed eyes opened wide and self-awareness flushed

past the flood gates of my closed mind with the

force of a thousand Red Seas.

Knowledge of self now leads me to believe.

**I Am the master of my fate.**

The setter of the attainable goals which I set out

to achieve.

**I have**

360 degrees of understanding.

**I Am**

A building block of my community.

**I Am**

*Somebody's eternal soul mate.*

***I Am***

*A protector of my loved ones.*

*I Am*

*Empowered because I know who and what I am.*

*ever again will I ask the questions. Who or what Am I ?*

***What I Am***

***is mentally free.***

*Roejay the Poet*

## Contact the author:

roejay1@yahoo.com
http://www.facebook.com/roejay1
http://twitter.com/Roejaythepoet
www.soundclick.com/roejaythepoet